Totally Bound Publishing books by Desiree Holt:

Crude Oil
Beg Me
Down and Dirty
Interlude
Intermission
Four Play
Game On
Swingtime
Party of Three
All Jacked Up
Top or Bottom
Rodeo Heat
Night Heat

Strike Force
Unconditional Surrender

The Sentinels
The Edge of Morning
Night Moves
Dark Stranger
Animal Instinct
Mated
Silent Hunters

Cat's Eyes
Pretty Kitty
On the Prowl

Corporate Heat
Where Danger Hides

Anthologies
Night of the Senses: Carnal Caresses
Christmas Goes Camo: Melting the Ice
Treble: Trouble at the Treble T
Subspace: Head Games
Bound to the Billionaire: Made for Him

NIGHT HEAT

DESIREE HOLT

Night Heat
ISBN # 978-1-78686-330-0
©Copyrightt Desiree Holt 2017
Cover Art by Posh Gosh ©Copyright September 2017
Interior text design by Claire Siemaszkiewicz
Totally Bound Publishing

NIGHT HEAT

Dedication

To my hero, my late husband David, who took
me to live in our own Bluebonnet Falls and made
both the flowers and Texas come alive for me.
And of course, as always, my magic team: Margie
Hager, Kate Richards, Janet Rodman.

Chapter One

Dumb, dumb, dumb.

Of all the dumb things she'd ever done in her life, this one ranked right at the top of the list. *How did I ever let myself be talked into it?*

Okay, so this was a great article she'd been selected to write. Maybe there'd be something that would help her make the leap from writing to reporting. Not that she didn't love her job, but she continued to look for ways to switch from magazines to news.

But career choices aside, the closer Jill Danvers got to Bluebonnet Falls, the harder butterflies tap-danced in her stomach. She hadn't seen Gabriel Carter in ten years. Not since the summer she'd given him her virginity and her heart and he'd trampled on both by marrying someone else. After that, she'd made a conscious effort to ignore the town and any news about it. She sure didn't want to read about how well Mr. and Mrs. Gabriel Carter were doing.

Still, no matter how hard she tried, she hadn't found a way to get him out of her system. Her secret guilty pleasure, the hot lover who invaded her dreams and left her breathless, sweaty and tangled in her sheets when she woke. Gabe Carter was the yardstick by which she measured every other man she met.

Now, in just a few minutes, she'd be face-to-face with him again. Just the memory of his hot, firm body made her nipples harden and a pulse throb between her thighs like a jungle drumbeat. The singing of the tires on the pavement was a counterpoint to the thudding of her heart.

"Get a grip," she scolded herself. "He's probably flabby, bald and missing half his teeth."

She only wished. Seeing him again would be a lot easier if he were, him being someone else's husband and all.

Yes, let's not forget the husband part.

She wheeled her Chevy Blazer up the Interstate 10 off-ramp and turned right onto the two-lane road into Bluebonnet Falls. Five more miles and she'd be facing her personal Armageddon.

"You can do this," she said, her words disappearing in the wind. "Smile, shake his hand, make your arrangements and get on with it." If she was lucky, maybe her homecoming wouldn't be a big deal to anyone. She could do her story and get away pretty much unscathed.

The notes for her *Life in America* assignment were tucked away in her Coach portfolio. She'd worked very hard to get where she was, scrabbling her way up the publications ladder to finally get the position at one of the country's top magazines. *Life* had been running her *Slice of Life* series of articles on small towns and large cities and she'd seen a lot of the country.

This time, she'd be focusing on Bluebonnet Falls and its upcoming bicentennial celebration. Normally, she'd be looking forward to this type of assignment.

'It's a good story,' her editor had pointed out. *'Besides, it's your hometown, so you ought to give it a special slant.'*

Then she'd learned Gabe was chairing the bicentennial steering committee. *How on earth can I handle seeing him again? Working closely with him?*

"Damn it!" she shouted into the breeze. "I don't want to do this."

Driving down Main Street, she thought how little the place had changed. Ten years later and every stone and storefront seemed exactly the same. Time had stood still.

She pulled into a space in front of the Hoechler Building where Gabe's office was, got out and fed coins into the parking meter.

"Jill? Jill Danvers? Is that you?"

At the sound of her name, Jill turned and squinted at the tall, willowy blonde who walked up to her. Her stomach knotted. *Jennie Foster, the biggest gossip in high school.*

Jennie pulled off her sunglasses and stared at Jill. "Well, this is quite a surprise. Long time, no see."

And with good reason. "How are you? You look great."

Jennie's stick figure had filled out so she now had curves. Her hair, now a lustrous shade of champagne instead of dishwater dull, framed her oval face and her outfit complemented her lightly tan skin. The whole ensemble screamed *money.*

"Oh, thanks, but you know, it's a constant struggle." She laughed. "Although three kids will keep you from sitting around too much."

"Three children?"

"Yes, indeed." She waved her left hand at Jill, the diamond wedding band and engagement rings flashing in the sunlight. "Married Jim Schroyer when we graduated A&M and the kids just started popping out." She laughed again, an easy, unselfconscious sound.

"It's good to see you," Jill said, surprising herself.

"Same here. I'll tell you, I wasn't sure we'd ever see you around here again. You know, the way your aunt and uncle swept you off after your folks died."

Jill wondered if anyone in Bluebonnet Falls had guessed the real reason she'd left and never come back. She and Gabe had kept pretty much to themselves so their big romance—or whatever it was—hadn't been front-page news. By September, things had changed. The death of her parents had provided her with a plausible excuse to leave.

"Well," Jennie went on, "are you planning to stay for the big celebration? It's not for a couple of weeks yet."

"Yes, I am. I'm doing an article about it for *Life in America*. I came early to do some research about the town's history and interview some of the people involved with the event."

"Wow! That's just too great." Jennie eyed her shrewdly. "I guess you'll be meeting with Gabe Carter about it, since he's the chairman."

"Yes." With an effort, Jill kept her voice calm. "As a matter of fact, I'm on my way to see him right now."

"Great. Good luck."

Good luck?

Jennie hugged Jill briefly. "Lordy, wait 'til I tell everyone. Jill Danvers back in Bluebonnet Falls. Wow."

Jill watched Jennie clip-clop down the street in her sandals, fishing a cell phone from her purse. The woman was busy punching in numbers and seconds later had the phone pressed to her ear.

So much for trying to keep a low profile. By tonight everyone in the Falls would know Jill Danvers was back in town. Smoothing imaginary wrinkles from her skirt with nervous fingers, she walked into the building. As she rode the elevator to the third floor, she counted to ten then twenty. Anything to calm herself.

In a minute, she would be facing the sexiest man she'd ever met. The one who still held her heart even if he didn't know it. She had to keep reminding herself he was married to someone else and out of reach. She swallowed a sigh.

Get serious. Gabe Carter is just another man.

Yeah, right. And the Grand Canyon is just another ditch.

Then the elevator whooshed open. She walked the few steps to his suite of offices and pushed open the door. And caught her breath.

Gabe stood at the reception desk, talking to the woman seated there. At Jill's approach, he looked up and smiled. "Hi. Can I help you?"

That deep voice rumbled from his chest and long-forgotten waves of desire washed over her.

Just her luck that after all this time he was more mouthwatering than ever. His tall, muscular body was still trim, his hair a deeper golden brown, the laugh lines on his face more prominent. The sleeves of his soft cotton dress shirt, ocean blue like the color of his eyes, were rolled back at the cuffs, exposing tan forearms with a light dusting of golden hair. Jill needed every ounce of willpower not to throw herself at him.

She swallowed against an instant panic attack and took a calming breath. "Hello, Gabe. Nice to see you again."

His eyes widened and he stared at her with an expression close to shock. He reached out and took her hand. "Jill? My God, is that really you?"

"In person."

His gaze raked her from head to toe. She knew what he saw. She was still slim but she had filled out so now she had curves, rounder breasts and hips that flared just enough. Her makeup was more sophisticated and she knew the green of her simple tailored outfit complemented her eyes and brought out the auburn highlights of her thick chestnut hair. She had taken great pains to create the image she wanted to project to him, to let him know what could have been hers.

She felt naked under his penetrating look. Ten years hadn't put out the blaze that roared through her the minute he touched her. Maintaining her professional poise took superhuman effort. *This might turn out to be a lot more difficult than I thought.*

His hand was warm against hers, reminding her of the last time he'd touched her in intimate places. The last time they'd made love. She'd never forgotten the feel of those slightly roughened hands gliding over her skin, touching her in intimate places, teaching her what love was about.

"Well." He released her hand with obvious reluctance. "You certainly have grown up, haven't you?" He grinned, a dimple flashing at one corner of his mouth.

"Haven't we all." She tried to match his nonchalance.

"Christy." He turned to the woman at the desk. "You may not remember Jill Danvers. She was a year or so ahead of you in school, I think. Jill, this is Christy Malone. The heart and soul of the office."

Christy blushed at the compliment.

Jill smiled. "Nice to meet you."

"Same here. Gabe's been looking forward to seeing you again." Her eyes flashed. "We're all so excited you're writing about the big event. Won't that just put us on the map?"

"Well, that's my intention." *So Gabe's been looking forward to seeing me, has he? If only it were for the right reasons.*

"Hold my calls until we're done," he told Christy. "Come on, Jill. Let's go into my office and talk."

His hand rested just at the small of her back as he guided her out of the reception area. Her skin burned where he touched her and images of his naked skin next to hers and his hands stroking her flashed through her mind. As memories aroused her body, her panties dampened and her nipples tightened.

Not good.

With an effort she blanked her mind.

The office reflected the man well, solid and with a strong sense of masculinity. Lots of leather and wood, with rich brown carpeting to soften footsteps. Western-themed art hung on the wall and appeared to have been selected to reflect the geography of the area. But the absence of any personal photos struck her as odd. Not of Robin, or their child or the three of them as a family.

Interesting. What does that mean?

She moved toward one of the chairs in front of the desk but Gabe motioned to the couch against one wall.

"We don't need to be so formal, do we? After all, we're not exactly strangers."

That's the problem. I wish we were.

"You're right," she said instead. "But it has been a long time since we've seen each other."

"Too long." He flashed his gorgeous white teeth at her again. "Lord, Jill, it's so good just to look at you."

"You look pretty sharp yourself." There. She had just the right tone of nonchalance. "I gather from these digs your law practice is flourishing."

He leaned back against the couch, one leg crossed over the other, one arm thrown along the back. "I have to admit I'm happy with the way things are going."

"And Robin? How is she these days?"

Gabe's jaw tightened and his eyes darkened. "Robin? She's fine, I guess. I'm sure she'll be interested to know you asked about her."

"Well, give her my best." *Along with a pint of hemlock.*

Robin Fletcher and Gabe had been a long-standing couple through high school and college. Before That Summer. Following her graduation from the University of Texas, Robin had taken off to spend three months in Maine with relatives.

'I think she's in a snit,' he'd told Jill when she'd asked. *'About?'*

'We're examining our priorities. I told her some days I feel swept along on an uncontrollable tide.' He'd grinned. *'A tide named Robin. She didn't take it too well.'*

So Gabe, with one semester of law school left, had been at a loose end. Without Robin in the picture, the summer had belonged to them. They'd hardly mixed with anyone at all, unwilling to share even a minute with anyone else. In those three short months Jill's life had turned upside down. She'd fallen in love with Gabe and her parents had been killed in a highway crash.

Even after ten years, the day of the funeral was still burned into her mind—and not just because of the grief.

* * * *

Ten years earlier

It seemed the whole town turned out for the Danverses' funeral. Afterward, they filled the house to express condolences and sympathy. Jill had stood graveside between her aunt Karen and Uncle Joe, numb with despair and craving the feel of Gabe's arms around her. When he walked into the house he gave her a brief hug, murmured soothing words and said he'd be there when everyone left.

She was in the kitchen pouring coffee for herself when she heard Robin's mother and another woman on the other side of the door.

"I see Robin's home."

"Yes, just last week. We wanted her to have this summer after graduation before she starts working."

"I guess she and Gabe will be announcing their engagement?"

"Oh, of course. I'm hoping for a December wedding. The holidays are a great time for a celebration, don't you think? Although for some reason Robin wants a quiet one right away."

The words ripped Jill's heart open. *How can this be true?* Forgetting the coffee, she went in search of the man who'd whispered exquisite words of love and the future to her, only to find him on the patio with his arms around Robin in a lover's embrace.

Sick at what she saw, she ran from the house, away from everyone, trying to swallow the flood of tears.

Even when he spotted her and called after her, she kept on running. *So much for all Gabe's wonderful promises.* Maybe to him it had been nothing more than a way to pass the summer until Robin got back. Maybe everything was a lie, couched to get her into bed.

Gabe found her sitting on a bench in the park.

"Get away from me," she snapped. "I hate you — you are such a liar."

"Jill, please." He crouched down in front of her. "There are things going on I can't tell you."

"Things that made you lie to me?" She spat the words out.

"They weren't a lie." His voice was low. "I promise you that."

"Then why are you marrying Robin?" She managed to hold back the tears.

"You'll find out soon enough, but I can't tell you now. Please believe me."

"Not any more. I believed you once. Look where it got me." She jerked away from him and ran into the deepest part of the park. She hoped he'd follow her then hoped he wouldn't. When she discovered she was still alone she stopped running and allowed herself the luxury of a good cry.

By the time she returned to the house, everyone was gone. Uncle Joe and Aunt Karen were waiting with worried looks and a note from Gabe that said only *We have to talk. I'll try to explain.*

Explain what? He'd said he couldn't tell her the reason.

"He's called several times," Aunt Karen said. "He waited for you as long as he could, but then he had to leave. He said he'd keep trying until he got you. Honey, I don't know what's wrong but shouldn't you at least talk to him?"

"I did." She stared at her hands in misery. "We have nothing left to say to each other."

"Jill." Aunt Karen put her arms around her. "This has been a tough week for you. Today you buried your parents. Maybe you're blowing things out of proportion. Whatever is wrong between you and Gabe, at least give the man a hearing?"

Maybe. And maybe not. She was still crying tears of anguish for her parents, but then to see Gabe with Robin that way, to overhear the conversation...

Jill crumpled the paper and threw it into the trash. "All right. If he calls, I'll talk to him."

She ran upstairs and curled up on her bed, tears welling again in her eyes and choking her raw throat. Somehow exhaustion claimed her and she dozed off. When she woke, her room was filled with darkness broken only by the shaft of light from the street lamp shining through her window. She splashed cold water on her face in her bathroom, blew her nose and pulled her hair into a ponytail before going in search of her aunt and uncle. She'd made a decision and she needed to act on it before she changed her mind.

"I'm going back to San Antonio with you," she told them when she had herself somewhat composed. "Can I stay with you until I find a place of my own?"

"Of course, honey," Uncle Joe told her. "As long as you like. But Gabe..."

"I'll talk to him. I said I would. But that's all. I want to leave here." The phone was ominously silent. *So much for his need to talk to me.*

She spent most of the night packing everything she could fit into her car, anxious for them all to get an early start. The faster she left Bluebonnet Falls, the faster she could get away from the pain of her parents' death and Gabe's betrayal.

When the doorbell rang, she figured it was her neighbor coming for the extra key. But when she pulled the door open, Gabe stood on the porch looking as if his night hadn't been much better than hers. His clothes were rumpled and his eyes were red-rimmed and shadowed. Deep lines were carved into his face and he badly needed a shave.

"Go away." She started to shut the door.

"Robin's pregnant," he blurted out. "Four months."

Jill stared at him, the pain in her chest like a sharp sword. "Get the hell away from me." She slammed the door and ran up the stairs, holding her hands over her ears as the doorbell rang again. "Don't answer it," she yelled. "Do not open that door."

Karen stared up the stairs as the doorbell rang again and a fist pounded on the heavy wood. "What shall I tell Gabe?"

"Tell him…oh, tell him to go to hell."

A week later, with a perverse need to enhance the pain squeezing her heart, she did an Internet search and in seconds a picture of the new Mr. and Mrs. Gabriel Carter stared up at her. When a magazine offered her a job as a travel writer if she'd spend a year in Europe, she took it. The only way to keep her fragile heart from shattering altogether was to stay as far away from Gabriel Carter as she could, and never see him again.

* * * *

So, of course, here she was, hoping time and distance had changed her feelings and realizing from the first moment what a false hope she held. She prayed she wouldn't disgrace herself by falling apart and demanding answers from him, answers she knew she didn't want to hear.

Jill shook herself from her unpleasant reverie. *Back to business.*

"So," she said in the brightest tone of voice she could manage, "the Falls is having its bicentennial. And you're the chairman."

"That's me. But it's a job I'm enjoying. I love this town, you know." He squinted through the big window facing Main Street. "I took a position with a law firm in Dallas after I passed the bar, but then my dad developed some heart problems and needed to retire. He and Mom built a beautiful place over near Blanco and I came home and took over the practice. You know what they say." He smiled. "Home's where the heart is."

"That's what they say." She pasted a smile on her face. "Didn't quite work for me, though."

A flash of something crossed his face. "You've never sold the house," he commented.

Ah yes. The house. Where they'd made glorious love in her bedroom whenever they had the chance. "Uncle Joe thought I should hang on to it and rent it out. Said real estate was going to go way up in the Falls."

"I'd say he's a smart man. Available land's pretty scarce around here. Developers are paying a fancy price for it." He crossed and uncrossed his legs. "I notice the house is empty now. Looking for new tenants? If not, I can hook you up with one of the developers and see what he offers you."

Renting it out would certainly be the smart thing to do. Better than what she was actually planning. She hadn't thought she'd ever want to set foot in it again. Now some perverse devil had nudged her into staying there during her time in the town.

"Not yet. The lease was up on the last tenants and I decided to camp out there while I'm in town."

His jaw dropped. "You're going to *live* in it?"

She frowned. "Is there some reason why I shouldn't?"

"No. Not at all." She wasn't sure if his face showed surprise or displeasure.

"All the furniture's still there, though I'm not sure what shape it's in." She gave him a rueful smile. "I guess I'll find out."

"Don't you think you'd be more comfortable in a motel?" he persisted.

"No. This is what I want to do." She needed one last chance to rid her mind of all the ghosts. Her cheeks heated and her heart skipped in an erratic rhythm. She dug deep for her 'journalist' face. "Why don't you tell me more about the big celebration and show me what you've got lined up? Then I can do some preliminary research before the event."

"Sure. I've got everything ready." The professional voice was back again.

He stood, unfolding his tall frame in a familiar way that made her heart ache, picked up a folder from his desk and brought it back to the couch. Sitting so close their thighs were touching, he spread the pages out on the coffee table.

Jill swallowed hard, feeling the heat of his body through her thin skirt, and forced her mind to focus. *Remember*, she told herself, *don't screw your assignment by falling into Gabe Carter's arms again. He's a married man. Keep that in mind.*

"The historical committee has pulled together a list of the important dates in the town's past," he told her. "Something special's planned to celebrate each one." He picked up a sheet of paper. "Here's a preliminary list."

His hand brushed Jill's as he handed her the schedule and she almost snatched it away.

Cool it. Remember. Poised and professional. He did what any honorable man would do, so show him you've been able to deal with it.

"This looks quite ambitious." She hoped her voice didn't sound as shaky to him as it did to her. "Will the committee be able to give me background on all of this?"

"Yes. As a matter of fact, they asked to meet with you." He pointed to the bottom of the sheet she was reading. "Ernie Hoffman is the chairman. There's his number."

"Okay. Good. Thanks." The scent of Gabe's aftershave drifted past her nose and she couldn't seem to get more than single syllables out of her mouth.

She looked up at the exact instant Gabe turned toward her. Their eyes locked and her heart stopped beating.

"Jill." His voice was low, seductive.

"Yes?" *Don't touch me or I'll fall apart.*

It happened so fast she had no time to think. He reached for her shoulders, the feel of his fingers on her skin like branding irons, and the room disappeared.

"Forget the celebration for a minute." His face was close enough to count his eyelashes. "I told myself I'd keep my hands off you, but I feel as if I've waited forever for this. I have to find out if you still taste as good as I remember."

He brought his mouth down to hers and she fell apart. All the resolve in the world didn't help her. The barest touch and she was on fire for him. His lips were soft but demanding and his tongue probed the seam of her lips.

"Open for me, Jill," he whispered.

Without thinking she opened her mouth to accept his tongue.

Ten years fell away and in her mind they weren't on the couch but back on a blanket under the trees at Bluebonnet Lake. Hidden away in a copse, the moon their lantern sending its silver light washing over their naked bodies. Gabe's mouth tasting her everywhere — her lips, her breasts, between her thighs. His fingers stroking her — inside her, opening her, driving her crazy.

Warning, warning! flashed in her brain. *Wrong, wrong, wrong.* But she was past thinking, past reasoning. All she wanted to do was feel.

She moved her tongue with his in a remembered dance. The kiss went on and on, sucking every bit of energy out of her. When he lifted his head, he shifted their bodies until her legs were draped over his lap, and looked at her eyes as if he were memorizing them.

"God, Jill." His words shocked her. "You have no idea how much I've prayed that, despite every bit of bitterness you had a right to feel, you'd still walk back into my life one day." He traced a line from her mouth to her jawline with feathery little kisses then moved to her neck and the place behind her ear that drove her crazy. As he teased the soft flesh with the tip of his tongue, he used his body to press her back against the couch, moving one hand easily to the buttons on her blouse.

I have to remember something important. What? What?

Then his hands were on her, gentle but insistent, and she lost all ability to think. Peeling away the blouse and opening the front clasp on her bra, allowed him to touch her breasts with a gentleness she'd never forgotten. He closed his mouth on a nipple, teasing it with his teeth then swirling his tongue around the hardened bud. Sensation washed over her, sparking her nerve endings, spiraling through her.

"Jesus, I've missed you," he whispered, his voice hoarse. "Not a night has gone by that you weren't in my dreams."

Jill clutched at him, feeling his powerful muscles beneath the soft cotton of his shirt, the heat searing her palms. Memories of how well their bodies had fit together played havoc with her mind and her senses. Suddenly his clothes were too much of an obstruction. With frantic movements, she tugged his shirt free from his trousers, desperate for his skin, to relearn the feel of him. The instant contact fogged her mind.

With one arm tight around her, Gabe moved his free hand in slow caresses over her body, as if he was mapping it, relearning it. He touched the familiar places, from her breasts to the curve of her stomach, down to her slim legs and up to the inside of her knees, her thighs. Beneath the thin fabric of the skirt, he used his fingertips to tease at the elastic edge of her lace panties. All the while he murmured soft words in her ear, words that inflamed her and made her writhe against him.

Without thinking, she opened her legs to give him greater access. He deepened the kiss as he reached beneath the scrap of silk to the soft curls covering her mound. She felt him now, touching, probing, her breath coming in shorter and shorter gasps.

Then the painful memory of his betrayal blasted into her brain along with the reality of the situation, shocking her. *What on earth is wrong with me?* She had no business doing this. There was too much bad history between them. She wasn't even sure she knew him anymore. Wrenching her mouth away from his insistent lips, she pushed at him with all her strength.

"Stop," she gasped. "Stop, stop, stop. Let me up, Gabe. Right now." She writhed in his grasp, trying to get free.

"What? What's wrong?" He blinked and shook his head. "Jesus, Jill. I'm so damn sorry. I didn't mean to grab you this way. The truth is, from the minute you walked in the door, all I could think of was making love to you."

She shoved at him, pushing away. "We can't do this. Please."

He leaned forward while she adjusted herself, raking his fingers through his hair. When he spoke again, his voice was raw with passion and frustration. "Help me understand here. We'd both be lying if we said what we felt so long ago isn't still there. Ten years haven't made a damn bit of difference." He drew in a sharp, ragged breath. "You may have hidden from me all this time but you can't hide the fact you feel it too."

She bowed her head, biting her lower lip as she struggled to fasten and rearrange her clothing. "It doesn't matter. We can't do this. It's wrong."

"Wrong?" He grabbed her chin and forced her to look at him. "Tell me what's wrong with it. It doesn't get much more right than this. It never did."

She knew he was going to kiss her again and she jerked her head away. "I don't sleep with married men, Gabe."

"Married?" He dropped his hand. "What in God's name are you talking about? Who's married?"

"You are." Defiance gripped her. "To Robin Fletcher. Remember?" Her made her voice mimic his from long ago. "'Robin's pregnant. Four months'. Has the little scene somehow disappeared from your memory bank?"

Gabe rose from the couch and stood before her, looming over her, his expression a mixture of shock and anger. "I'm not married, Jill. Maybe if you'd bothered to keep in touch, you'd have found out. Robin and I were divorced two months after the wedding."

Chapter Two

Jill stared at him, wondering if she'd been dropped into the middle of a bad dream she couldn't wake up from. Or been plunged into another time warp. *Did I hear right?* Of course he and Robin were married. And they had a child. Would she have turned her back on the town where she grew up otherwise?

"What are you talking about? She was pregnant. You told me yourself."

Gabe clenched his fists at his sides and blew out a breath. "Listen to me, Jill. I. Am. Not. Married."

"B-But the baby…"

A brief slash of pain crossed his face. "She lost it a month after the wedding. I was out of town and her folks were away, so she had to go through it by herself. One of her girlfriends helped her. When I got back, we just sat and looked at each other, unable to ignore the sadness. And something else. If she'd had the baby, we'd probably still be married, but it wouldn't have been good. After eight years together, we were more like a pair of shoes on their way to being worn-out than two people who should be married to each other."

Jill cast her gaze down at her hands folded in her lap. "I'm sorry, Gabe. Terribly sorry."

His body was rigid with tension. "Maybe you'd have known we were divorced if you'd bothered to keep in touch with me. Or anyone in this town."

"You could have come after me. Found me."

"I did."

The words were so low she almost didn't hear them. "What?"

"I was afraid your aunt and uncle would have me arrested as a stalker, I pestered them so much. They told me you didn't want to see me and that was that."

And she hadn't. She'd made them promise. No contact, no matter what.

"It doesn't matter now. It's over."

Gabe reached down and hauled her to her feet, his grip perhaps a little too tight. "No, darlin', it's far from over. I haven't had a good relationship in more than nine years. And do you know why?"

"No."

His fingers on her arms were like steel. "Because the one woman I wanted to marry wouldn't even let me get in touch with her."

It was true. She had avoided him, unwilling to listen to whatever excuses he might make. Or worse yet, see him 'for old times' sake'.

"Well?" he pushed.

"I-I don't know what you want me to say."

"I want you to tell me why you wouldn't at least take a call from me? Circumstances got in our way, but I thought we had something very special going for us."

"You got married."

"And divorced."

"Please." She wet her lower lip. "You're hurting me."

He let her go so fast she fell back onto the couch.

"Things were a mess after the miscarriage. Robin left for Atlanta and I went to work for a firm in Dallas after graduation."

She drew a breath. "So. Do you ever see Robin anymore?"

He shrugged. "Now and then. Every once in a while she comes home to visit her folks and we have dinner together. She spends most of her time in Atlanta, decorating people's houses."

"Oh." Jill waited a beat. "I'm surprised she never remarried."

"She did. Twice." He turned and looked out of the window, his hands in his pockets. "I hear this second one's on shaky ground. I guess she can't figure out what she wants."

Oh, I know what she wants all right. And so do you, if you'd admit it.

"You never remarried, either."

Gabe turned back to her, his eyes darkening. "The person I wanted to marry wasn't around. I spent months—no, years—keeping track of you, trying to contact you. Tell me, Jill, did you leave the same message every place you went? Hang up on Gabe Carter?"

Yes. I had to.

As she'd moved from job to job, the message she'd left at the switchboard was always the same. *'If a man named Gabriel Carter ever calls, don't put him through. And don't tell me about it.'*

"Gabe…"

"When I knew you were coming here, I thought maybe we had a chance to try to build something again."

"Gabe, we're not even the same people anymore." She managed to pull herself together. "What's done is done. Let's leave it at that."

"Don't tell me you were faking what just happened here." A muscle twitched in his cheek. "Or almost happened. It's still there, Jill. Just like it was from the beginning. But I guess I don't get more than one chance with you, right?" He slammed his fist on his desk. "God damn it, anyway. When I told you I loved you, it wasn't some big line. I never expected what happened to happen. You have a right to be bitter, but maybe if you'd at least talked to me we wouldn't have wasted the last ten years."

He was so angry at her she didn't know how to handle it. She had to get out of his office right now and try to get some perspective on things. She rose from the couch as with as much grace as possible and adjusted her clothes then bent to shuffle the papers back into the folder.

"I think we should schedule another meeting, probably in a more public place. In the meantime I'll get myself settled, call Ernie Hoffman and arrange to meet with him."

Gabe stood in the middle of his office, hands thrust into his pockets, rage still stamped across his face. "Fine. Go ahead. Go on, run. Just like you did ten years ago. Get the hell out of here."

Her head spun and her hands trembled as she gathered her things. Her legs were not quite steady as she made for the closed door. She had turned away from him and reached for the door knob when he spoke again.

"What are you afraid of, Jill? And what were you afraid of then? How far will you run this time?"

She opened the door and walked through it, keeping as much of her dignity intact as she could.

* * * *

Gabe wanted to pound more than his desk. He didn't remember the last time he'd been this angry. All the anguish he'd kept buried for so long was bubbling to the surface and consuming him. When he'd received the letter from the editor of *Life in America* he'd been excited at what it could mean for the town. His town. Discovering that Jill would be doing the story was a bonus, an opportunity for him to talk to her face-to-face after all this time, tell her he'd never stopped loving her. Ask for another chance.

His intention had been to greet her with polite warmth, get to work on her article with her and try to pick up the pieces of their relationship he'd shattered in such an abrupt manner. She'd closed the door on him with such ruthlessness he wasn't sure if she'd even be willing to try again. He was leery of putting himself out there until he saw how she felt.

But the minute he'd laid eyes on her, that all had flown out of the window. Gone, like a puff of smoke. He wanted her with the same ferocity which had gripped him that entire fateful summer. All the women since then hadn't quenched the desire the slightest bit.

Even lying in his bed at night with his eyes closed, he could imagine the feel of her soft satiny skin with its golden tan. His fingers itched to touch the silken threads of her hair, rich with highlights. But most of all, he wanted to bury himself again in that sensuous, lush body that she'd given to no one but him. To feel her slick walls close around his erection as he stroked her heat, carrying them both to climax. See the blaze in her emerald eyes in the afterglow of joining as their bodies eased down from an incredible high.

It had been the worst coincidence of fate that, as Jill had been grieving the tragic death of her parents, Robin had hit him with the news of her pregnancy and everything had blown up. But not even to accept a phone call from him all these years… Yes, he'd hurt her. He'd known it then and he knew it now.

Go slow, he'd warned himself. So what had he done? Attacked her with no finesse at all, then started a fight with her. *Way to go, Gabe. Very smooth.* How in hell would he ever get a chance to make it up to her if she kept running from him?

Would she call her editor and ask to have someone else assigned to the article? The thought lay hard and cold in his stomach.

He blew out a breath.

God, he couldn't believe how much he still wanted her. He had more to concern him, however, than the possibility of her rejection. The sex had been great between them from the very beginning — hot and demanding. But in ten years, his sexual tastes and habits had grown and changed. Become more insistent and sophisticated. That meant holding back a lot if he got the chance to make love to her again. *Can I do that? Damn straight, if it means being with her again.* He'd call on every bit of control he had. At least for a while. Maybe for a long while.

If he acknowledged that, he also had to recognize that his pride would have to take a back seat. Angry words and a shouting match weren't going to win him any points.

He wouldn't call her. The phone at the house was probably not connected. He had her business card with her cell number, but he wasn't sure she'd pick up. *This calls for a planned attack. In person.*

But first he had to deal with Gary Armstrong, a recent client who wanted to know why his investment in the newest development in Falls wasn't returning any money.

* * * *

Jill backed out of her parking space with slow deliberation and turned down Main Street.

Not married. Not married. Not married.

The words played over and over in her head like a bad song that wouldn't fade away. Gabe had been right. If she'd just forced herself to talk to him when everything had happened, she might have known this a long time ago. But her stupid pride had made her do some very dumb things. Now Gabe was as angry with her as she'd been with him then.

Well, doesn't this really suck?

But just as she'd told him, they were two different people now. Their lives had changed. If they still had feelings, the episode in Gabe's office aside, could they be anything more than how good they were together in bed? When he'd broken her heart, she'd purged him from her life with ruthless efficiency. Could she find a way to maintain that distance?

She reminded herself that she really knew nothing about the Gabe of today. What was his role in the community? Who were his friends? What did he do in his free time? How had he become so successful? With all those questions tumbling in her brain, she gave herself a mental smack. She'd come back here to find answers and now she wasn't sure she even knew the right questions to ask.

Realizing she'd get nothing more done today with her mind in such turmoil, she decided to focus on settling herself in at the house. The big backyard, always a peaceful haven, was just the place to let her mind air out. She'd help it along with some nice white wine.

When she stopped at Majors' Market to pick up some groceries, the gossip line had already begun its work. Allie Majors was more direct and forthcoming than Jennie had been. She wanted chapter and verse on Jill's life since she'd left and every detail of what she was doing in town after all these years. Of course the other customers had their own questions, as much about her personal life as the article she was writing. Using all her public relations skills, Jill managed to escape, answering as few questions as possible. She wasn't ready just yet to share her life with the town.

She smiled when she pulled into the wide driveway beside the old two-story house, happy to see the building still had a Victorian and queenly air, despite its age. She'd had it painted the previous year and a landscaping service kept the yard maintained. When she unlocked the front door a wave of musty air smacked her in the face, so she went about opening windows to let the breeze blow through. She'd turn the air conditioning on later.

The tenants had not done much damage to anything, thank heavens. And she was grateful they had made at least a haphazard effort at cleaning before they'd moved out. A little elbow grease and some good household products would take care of the rest. In less than an hour she had the house well on its way to being aired out, fresh linens on the beds and she was relaxing in the backyard in shorts and a T-shirt, sipping a glass of wine. Maybe she could sit there long enough to stop thinking about anything and tomorrow she'd have better control of herself. She did have a job to do, after all.

But hanging out in the yard didn't help much. Every place she looked had memories of time she and Gabe had spent there. Why didn't he understand how hurt she'd been over what she saw as his betrayal? The pain she'd clutched to herself all these years was the only thing she had to remember her feelings for him.

And how sick is that?

Three glasses of wine later, the sun had dipped below the horizon and evening shadows were streaking the trees when a cough woke her from the light doze she'd fallen into. She jerked upright, wine sloshing onto her hand, and turned her head.

Her eyes widened.

Gabe Carter stood at the gate to the yard wearing jeans, a clean chambray shirt and a hopeful expression on his face. In his hands he held a bouquet of seasonal flowers, a large box of chocolates and a six-pack of wine coolers. She burst out laughing. She couldn't help herself. He had recreated every detail of his arrival for their first real date. At first she wanted to tell him what he could do with his peace offerings, but he looked so mouthwateringly good she thought twice about cutting off her nose to spite her face.

"I think I need to apologize for my earlier bad behavior." His lips turned up in a tentative grin. "Is it safe to come in?"

"At least for the moment." She rose from the lounge chair and went to unlatch the gate, almost afraid to be near him again. "I'll take the presents, anyway."

He followed her into the yard, to set the wine coolers and candy on the low table next to the lounge and hand her the flowers.

"They smell wonderful." She glanced up at him, her voice a little unsteady. "Let me just put them in water and get another wineglass. Have a seat."

"Jill?" There was no teasing humor on his face now.

"Yes?" She raised an eyebrow, watching him.

"I'm sorry. About ten years ago. About today. About a lot of things."

Sorry. She was sorry too. *For a lot of things.* And underneath it all she didn't want him to leave. Too bad she had no idea exactly what she *did* want.

Her hands shook as she found a vase in the kitchen, filled it with water and arranged the flowers. She hadn't expected this at all. Gabe, here in her backyard. Waiting for her. What did he want? After the blowup in his office, she had dreaded seeing him again. She was damn glad the wine she'd drunk had relaxed her, but she couldn't afford to let her guard down. One wine cooler and she'd send him on his way.

Yeah, right.

Yes, right. Be smart.

She held out the vase of flowers.

"I thought I'd bring these out here until later. I can't look at them if they're in the house."

Gabe rose to take the vase from her and their fingers made light contact. They stared at each other, both seemingly shocked by the intensity that ghost of a touch generated. With great care he lowered the vase to the table, his eyes never leaving hers, then pulled her against his body.

For an instant she stiffened, remembering her promise to herself to be careful of just this kind of thing. There was so much bad history coloring everything. She should be sensible. Guarded. Controlled. But the damn magic was still there, even after all these years, and her brain just disconnected from her body. Calling herself all kinds of a fool, she leaned into him. With their bodies glued together, she felt every inch of him, from his broad shoulders to his firm belly to his strong thighs and the bulge of his cock pressing against the fabric of his jeans. He bent his head toward her, waiting a fraction of a second, perhaps to see if she objected before he captured her mouth with his.

His lips were warm and firm brushing against hers and his teeth nibbled gently. When he pressed his tongue against the seam of her lips, she opened for him and he swept inside, touching every inch of wet flesh. Gripping her shoulders, he held her tight against him while he devoured her mouth.

He skated one hand down from her shoulder to cup a breast through the thin material of her T-shirt, the nipple resting in his warm palm. It hardened and strained against the fabric as if seeking a permanent home in his hand. When he gave it a gentle squeeze she moaned into his mouth, a soft sound. Then he was stroking her back and reaching down to palm her buttocks, kneading the flesh with his long fingers.

God, how she remembered that touch. Her body craved it now as much as it had then. When she pressed herself harder against him, he eased his hand upward and into the waistband of her shorts. The thickness of his hot erection burned into her and she rubbed her mound against him, wishing the jeans would disappear.

Gabe lifted his head an inch, still so close his breath dusted her face. "Don't send me away. Please. I've waited all these years for a chance with you again."

"W-Waited? Really?" *Can I believe him?*

"Damn straight, which you'd know if you'd ever taken my calls or read my letters." Desire flashed in his eyes, and need. "Jill, either tell me to stop, or we're taking this into the house. No way am I going to do what I have in mind out here on the lawn so the neighbors can have a show."

Tell him to stop. Now. I cannot lose control, not with everything that stands between us. No, no, no.

"I-Inside," she whispered, as needy Jill took over.

He nodded and picked her up in his arms to carry her into the house as he had done so many times that long-ago summer. It seemed the way to her bedroom wasn't something he'd forgotten. He snapped on the lamp and stood her beside the bed, studying her for a moment with a hot, hungry look in his eyes before undressing her with slow, deliberate care.

She shivered in anticipation as he removed each item of clothing, the gentle movement of air drifting in from the open window raising gooseflesh on her exposed skin. He touched every inch of her — her shoulders, her breasts, her nipples, the indentation of her waist. He skimmed her navel, a light dab with the tips of his fingers, before following a path to the curls covering her mound. With a gentle stroke, he followed the line of her cunt, nudging her thighs apart to give him easy access.

How many nights during that summer had they spent in this room while her folks had traipsed around the country in their RV or were off on golf weekends? They'd explored each other's bodies, learning the many ways to give the other pleasure. She wanted to be angry with him, to tell him of the misery she'd suffered, to make the blame all his. But he'd come calling tonight with flowers and chocolates and a kiss that had seared her down to her toes.

And just like that the years were gone as if they'd never happened.

So much for my resolution not to do this.

At least for one moment in time she could be with him.

She stood there, trembling, naked to his eyes and his touch, eager for him to take her once again to a place of unbelievable pleasure.

"You," she whispered. "I want you naked, too."

She unfastened the top two snaps on his shirt but he brushed her away with an impatient gesture. In seconds, his clothes lay in a heap on the floor and the two of them were skin to skin for the first time in years. As he had done to her, she ran her hands over his body, marveling at the feel of tight muscle and hard planes. Of soft curly hair matting his chest and arrowing down to a magnificent erection. She nearly swallowed her tongue when she saw his penis jutting proud and straight from his groin.

He cradled her face in his big, warm palms. "You should now something before this goes any further."

"What is it?" She was almost afraid to hear the answer.

"I'm, ah, a lot more adventurous in the kind of sex I like these days."

She had to swallow a laugh. *Wait until he discovers how adventurous I am now.*

"Show me," she whispered.

He kissed her again then lifted her. "I want to see you," he told her in a soft voice. "I have to see you. I feel like a man who's been starved and now the banquet awaits him."

He placed her on the bed with sweet care, positioning her on her back so her knees were bent and her legs wide apart. Then he kneeled on the floor in front of her, used his wide shoulders to separate her thighs even more and gently opened the lips of her cunt as if unwrapping a special package. He knew her body as well as she knew his touch and every dormant nerve rose and fired.

He drew in a breath as he stroked her and his heated gaze rested on her. The roughened pads of his fingers against her sensitive skin sent tiny sparks of electricity through her. When he rubbed the juices from her slit into her tender asshole, she jerked with the touch.

"You used to love this, you know. Remember the first time I slid my fingers inside this hot pussy of yours, felt your cream coating them, stretched you to make you ready for my cock? I almost didn't make it in time—the feel of you in my hands was so good. And now it's even better. Wetter, slicker, more vibrant. I can't decide what I want to slide into you first—my fingers, my tongue or my cock. God, you are an exquisite delight, Jill Danvers."

He slipped his fingers inside her, moving back and forth in a motion so familiar it might have been yesterday instead of all these years later. He reached for that spot so high… *There, no, yes… There…there!* Her muscles clamped down on his touch and her pelvis began to rock.

"Easy, sweetheart. This is just the opening act. The first scene. I want to see every single bit of this gorgeous cunt and ass. Feel it, taste it. Jesus! I've dreamed about this for so long. You can't even begin to imagine the things I want to do to you."

What things, Gabriel? Should I tell you the things I've learned since last we made love? Things I like? Maybe even crave? Things I'm willing to bet they don't do in Bluebonnet Falls. Things I want you to do to me.

With an effort she forced her mind away from unbidden images, visions that heated her blood and made her pussy quiver even more. Oh, God, how she wanted those things with Gabe, but there was no way she could even suggest them.

She made herself lie as still as possible while he probed her, touching every inch of her inner walls, the light rasp of his breath drifting in the air. When he pinched her clit between thumb and forefinger she arched into him, desperate for the rubbing motion she knew would bring her to climax. Her stomach clenched and her juices ran onto his fingers and palm.

Gabe leaned forward and blew a gentle puff of air on her waiting pussy, the soft breeze as erotic as the touch of his hand. When he spoke, she was surprised at how unsteady his voice was.

"Would you like to come, darlin'? Remember how good I always made you feel? I'm going to make you come all right. More times than you can count. And more ways than you can imagine." He drew in a breath and let it out. "I wish…"

He stopped.

Jill raised her head a little, trying to see his face. "What? What is it you wish, Gabe?"

He shook his head. "Nothing. I wish the last ten years belonged to us, that's all." Then he set to his task in earnest.

He stroked his fingers in and out while using his other hand to massage her clit with a touch so light she wanted to scream, *More, more, more.* But she remembered his relentlessness, his gentle but demanding need to always take her as high as he could. Her hips shifted and her pelvis rocked against his hand, his fingers. Every nerve in her body seemed to be centered on her clitoris, vibrating and throbbing.

Back and forth he caressed with his thumb, a tiny pendulum never missing a beat, his fingers exciting her. *More,* her hips urged. *Please, more.*

Then, just as it had so long ago, the release swept up from her lower abdomen, through her heated center. The shudders overtook her as her climax roared up through every part of her body. Gabe pushed her harder and harder, but then at the top of the slide he removed his fingers and held her lips wide open.

She moaned, a long sound of pleading, knowing what he wanted. The first time he'd done this they'd been on this very bed and he'd been kneeling between her thighs and bringing her to climax with his hands, just as he was doing now.

'Let me see you,' he'd begged in a hoarse voice. 'Let me watch when you come, see you quiver and throb and all that wonderful cream pour out. You don't know how many dreams I've had about that.'

She shook as the orgasm overtook her, intense but leaving her unfulfilled. Since that first time together, Gabe had been obsessed with watching her. Knowing his eyes had been on her center as she'd come had only increased the intensity of her release, even as it left her begging for more. *Is he going to do that now?*

"God, your cunt is so beautiful when you come," he whispered. "All deep pink and pulsing and wet. I've dreamed about seeing it just like this for years." He paused. "I…"

"What?" she asked in a strained voice. She wanted to tell him to stop talking and make her come. Why was he talking, when she was so close to falling over the edge? "Is something wrong?"

"No. Everything's just right."

He scraped his fingernail over her swollen nub and she exploded. Her thighs squeezed his broad shoulders, her hips rocketed off the bed and her entire body convulsed. With his upper arms, he pressed her thighs apart, her inner muscles clenching on empty space, seeking something to fill her. Her juices poured out of her and down into the cleft of her buttocks.

He was relentless, as if trying to make up for lost time all at once, driving her, driving her, torturing her clit until she fell back, panting and exhausted, a fine sheen of perspiration covering her body. Tiny aftershocks still rumbled through her sheath and spread into her abdomen and thighs.

Gabe lowered her legs and scooted her farther up on the bed, tracing little feathery kisses along the insides of her thighs, along her belly, across her waist, every place he came to as he moved to lie next to her.

"You taste better than I remember." His voice was heavy with emotion. "Vanilla and spice and woman. I may never let you get to sleep tonight."

They still had so much left unsaid between them, but Jill pushed it out of her mind. Tomorrow she could sort it out. Tonight she just wanted to feel.

Chapter Three

"I fantasize about your breasts."

Gabe was propped up on one elbow, lying full-length beside Jill, holding one breast in his hand, rubbing the tip of one finger back and forth against a berry-red nipple, diamond-hard at his touch, her skin so soft beneath his palm. He kept waiting for her to push him away, to leap off the bed and tell him to get the hell out of her house. But it seemed whatever switch he'd flipped had taken her right back to that summer when they'd been so good together.

Her breasts had been the first part of her body she'd allowed him to see naked, her face shy as she shrugged out of her blouse when he'd unbuttoned it. Her eyes downcast when she let him unclasp her bra in the front seat of his car. The shafts of moonlight slanting in through the window had bathed them in silver. He remembered his mouth had gone dry at once, speech deserting him as his eyes had feasted on the two perfect globes.

He'd touched them with reference, awed at their beauty. At twenty-five he'd been no novice at sex by any means. He'd 'made love', screwed, fucked – the verb depended on his bedmate and the degree of sophistication he'd employed. But there had been something about looking at Jill nude that had been almost sacred.

Seeing her breasts now, after all this time, he was overcome with a desire to suck them dry. He took one ripe bud into his mouth, swirling his tongue around it, his body reacting when she arched up to him. He remembered her breasts being very sensitive, so much so that he could often make her come just by licking and nibbling at them.

His hand on her body registered the even pace of her breathing, slowed now from its frantic speed. He wanted to ravish her in every way he knew and some he might not even know yet. He'd always loved the taste of her cunt and the feel of her sheath as he teased at it. But where before it had been anticipatory foreplay, tonight he was driven by a perverse desire to withhold satisfaction, to bring her to the edge but never let her rocket over it until she begged for release. Until she knew that only he could bring her fulfillment.

There were so many things he wanted to do with this woman. Ten years had brought a lot of changes in his sexual needs and behavior, things he was reluctant to tell her about. The memories they shared were of tender sex, even at its most heated. Not that Jill had ever been averse to trying anything he'd suggested. She'd been far less experienced than he was, but what she'd lacked in knowledge she'd more than made up for in enthusiasm and responsiveness. Whatever he'd wanted to try, she'd been a willing partner, giving as much pleasure as she received.

Would she feel the same way now, if she knew what he longed for? The things that excited him? He had no idea how sophisticated her outlook on sex was now. God, just imagining her in some of the scenarios that ran through his head made him so hard it was painful.

But tonight he just wanted to concentrate on pleasuring her, coaxing responses from her until he'd wrung every last orgasm from her. He wanted to see her skin flush with pleasure and her eyes slumberous with desire, feel that vibrant body come alive under his hands.

A thought pierced him from out of nowhere. In all this time she must have known other men. Right? Slept with them. Men who'd put their hands on the person he'd once claimed as his own. Had their cocks fit the tight glove of her cunt the way she had clutched at his? The thought of her with another man made his gut clench. He wanted to scream with rage.

She's mine! She's mine!

He had to work hard to suppress the urge to manacle her wrists with one of his hands and demand every last detail. Except this was a story he just didn't want to know.

He continued to nuzzle her breasts and palm them, licking and teasing the nipples, grazing them with his teeth. Her breathing, which had slowed from its accelerated pace, was picking up again and delicious little moans escaped her lips, which were bruised from his kisses.

He moved one hand between her thighs, feeling her juices drying on her skin and the neatly trimmed curls at the top of her mound. Watching her with fascinated eyes, he slipped one finger into her heated folds. At the same time, on impulse, he bit down on one nipple, hard but in a playful way. He was stunned at her response, arching up to his mouth and flooding his hand.

So. The grownup Jill likes the bite of pleasure-pain. What else might she like? As he thought about it, his cock hardened even more and he had to dig deep for a measure of control. Tonight he would play. Test her. He wasn't ready to lead her into a more intricate dance until he discovered more about the person she'd become.

Her nipples were now dark red and puffy from his sucking and licking, especially the one he'd used his teeth on. He slid his hand from Jill's hot sex and rubbed the juices on both nipples, pinching the one he hadn't bitten with some force. Again Jill moaned, a cry for more pleasure.

Her body told him that all the attention to her breasts had brought her to a high state of arousal. He coated his fingers again with her cream and painted her lips with it.

"Taste yourself. Just like the finest nectar of the gods."

She licked her lips obediently, eyes half-open and glittering with lust. "I want to taste you, too."

One corner of his mouth turned upward. "You will. Oh, yes, before we're done tonight, you'll have all of my cock in your lovely mouth, those rosebud lips closed around it while your tongue licks at it. But not until I make you come a lot more. Holding back makes it that much better for me."

He shifted to kneel in front of her again, spreading her legs and lifting her pelvis with his large hands. "Time for the second course, darlin'."

He leaned forward, pulled her labia far apart to give him access to inner lips and opening and drove his tongue as far into her as he could get it. Stabbing in and out in a steady motion, rasping it against her silken inner walls, he tasted her cream as it surged into his mouth.

A long, low cry of ecstasy drifted from her and she tried to shift against him, but he held her firm, sucking at her without mercy. When her inner walls began to spasm and her breathing sped, he knew she was close. With deliberation he backed off. He wanted to bring her to the edge again and again before taking her over and giving her the release she craved.

"No…" The sound escaped her in a long, low wail. "Don't stop."

"Easy there."

He licked the entire rim of her opening, just brushing the sensitized skin with the tip of his tongue, drawing more moans and pleas from her. Her flesh was so wet and heated, so delicious-tasting, he wanted to feed on it forever. He nipped a row of little bites, holding her immobile for his mouth to plunder. Whenever she rocked her pelvis he tightened his grip and licked a little harder.

When her tiny inner muscles began to flutter against his tongue, he lifted his head. In protest she pushed against his hands holding her, trying to twist her hips this way and that.

"Please, Gabe." Her voice was tight, her breathing erratic and he knew she was close to the edge again.

"Please what? Tell me what you want."

"Please let me come. Please, Gabe."

"But you already came once," he teased, his own voice none too steady. "Do you want to come again?"

"Yes." Her stomach muscles clenched. "Yes, I do."

"Yes, what?"

"Yes, I want to come again. Now. Please."

"Of course, darlin'. All you had to do was ask."

He leaned down and with slow strokes licked the length of her slit, touching every inch of cream-covered flesh. Her legs, pressed against his shoulders, shook with tension and the muscles of her body flexed as he took her one tiny bit at a time up the spiral.

She rocked against his grip with an increasing tempo that matched his movements. When her whole body tensed, he stiffened his tongue, plunged it as deeply inside her as he could get and pinched her clit with thumb and forefinger. If he hadn't been holding her she would have jackknifed over him as the climax hit her, shaking her body, her inner walls clutching at his tongue.

He licked and stroked her and tugged until the last tiny shiver died away and her body lay limp in his hands. Then he eased up to lie beside her again, pulling her against him and cradling her to his chest.

"Ah, Jill, I've missed this so much. Missed *you*." He kissed her forehead, her cheek, pressed light kisses to her nose and her chin.

And now that you're here with me again I'm not letting you go.

She curled into him, still shivering from her orgasm, her breath little puffs of air against his chest. He smoothed down her spine and the curve of her buttocks, squeezing the globes with a gentle touch, insinuating his leg between hers to provide friction for her swollen pussy.

How have he lived this long without her presence? Maybe the better question is why? She might have hidden behind her hurt and pride, but he hadn't done much better. He managed to talk down opposing lawyers in court. He could have breached her wall of protection if he'd made a strong effort, but he'd used his own pride as a shield.

Now that he had her, he didn't plan to let her go again. Ever. Before long, when he was sure they were on solid footing, he would take the chance and introduce her to sexual pleasures that would make the orgasm she'd just had seem like child's play.

Jill pressed her hands against the soft pelt of hair on Gabe's hard-muscled chest, sliding them back and forth across the fine curls. As exhausted as she was, her body was still craving more. More of his touch, more of his caresses, more of his hands and mouth on her. They had so much time to make up, so much lost to pride and anger.

So much for keeping my cool with him and not giving in. But who am I kidding anyway? Whatever this thing is between us hasn't faded even one single bit in ten years.

His cock, thick and pulsing, pressed against her abdomen as he held her close to his body. Despite the distance of years since he'd last been inside her, she remembered the feeling in vivid detail. How many sleepless hours had she lain there, images of the nights they'd spent together in this bed racing through her mind?

What would Gabriel Carter say if he knew the only way to relieve the aching need those visions created was for her to touch herself with her own fingers and pretend they were his? Would he be turned off by the knowledge that she brought herself to orgasm stimulating her clit and sliding her fingers inside herself?

What if she told him about her selection of vibrators and other toys she'd accumulated? She hadn't been an idiot during the time they'd been together but giving her virginity to Gabe had seemed like the most natural thing to do. Romantic that she was, for her it had been an act of love and the reason his betrayal had hurt so much.

Was it possible they could start over again now, with the shadow of his marriage and the price of her pride hovering in the background? At the moment she didn't know. She only knew her body wanted his as if it was a drug. For now, that would have to be enough.

With slow movements, she slid her hand down, tracing the line of his rib cage, mapping the structure, and down the hard plane of his abdomen, relearning him. At twenty-five, he hadn't been a boy by any means, but this was definitely the body of a mature man. She followed the fine arrow of soft hair to the rigid penis that she'd known in all its magnificence and closed her fingers around the silken skin over the hard steel. With a gentle hand, she slid one fingertip back and forth across the broad head, gathering the bead of moisture she found there and spreading it across the baby-soft skin.

His cock jerked at her touch and a quick shudder raced through his body.

Brushing her free hand across his chest, she touched his flat nipples and they ripened under her caress. She moved her head enough to take one into her mouth, loving the taste of him and the feel of the hard bud against her tongue. When she bit down, just a light touch, he sucked in a breath and pushed his cock harder against her. She wanted to wrap her lips around that thick shaft, but she could tell he was close to the edge and more than anything she wanted him inside her when he came.

Tonight, after you fuck me blind, I'm going to take your magnificent cock into my mouth and suck you dry. You'd be amazed what I've learned in ten years.

"Slow, Jill." His voice sounded like gravel hitting steel and he closed one of his hands over hers as it held his erection.

When he moved his leg, his thigh rode higher against her cunt, pressing against the lips covering her opening. The well of honey, he'd called it. She moved against him, catching his rhythm and stroking his flesh, the hair on his thigh stimulating her sensitized labia so that her juices slicked his skin. One hand found a nipple nestled in the curls and she teased it with a fingertip.

"Jesus, Jill," he rasped, tightening his hold on her.

Resting her head against his shoulder, she licked the line of his jaw. He tasted salty and sweet and the remembered spice of his aftershave tantalized her nose. His skin was smooth, indicating he had shaved before coming over tonight.

Insistent, he nudged her legs apart, rolling her onto her back. He tightened his hand over hers and lifted it from its grip on his cock to move to her mound. Fingers twined in hers, he pushed between her outer lips so her own fingers touched the slick, wet surface of her pussy. He ground the heel of his hand against her clit, sliding back and forth so every nerve connected to that throbbing nub was firing. When she sucked in a breath, she twined his fingers with hers and slid them so they were both in her channel.

"Fuck yourself for me, darlin'," he whispered, moving their hands together.

Jill's circuits went into overload.

"You like that, don't you." The gravelly voice was rough against her ear. "Can you feel my fingers locked with yours? See how it fills you up?"

"Yes," she breathed, moving her hips in infinitesimal thrusts.

She couldn't believe how erotic it felt, but if she'd thought her blood was heated now, his next words raised the temperature even higher.

"Fuck yourself for me, Jill." Using the tip of his tongue, he traced a line from cheekbone to jaw. "Let me feel you do it."

Tiny shock waves cascaded through her. This wasn't the Gabe Carter she'd had such spectacular sex with ten years ago. She didn't even want to think about how and when he'd gotten so good. Then he wiggled his fingers a tiny bit and all thought disappeared, replaced by a surge of sensual heat.

"Come on, baby," he urged. "Move your fingers with mine. Let me feel you finger-fuck that sweet little pussy."

As he moved their joined fingers in and out, back and forth, he used the heel of his hand to torment her clit. Her lowered eyelids shut out everything but sensation as the need grew inside her.

"Open your eyes, Jill." The sound of his voice was uneven and harsh. "Let me see every expression when you come."

He braced one arm against her, his body hot and hard, his warm breath fanning her cheeks, their twined hands moving as one.

Jill couldn't drag her eyes away from his, eyes which were filled with hunger and need and savage want. The tremors began in a slow rhythm then rose in intensity. The orgasm erupted, spreading through every part of her body. Her inner walls clamped down with force on their joined fingers, a rainbow of lights flashed and everything faded way but the here and now. Her. Gabe. This erotic moment.

When the last of the tremors weakened, Gabe reached for the foil packet he'd dropped on the bed earlier, ripped it open with his teeth and sheathed himself with one hand. He moved over her, shifting her still trembling legs to give himself greater access. Then he nudged the head of his shaft against her opening and began a leisurely glide past her swollen outer lips. Her inner muscles, still trembling with aftershocks, gripped him hard.

"Gabe," she moaned.

"Ssh, darlin'. It's all right. You are so ready for me and I can't wait any longer."

He was thicker and harder than she remembered, but the first stroke took her back to that familiar place. At first she just lay there, absorbing him, her body still drained from three powerful orgasms. But then moved with him, slowly at first, savoring the feel of him inside her. His enormous erection rubbed the walls of her channel as with the languid movement of his hips he thrust in and out.

When he shifted position and the broad head found a certain spot, the pulsing began low in her body again. She lifted her legs higher, locking her ankles behind his back and pulling him closer to her, harder, hips moving and thrusting to meet him.

Thrust and retreat. Slowly, slowly, as he built up the need in her again. His forehead held a sheen of perspiration and his jaw was rigidly clenched, evidence of the tight control he was exerting. When he lowered his head and pulled one nipple into his mouth, biting down on it, she screamed at the intensity of the pleasure-pain. Still braced on his forearms, moving his hips in a smooth, steady motion, he sucked hard at one breast then switched to the other.

"Oh, God." She tossed her head back and forth and lifted her hands to grip his shoulders so tight her nails bit into the skin. "Oh, please, Gabe. Harder."

His chuckle was low and strained. "Make it last, sweetheart. Hold off. It'll be worth it."

But no amount of urging on her part could alter that slow, inexorable rhythm, until his control fractured and he increased the tempo. The friction of his cock against her sore flesh only enhanced her pleasure. He increased his pace, faster now, and reached between them to find her clit. Pulling on it between thumb and forefinger, he bit down on her nipple again.

She screamed and convulsed around him, her legs locking in place like a steel vise, the slap of naked skin to naked skin and the harshness of their breathing the only sounds in the room. Then she flew into space, whirling, spinning, tossed in the grip of erotic turbulence. She felt Gabe's final plunge and heard his heavy sounds of completion. Just as she was sure her body would snap in two, the spasms subsided, leaving her limp.

Gabe lay on top of her, his forehead pressed to hers, his uneven breathing rough in the silence. After long minutes, with his cock still inside her, he rolled to one side, taking her with him and holding her against his sweat-slicked chest.

"Jesus," he said.

They were lying in the tangle of bedclothes, sweat cooling on their bodies, breathing labored. Gabe's cock was softening inside her but he left it wrapped in the heat of her cunt, as if breaking the connection might make everything disappear. He kissed her eyelids, her cheeks, her jawline and then soft touches to her lips while his fingers lightly stroked the curve of her spine.

Jill rubbed her face against the damp curls of his chest, inhaling his rich, musky scent. *Has he missed this as much as I have?* Her love life in the intervening years had been carefully controlled because she'd been unwilling to put herself in the position of losing her heart again. But two long-term relationships had at least taken her to new areas of sexual activity and satisfaction. *How will Gabe react if I want to introduce him to some of those things? Will it shock him, or does he still cling to the image of the untutored virgin of the past?*

She sighed.

Gabe pushed her hair back from her face, tucking it behind her ear. "Everything okay?" He asked it in a casual tone of voice, but his voice held an underlying anxiety.

Jill smiled up at him. "Everything's just fine. Better than fine." She laughed, a low, soft sound. "Even better than great."

"Good." He tucked her head under his chin. "How about a little nap? Then we can rustle up some food and…see what else the night turns up?"

"Mmmm. Sounds good." Her eyes were already closing.

Chapter Four

Somehow they slept right through the need for food or anything else. When Jill woke she was tucked beneath the covers, the blinds had been adjusted to permit a minimum of light and Gabe was gone. She held the sheets against her nose, seeking his lingering scent and rubbing it against her.

No goodbye? Not even thanks for a great night? Is this all that remains of what we once had?

Then she noticed the note, stuck to her night table lamp with tape.

Ran home to shower and change for an early client meeting. If you meet me at Danny's Roadhouse for lunch I can thank you properly for last night. Noon. Be there.

It was signed with a large *G*. No *Love, Gabe* — just the initial. Oh, well, at least he'd left the note.

She threw back the covers, swung her legs over the side of the bed and opened the drawer to drop the note into it. Her lips curved into a tiny smile as she looked at the contents, wondering what Gabe would have thought if he'd seen them last night. How would he have reacted to her assortment of intricate vibrators and wands, to her set of butt plugs? The oil that stimulated her with such intensity her climax extended almost beyond the range of tolerance? The handcuffs and the flogger?

Her four-year relationship with Mike Halloran hadn't produced a deep and abiding love, just a really good relationship and an introduction into sexual experimentation she'd only read about. Maybe it had been her reaction to the absence of Gabe in her life that had led her down that path, but then she'd discovered how much she enjoyed it. He'd been a talented lover, patient and sensitive, overriding her fear of the unknown. Little by little, she'd let him move her along, bringing her orgasms of shattering intensity, until now she found it hard to have sex without them.

Except that after Mike, no one else had interested her and the memory of Gabe had always lingered in the background. So here she was, with her first love after ten years of separation, wondering what he'd say if he knew the truth about his little virgin.

And, she reminded herself, no matter how glorious last night had been, he hadn't told her he still loved her. Or anything close. Maybe all they had left between them was sex.

She sighed and closed the door. At least Mike had taught her how to bring herself to fulfillment when she was alone so she didn't always walk around frustrated and horny.

Before she showered she called Ernie Hoffman, endured the expected long-lost greeting and arranged to come by and see him in an hour.

* * * *

Gabe pushed the yellow pad he'd been scribbling on away from him, tossed his pen onto the desk and leaned back in his leather desk chair. The meeting with Gary Armstrong had run long and he was frustrated because at the moment he didn't have any answers for the man. Armstrong had been introduced to Bob Dolman, a land developer, by mutual friends. He'd been convinced to invest a substantial amount of money in the builder's new project, a planned community on the outskirts of Bluebonnet Falls that everyone was excited about.

Dolman, a Dallas native, had spent the better part of two years acquiring the land and the permits and put together a consortium of investors to pay for the actual development. But nothing seemed to be happening and Gary Armstrong didn't like all the waiting around. Dolman had a whole string of clever explanations that Armstrong had now started seeing as excuses. Out of patience and tired of the whole business, he'd hired Gabe to check it out and see if there was cause for legal action.

Gabe had been curious himself, more so than otherwise since somehow the subject kept coming up in the bicentennial committee meetings. Nearly everyone wanted to tap Dolman for sponsorship and half the people wanted to urge him to make an announcement at the opening ceremonies. Gabe had already begun to put his own information together when Gary had asked him to look into things. Since he seldom had time to do any of the investigating in his cases, he had a list of freelance investigators he frequently used. He just hadn't settled on which one to assign yet. His trouble was that, at the moment, he couldn't make his brain function. Every time he closed his eyes he saw Jill's naked body stretched out next to him, smelled the scent of peaches on her skin and felt the velvet touch of her hair. The hardening of his shaft pressing against his fly did little to help maintain his discipline.

He couldn't believe he'd embarrassed himself by falling into such a deep sleep. But when he'd slid his throbbing cock into her familiar wet heat, his climax had been so powerful it had drained every bit of energy from him. Today, when he needed to be sharp, he was lethargic and sore, every muscle in his body aching.

How many nights over the past years had he lain awake torturing himself with memories of the sweet, sweet love they'd made, over and over again? He'd been humbled by the gift of her virginity and cherished the love that blossomed between them. He hadn't been sorry when Robin had told him she was going away for the summer. It had put some needed distance between the two of them, giving them a chance to evaluate what had never been a burning relationship to begin with. He had no longer been sure he wanted to spend the rest of his life with her. By the time he and Jill had found themselves alone picking up pizzas one night, he'd already been formulating his speech to end the relationship.

Surely Robin wouldn't have minded. She'd been so indifferent that she'd been unaware their lovemaking had become perfunctory and their conversations almost dull. After so much time together, a couple was either committed for life or sniffing at greener pastures. Gabe had definitely been sniffing, only he hadn't expected to fall in love...*really* fall in love...with Jill Danvers.

But there they'd been, two people at loose ends, Gabe clerking in his father's law office and Jill running the bookstore while her parents traveled the country in their RV. It had just seemed so natural for them to grab a sandwich together, see a movie, even have a casual picnic in the evening down by the lake. A picnic that had changed their relationship forever. Then Jill's parents had been killed and Robin had returned with the announcement of her pregnancy.

Fuck.

He'd managed to screw up his life in a big way because he hadn't kept his screwing under control. He was so sure he and Robin had used proper precautions, although the advertising always disclaimed that nothing was one hundred percent safe. *Well, no shit.*

Now, after all the years of separation, Jill had walked into his life again and he had one shot at putting things back together. That first kiss in his office had rocked him back on his heels. The invisible but powerful thread that bound them hadn't diminished. He wasn't fool enough to think the sex last night meant she'd be ready to forget the past. But the attraction still hovered, stronger than ever.

And in the intervening years, he'd learned a great deal more about sex and its many facets. How would Jill react if he told her he wanted to cuff her to the headboard while he licked her pussy until she couldn't take it anymore? Or decorate her nipples with clamps that caused just the right amount of pain to heighten pleasure? What if he said he wanted to slide his cock home in that cute little ass that he was sure was still untouched? How far would he get then? Or would she run back to San Antonio as fast as she could?

What if he told her how he still felt after all these years? She'd said they had both changed, but had their feelings for each other disappeared altogether?

Well, he wasn't solving anything just sitting there. Not his client's problems nor his dilemma with Jill. Checking his watch, he realized it was almost noon. *Time to meet her for lunch. If she shows up.*

* * * *

"Well, Jill." Ernie Hoffman gave her a hug then put her away from him for a better look. "If I said you're all grown up, I'd sound like a character from a bad movie, but you sure are."

"And you aren't a day older," she teased. "How are you, Ernie?"

"Best I can be." He sat back down in his chair and indicated she should take one across from him. Ernie had been selling real estate in the Falls since he'd graduated from college. Now he was considered the local expert and the plush appearance of his office spoke of his success. "How about you? What's been happening with you in all these years? We sure have missed you around here."

Jill gave him the abbreviated version she'd been practicing and managed to steer him around to the topic of the celebration.

"I'm sure you've got a bunch of questions, honey. Let's hear 'em."

Jill opened her portfolio and extracted the list Gabe had given her. "I'd like to go over each event and get as much background from you as possible. I can research history in the library, but I'd like to know how the committee made these specific choices."

"Well." Ernie leaned back in his chair, ready to pontificate. "The opening festivities are on Founders Day, the official date Bluebonnet Falls came into existence."

With a skill long perfected Jill guided him away from an endless stream of narrative to the exact items she needed. Opening night would be a big public buffet at Bluebonnet Community Hall with speeches by the appropriate people. As she made notes, Jill hoped someone was timing those speeches before everyone fell asleep. Then a short skit dramatizing the founding of the community would be followed by a street dance. All the committee members and their helpers would be dressed in outfits from the early 1800s.

As she jotted down notes, she forced herself to focus on Ernie's answers, but images of Gabe kept intruding and distracting her. She hoped the involuntary flush that kept suffusing her face didn't turn her skin red and that Ernie wouldn't notice the tiny tremor in her hands.

Her watch showed almost twelve by the time she was able to wrap up the meeting. Ernie would have talked until dinner if she hadn't shut him down, but she was grateful for the information he'd given her. She arranged to come to the committee meeting the next night and talk to everyone there.

* * * *

Gabe was sitting in the back booth at Danny's when she flew in, tucking a loose strand of hair behind her ears and shoving her sunglasses to the top of her head.

"Sorry if I'm late," she said in a breathless voice, sliding in next to him.

"You're fine." He wrapped his arm around her and kissed her cheek. "I'll take you any way I can get you."

The words were innocuous but they set up a faint throbbing deep inside her body. She wished they were someplace really private so she could yank off her clothes and straddle Gabe's lap.

My God, I'm turning into a sex maniac.

Danny's was one large room, usually dark in an attempt to create atmosphere. A heavy oak bar ran the length of one wall. At the end of it, the room made a tiny dip, creating an alcove with one booth — the one they were sitting in. Jill wondered how Gabe had dodged Danny's questions about why he'd chosen it.

Speak of the devil — Danny himself appeared before them, carrying two drinks. "Nice to see you again after all this time, Jill. Y'all give a holler when you want more drinks or you're ready to order." He smiled and headed back to the bar.

Jill raised her eyebrows at the glasses.

"A drink to celebrate your return. I didn't think we'd need a note from the teacher to have a drink in the middle of the day." He pointed at the wineglass. "Riesling, right?"

"I can't believe you remembered."

"I remember a lot of things, Jill." His voice had a low rumble. "You'd be surprised." He touched his glass to hers. "To new beginnings."

The butterflies were waking up in her stomach as she nodded. "New beginnings."

The white wine was smooth going down, as always. She'd never yet found a drink she enjoyed as much.

"So how was your morning?" he asked.

"Good. I met with Ernie and got some great background on the events. Lordy, he still talks as much as ever."

Gabe chuckled. "That he does."

"And you? How did it go with your client?"

Gabe shrugged. "So-so." Then he grinned. "But I didn't ask you to lunch to discuss business. I've got something very special planned."

Jill cocked an eyebrow. "Special?"

"Mm-hmm." He touched his glass to hers again. "To special things for special people."

Before she realized it she'd finished her wine and Gabe had called for refills.

"Hey, I'll be too drunk to walk out of this place," she protested, smiling.

"Not to worry," Gabe rumbled. "I'll carry you." He ran the tip of his finger around the shell of her ear then leaned over and followed the path with his tongue.

Jill shivered, little tremors cascading down her body.

"Gabe—"

"No one can see us here, darlin'. Feeling a little daring?" He tilted her chin toward him with one finger and captured her mouth in a slow, sensual kiss. His tongue was hot as he licked the surface of her lips, rubbing back and forth, nipping at the soft flesh with his white, even teeth. When she opened in a moan, he thrust his tongue inside and swept it over every inner surface.

"Do you know I could hardly think about anything but you this morning?" His deep voice sent shivers down her spine.

"Me, too," she breathed, inhaling his spicy scent. *More fool me.*

He inched her around on the bench until she faced him and slid one hand between their bodies. With a gentle touch he walked his fingers up her rib cage to her breasts, lightly twisting the nipple through the fabric of her blouse. Her nipple hardened at once to an almost painful point, begging for more, begging for him to pinch her the way he had last night.

Another moan drifted past her lips as she pushed her breast into his heated palm.

"I love your breasts," he whispered, his mouth pressed to her ear. "I love their fullness, the way they just fit my hand and the way your nipples get so hard when I touch them. If we were some place more private, I'd take off that blouse and that scrap of lace you call a bra and lick every inch of them until I made you come. Last night I almost made you come just from sucking them, didn't I?"

She nodded, unable to make her mouth form words. The smooth drink had warmed her blood and settled her nerve endings. She had a vague feeling she shouldn't be doing this but for the life of her she couldn't figure out why.

Gabe moved his tongue back to her ear, sending more shivery feelings down her spine, and slid his hand beneath the slim skirt she was wearing. His fingers glided along the flesh of her inner thigh, a whisper of a touch, and she shifted in her seat to give him greater access. Sparks of electricity shot through her body when he brushed his knuckles across the trimmed line of curls at the top of her mound.

"Gabe." She tried to rouse herself, knowing she was falling deeper into a pit, but her body didn't seem to be hers to command.

"Ssh," he soothed. "I told you. No one can see us. Tell me, sweet Jill. Did anyone ever make you come like this in a public place, when you couldn't cry out, couldn't do anything but sit there and let it rock your body?"

Yes, but I'm not telling you. Not yet, anyway.

"If you want me to stop, just tell me." He danced his tongue over the surface of her neck. "Well?"

"Don't stop," she whispered as he touched the edge of her thong and tugged on it.

"Good. I wasn't going to, anyway. Want to try a little adventure?"

She nodded, powerless to do anything except sit there, praying he'd plunge his fingers into her and ease the building ache.

He tightened his arm around her, holding her with a firm grip against him as he insinuated one finger under the scrap of lace covering her mound and slowly stroked her clit. She jerked at the first touch, but his arm held her in place and his murmurings soothed her.

"I love the feel of your thighs. They're so soft, like satin. Just touching them nearly makes me come."

The proof of her arousal seeped from her outer lips and trickled onto her thighs.

Gabe drew in a breath. "I can smell you, darlin'. You're hot as a pistol, aren't you?"

He kept up the steady pace, tracing a pattern with his finger from knee to pussy and back again, taking his time. All the muscles in her sex were fluttering with their own primal rhythm and she wondered if Gabe could tell what was happening. The slow smile that spread over Gabe's face told her he knew just what she was feeling.

He kissed her eyelids, her cheeks, her jawline and finally soft touches to her lips. And all the time he used his clever finger to trace the lips of her sex, smoothing the trimmed curls, rubbing the clit now so sensitized Jill was sure the next touch would send her off into outer space.

"You're so wet." Gabe's voice held the purr of a jungle cat. "I wish we were alone so I could strip us both naked and plunge my cock inside you. I'll bet it would slide right in. I'm so aroused I'd need every bit of that wonderful cream to ease my way."

She was getting closer, her orgasm building and taking over her body. She opened her thighs as much as the slim skirt would permit and tried to rub against Gabe's touch.

"Uh-uh-uh," he cautioned. "Your part of this is to stay absolutely still. Not move, not say a thing. Okay?"

She nodded. He slid his finger back and forth over her clit again, scooping the juices that were slicking the flesh just inside her outer lips and drenching that swelling nub. When he pushed a long lean finger inside her, she nearly leaped off the bench but forced herself to stay still. Being immobile made every sensation twice as intense.

"Now," he went on. "Bring one hand up—easy does it—slip it inside your blouse and pinch your nipple. Hard."

When she did as he'd directed, heat arrowed straight to her cunt and she flooded his hand.

"Keep pinching it, darlin'. That's it." He slipped one finger in and out of her while he used another to tease and torment her pulsating clit. "Now. Listen to me. In a minute I'm going to make you come and you won't say a word. Not a sound. Got it?"

"Y-Yes." Her voice sounded far away.

"All right, then."

He dragged his thumbnail over her clit, pinched it once and pulled her over the edge. Her body shook as the spasms overtook her, but she glued herself to the seat, teeth clenched to prevent any sound from escaping. As her body convulsed Gabe kept stroking her swollen sex, pulling and scraping and tugging until he'd wrung every last drop from her.

He leaned against the back of the booth and brought his fingers to his mouth, his eyes glittering as he licked them. "You taste better than any gourmet dish, sugar. You surely do."

Her breathing was finally returning to normal although her body felt like jelly. *Where did Gabe learn this little trick and with who? And what else does he have up his sleeve?*

As if he heard her thoughts, he leaned over and kissed her full on the mouth, taking one smooth lick. "Did you like that, sweetheart? Did it excite you? There's a lot more where that came from." He studied her eyes. "Am I scaring you off, Jill? Is this too much for you?"

She shook her head, not trusting herself to say a word. This was a Gabe who spoke to her wild side, a side she hadn't even known she had before Mike Halloran.

"All right, then." He picked up one of the two menus lying on the table. "What do you think you'd like for lunch?" He winked. "Gotta keep up our strength."

Jill couldn't believe that after what they'd just done, they were going to sit there and eat lunch as if nothing had happened. Only the wicked smile Gabe kept flashing her reminded her the whole thing wasn't just something she'd imagined.

Somehow she got through the meal without falling apart, but she was sure she'd have melted to the floor if Gabe hadn't kept her pulled tight against him on the walk to the parking lot.

"What's on your agenda for the afternoon?" he asked.

"I want to drive around town, see what's changed and what hasn't. Then start to do some research at the library on all the details of the Falls history. Just so I can give myself some perspective."

"I have a late meeting this afternoon or I'd ask you to meet me for dinner. Can I come by the house when I'm through?" A shadow of a grin flitted across his face. "When I knew you were coming back here, I bought you a couple of presents I want to give you."

"Presents?" She shifted, uneasy at his words. "Oh, Gabe. I don't think —"

"That's right. Don't think." He stroked her cheek. "Let me come by, Jill, okay? Aren't you even curious about what I got for you?"

She burst out laughing. "Okay. Yes, I am."

"Good. I'll see you about eight o'clock."

* * * *

Jill prided herself on her research abilities. Every story she'd ever done had begun with an intensive study of the subject. Since she'd grown up in the Falls and knew a fair amount about it, she'd been able to do her preliminary outline. Now what she wanted was the nuggets of its history and stories of the people who made the town what it was.

Yet try as she might, she couldn't focus on one thing she was reading. Her mind kept drifting back to Danny's and the quiet way Gabe had made her come, not allowing her to do anything but sit there in a public arena while wave after wave of sensation rolled over her.

Now he was coming to her house again tonight. She should have said no, told him they needed some distance. It still bothered her that he'd said nothing about his feelings, if he still felt anything for her except lust. What did he think of her quiet acquiescence today? What would he say if she told him he wasn't the only man she'd done this with? Did he still expect her to be the same person in bed she'd been ten years ago?

But she reminded herself again that Gabe had picked up a few tricks of his own.

He was bringing presents, he had said. *What kind of presents?* She shivered in anticipation of the unknown, of what the night would bring.

Unable to concentrate on the books in front of her, she closed them and left them on the table. Maybe a drive around town would clear her head and help her think straight, but she doubted it.

* * * *

Gabe was beginning to think the meeting would never end. He'd been stupid to schedule it during dinner, giving everyone the opportunity for before-dinner drinks and bullshit conversation. But it was tough getting the director of Planning and Zoning, the chairman of the City Council, the local bank president and the mayor together without offering them food and drink.

A treatise on our local political climate.

"Gentlemen." He rapped a knuckle on the table. "Can we come to some kind of conclusion here? My client is getting a rash over this."

Mayor Larry Hofstra finished the last swallow of his bourbon, looked at the empty glass with regret and set it back on the table. "Gabe, I just don't know what to tell you. We're trying to get everything done as quickly as we can, but there's all these environmental restrictions and so many groups to answer to."

All of whom vote for you, you insufferable ass.

"George?" He looked at the P&Z director.

George, as political a creature as the mayor, just shrugged. "As soon as the committee meets again and checks to see if Dolman's complied with the last set of requirements, we're hoping to move forward."

"You need to keep on top of this," Gabe reminded him. "Gary Armstrong's getting a little antsy."

"He's not the only one," George interjected. "We just don't want to piss him off at this point, though."

"You know, this will mean a heavy infusion of cash in the town as people buy homes and move here," Larry pointed out, reaching for his coffee. "And more businesses will open. That means more tax money."

"At least he's earning interest," the bank president pointed out.

Gabe had begun to have his own ideas about the situation but he wasn't going to lay them on the table until he'd looked into it a lot more. He had also contacted attorneys in other towns where Dolman had developments, to get feedback on the process there. He couldn't decide if Dolman was a crook in expensive clothing or someone he needed to get to know better.

What he wanted was the whole story and he had the feeling at the moment he only had disjointed pieces.

"Interest? Small comfort when he's marking time on the real return on his investment."

"You mean the sale of lots to builders?" George asked.

Gabe nodded. "Doesn't it seem weird to you he'd be willing to settle for what, in his scheme of things, is a small if steady income stream when there's so much more out there?"

Larry swallowed the last of his coffee. "I think he's just being careful with his planning. Let's give him some breathing room. We don't want this thing to fall apart. Bad for Bluebonnet Falls all the way around."

Gabe swallowed a sigh. Sometimes dealing with this crowd stretched his patience to the breaking point. Tomorrow he'd get his investigator on it first thing and find out just what the hell the real situation was.

"All right, folks." He signaled for the check. It was after seven and he still had to run by his house, shower, change and pick up Jill's present. His cock hardened as he thought of what was in the gift-wrapped box. How would she react? Would she be excited or throw him out of the house?

He hadn't said a word to her about his real feelings yet, waiting to see if she'd accept him as he was today, not pining for the very young man he'd been. *Changes.* He'd been through a lot of them. *She says she has, too. Is that true?*

"One week," he told the men at the table. "In one week I want a firm construction schedule and I want to see some activity on that site. I don't want to go to war in my hometown, but I will if I have to. The last thing we need is for people to hear that Bluebonnet Falls is a losing proposition for investors."

Climbing into his car, he forced himself to wipe the meeting from his mind. He needed to focus on the night ahead.

Chapter Five

Jill opened her eyes with a start. The rosebud-painted clock on the bathroom counter read ten minutes to eight. *Damn!* She'd fallen asleep in the bathtub and Gabe would be here in ten minutes. But the scented water, the candles and the soft music playing from the portable CD player had been so soothing that her eyes had closed without any resistance from her.

Her mind was still whirling. Lunch had been many things—arousing, startling, amazing. It had left her body in a state of near arousal and her mind in a state of confusion. She still had no idea what was going on between her and Gabe. She couldn't seem to make the bitterness of his betrayal with Robin disappear altogether and he'd said nothing to indicate what his feelings were now. Today. That minute in time. He'd said he'd been waiting for her all these years but that brought up another question. Was it the Jill he knew or the Jill she'd become?

Changes. So many changes.

Nothing ever stayed the same. Was there enough left between them besides sex to move forward? What would he say if he discovered how her tastes had evolved in all this time? Discovered the games she liked to play? Would he be turned off? Excited? If she revealed the person she was now, would he still want her? Lunch today had made her think he would. That he, too, enjoyed adventurous sex. Still…

"Are you waiting for me to help you finish?"

Gabe's deep voice made her jerk and nearly slip beneath the water.

"How did you get in?" *Did I leave the door unlocked?* That didn't give her an easy feeling.

"Your doorbell doesn't work. You didn't answer my knock, so I tried the back door to see if it still opened when you jiggled it." He winked. "Here I am."

Jill started to rise from the tub, reaching for the towel folded on the floor beside her, but Gabe shook his head.

"Stay where you are. Let me soap you all over." He wore a strange look on his face and there was a hunger in his eyes that was deeper and more intense than anything she remembered. A wicked smile curved his lips. "Remember the first time I did this?"

She swallowed hard and answered in a soft voice. "Yes. I do."

It happened in this very tub. The last time anyone had bathed me I was a child, but that episode had nothing childlike about it.

"I've gotten a lot better at it." He raked his gaze over her, smoldering heat flaring in his eyes. Then he kneeled beside her and reached for the bath sponge on the ledge. He dipped it into the water, squeezed out the excess and began to stroke it over her shoulders. "You always had the softest skin, Jill. I never could understand how a grown woman could have skin like a baby's. I couldn't ever get enough of touching it."

He cupped the back of her head in his palm to draw the sponge along her neck and the tender area beneath her jaw.

She shivered at the gentleness of his touch. "You haven't lost your technique."

"Good to know." He leaned forward and dusted a light kiss on her forehead.

Then he turned to her breasts, first one then the other, his motions unhurried. As he reached each nipple, he placed the sponge directly over it and squeezed. A hissing breath escaped her mouth. Jolts of lightning raced through her and she shifted a bit in the tub.

"Feel good, darlin'?" His voice had a deep, husky sound to it. "I plan to make you feel a whole lot better."

He smoothed the sponge over her abdomen, rubbing it against her navel before dipping lower. When he nudged at her thighs, she opened them for him. As he pressed against her sex and brushed her clit with teasing strokes, she was conscious of a fluttering in her pussy. Without thinking she lifted her hips toward him.

He let the sponge float away, replacing it with his fingers, brushing at the curls covering her mound. The scrape of his nails brought a tiny bite of pain that made her clench her inner muscles. His mouth close to her ear, he asked, "Do you have fantasies, Jill? Things you dream about? Wish for? Secrets that you hug to yourself?"

In an instant her mouth went dry as a stream of erotic images danced through her brain. "Fantasies?"

"Mm-hmm. Dark secrets."

"I-I have fantasies." *Maybe even more than you expect, Gabe Carter.*

"Would you like to know what one of mine is? What I dream about more nights than I can count? A dream that makes me so hard it's painful?" His fingers continued to drift through her tiny curls, just brushing the skin of her sex.

She nodded, her eyes locked with his.

He leaned in close, strumming her clit with those very clever fingers. "I dream of seeing your cunt completely naked. Bare, with not a single hair on it. I would give anything if you would let me shave off this little patch you keep so neatly trimmed." He traced the inner shell of her ear with his tongue, the light touch sending shivers skittering through her body. "Would you let me do that? Shave you 'til your pussy is naked for me?"

Oh, yes. I would.

Jill swallowed hard and nodded. Was this really Gabe asking her this? The muscles in her pussy rippled.

"Say it, darlin', so I know you mean it."

She had to swallow twice before she finally got the word out. "Yes."

"Yes what, Jill?"

"Yes, I want you to shave my pussy."

Am I really having this conversation with him? What has he done since the last time I saw him to become such a talented lover with new, sophisticated tastes?

His eyes darkened and a muscle jumped in his cheek. He cupped her chin and brought her mouth to his as if tasting her lips with his tongue before thrusting it inside. "All right, then," he husked when he lifted his head. "Tell me where your things are."

Hardly believing she was doing this, she told him where to find her razor and the soothing gel she used. Then he helped her from the tub, picked her up and carried her to her bed, snagging the towel to place under her as he lowered her. She was shaking from anticipation of the unknown.

Gabe leaned down and placed an openmouthed kiss on her abdomen just below her navel. "Don't worry, baby. Just think how much more sensitive you'll be when we're done here."

He placed the razor and gel beside her on the bed then fetched a small satchel he'd brought with him. "I have some presents in here for you, for later. But I also wanted to make sure we didn't run out of protection." He winked and extracted a large box of condoms. "I'll just put them in here to keep them out of the way for now."

He started to open the nightstand drawer and Jill bolted up from the bed, reaching for his hand. "No!" She was almost shouting. "No, don't put them in there."

But he already had his hand on the knob and was pulling it open. His eyes widened and heat crept up her body from her toes to her hairline.

Gabe looked at her then back at the drawer. "Holy shit!"

"Um…" Jill licked her lips, searching for a way to explain her toys.

"I can hardly believe all this." His mouth turned up in a wicked smile. "This is some collection, sugar. *Vibrators. Butt plugs. Bondage toys and other items. I know until yesterday we hadn't had sex in ten years. But I'll tell you, even in my wildest dreams I'd never imagined you'd be testing the waters of kinky lovemaking."

I should have hidden them, but who knew he'd show up like this?

"Well," he said. "And here I was worried that I might do something to offend or frighten you."

Jill tried to slam the drawer shut but Gabe held it open, one hand closing over hers. "No, don't. I want to see these." He took her hand and placed it over the hard erection straining against the fly of his jeans. "See what just the thought of you and these toys does to me?"

"Gabe, I..." She lifted her hands in a helpless gesture.

He leaned down and kissed her — a tender kiss — and ran his tongue over the soft flesh of her lips. "It's all right, darlin'. You don't know how relieved I am to find this." He stroked her cheek with his thumb. "My own tastes have changed a lot over the years. I was scared to death I'd chase you away if I tried to introduce you to some of the things I want with you."

Jill exhaled a long breath and relaxed. "I was afraid you'd think I was, you know…"

He laughed. "What I think is how lucky I am you walked back into my life yesterday. Now how about you lie back and let me get to my work here, okay?"

She nodded, swallowed and lay back on the bed.

Gabe dropped to his knees, placed her feet flat on the bed and pushed her knees as far apart as they would go. He licked his lips as he studied every inch of her sex.

"I have an idea. Don't move."

As if I could.

He opened the drawer again and studied its contents for a long moment. Then he selected a toy and licked it before sliding it into her opening.

Clenching her fists for some measure of control, Jill managed to hold herself very still.

"Easy, sweetheart." Gabe caressed her thighs and her belly, soothing her with his voice and touch. "I thought

I'd give you a little pleasure while I enjoy my task. But you have to stay completely still. This is delicate work here."

He turned the control at the base of the vibrator to its lowest setting.

Oh, God!

Jill lifted her hips once then settled down.

Gabe took her hands and placed them over her head. "Don't move them," he ordered. "Close your eyes and just feel, okay?"

She took a deep breath, nodded, her muscles losing their tension.

The gel was cool on the skin of her mound, the touch of his fingers as he smoothed it in a heated contrast. Then he began, tugging her outer lips to the side to give him access to every inch of her as he made clean strokes with the razor. After each sweep came the clink of the razor against the glass of water as he cleaned the blade. Every time he pinched the outer lips he made sure his thumb brushed her clit. *Holy hell!* Holding herself still was becoming impossible.

Increasing the sensations was the realization that this new Gabe Carter would be taking her on what she believed to be the most erotic sexual journey of her life.

Finally, he was finished, cleaning away the last of the gel with a warm cloth that brushed her sensitive clit with each stroke. Keeping still was pure torture, yet at the same time so erotic that she had a hard time clamping down on her arousal.

Gabe set the razor and bowl on the nightstand, leaned forward and placed kisses on the inside of each of her knees. "Good girl. Now it's time for your reward. Remember, keep those hands over your head."

He reached down to adjust the setting on the vibrator and the hum grew louder and more forceful. Her inner muscles clenched, her breath was caught in her throat and the sensations were only increased by the sight of Gabe holding her legs apart and watching her.

"Beautiful," he breathed. "Jesus, Jill, you have no idea the things we're going to do that I'm going to enjoy watching."

His words triggered her release and the orgasm crashed through her. She bucked her hips, clenched down on the vibrator and rode it hard as it buzzed and shimmied within her. Gabe shifted one hand to push at the bottom of it, keeping it seated all the way inside her, and the force of the spasms increased, shaking her even harder.

She struggled for breath, her heart hammering and air seesawing in and out of her lungs, until the shudders eased. She lay there, panting, her entire body loose and limp. When the aftershocks had subsided altogether, Gabe removed the vibrator and licked it again.

"You have the sweetest-tasting cunt in the world, Jill." He ran his tongue over his lips. "I could feast on you forever." Then he put the vibrator to the side and helped her to sit up on the edge of the bed. "Keep your legs apart so that naked pussy is exposed. I'll be right back."

"Where are you going?"

"To get something else I brought with me."

Jill sat as he arranged her, the air of the room cool on her now bare skin. She was still weak from the orgasm that had built and built while Gabe shaved her with meticulous care, yet she was more aroused than ever.

She was shocked to discover that Gabe was into erotic sex too. Never in her life would she have expected it from him. She didn't even want to know where or with whom he'd learned all these things. Whoever would have thought that they both would have undergone such changes in their sexual tastes? But where did that leave them now? Back together just for a wild time in bed while she was in town? Or could they pick up where they'd left off so many years ago? Did she want to risk it again? She had no idea about Gabe's real feelings for her now, except it was obvious he wanted to fuck her in every way possible.

She was still batting questions around in her brain when he came back into the room carrying two goblets and a wine bottle.

He held it toward her to see the label. *La Rochelle Winery, San Jose, California.*

"It's a boutique winery owned by Mirassou Wines. The original vine cuttings were brought over in the 1800s from La Rochelle, France. A client in California turned me on to it when I was out there a while ago. Beats anything you can import from France."

"Nice."

He filled both glasses and handed her one, then touched his glass to hers as he had earlier in the restaurant. "To us, darlin'."

She took a small sip. "Is there an *us*, Gabe? I mean, beyond this? Are you really over Robin?"

Gabe put his glass down on the nightstand with a careful motion, staring at the liquid.

"Jill, if I wanted Robin back, I could have had her any time since the divorce. I know this sounds arrogant and cold, but Robin had become a habit to me. I think I was actually relieved when it was over."

She wanted to believe him with a desperate need. Maybe this was yet another turn in their lives, a new beginning for them, something she hadn't dared hope for when she'd taken this assignment. As she sipped at the wine, trying to find some level footing in the maelstrom of her emotions, she decided to worry about it later. She and Gabe were exploring new sexual boundaries together and she wouldn't let anything get in the way of that. But could she be happy if that was all they ever had?

Cut it out, Jill.

She'd give him her body, but she taken great care to guard her heart. When her assignment was completed, she'd see where they were.

She smiled up at him. "All right, then. To us." She shivered at the heated look in his eyes as he raked them over her, focusing on her bare pussy, the evidence of her arousal soaking into the towel beneath her.

Gabe reached into the satchel he'd placed on the bed and took out a small box. "Stand up," he ordered, his voice soft. "And come over to me."

Jill pushed herself to her feet. As she walked, the friction of her naked labia rubbing against each other set up a tiny throbbing deep inside her. *Oh, Lord!* When she reached Gabe she stopped, hands at her sides, waiting.

He bent his head and took one nipple into his mouth, pulling at it with a gentle tug, sucking it. Heat streaked through her body. Then he closed his teeth over it, biting down, and liquid seeped from her again, wetting her thighs.

"God, Gabe." She clutched at his arms with both hands to steady herself.

He lifted his head to look at her then moved to the other nipple, repeating his actions. Back and forth he went, from one swollen tip to the other, not touching any other part of her breast. As he pulled and tugged and bit, the tiny buds became swollen and elongated and her knees weakened, in danger of not holding her up. Gabe was right. He could bring her to orgasm touching no other part of her body except her nipples.

"Gorgeous," he breathed and rolled them between thumbs and forefingers. "I could suck on them forever." He picked up the box he'd taken from the satchel and opened it.

To Jill what lay inside looked like a pair of chandelier earrings, but Mike had given her a similar pair so she knew what they were. *Nipple clamps.* Her inner muscles tightened in anticipation.

Gabe held one up. "You know what these are."

"Yes."

"Someone else gave you a pair."

"That's right."

For a moment jealousy turned his eyes the color of a stormy sea and a muscle twitched in his jaw. Then it was gone. "Throw them away. These are the only ones you should have."

He took one nipple, stretched it and slipped the thin circlet at the top over it. He squeezed until the metal bit into the tender skin. When she was unable to control the tiny flinch, Gabe eased back just a little, tightened again, then rubbed the tip of his finger over the pebbled surface.

"These were made for you, sweet thing. By the time tonight is over, these little buds will be so tender and swollen I'll be able to make you come with just the lightest touch."

He repeated the process with her other nipple. "How do they feel?"

"Good." She pushed the word through her dry mouth. "They feel good."

Then she was lying on the bed again, legs splayed.

Gabe began unbuttoning his shirt. "Rub your hand over your cunt. Feel all that soft, naked skin. Do you like that?"

"Yes," she moaned, touching her shaved area.

"Good. Now take your fingers and pull your cunt lips apart so I can see all the way inside you. Do it, Jill."

She did as he asked, feeling more exposed than she'd ever been in her life. Gabe shucked his shirt and dropped it on the floor, then unfastened his jeans. She tracked his movements as jeans and boxers joined his shirt and he toed off his shoes. The erection that sprang from the golden nest of curls made her breath catch.

Gabe closed one fist over the thick shaft, sliding it from the base to the wide purple head. His eyes never left Jill. "Rub your clit for me, Jill. Just lightly, with the tip of your finger. Use your other hand to keep yourself open so I can see all that sweet, sweet cream."

Jill knew how wet she was. She couldn't remember the last time she'd been so turned on, not even with Mike, who had taught her many ways to achieve physical satisfaction. The more she teased at her clit, the more her liquid seeped from her and trickled down into the cleft of her buttocks.

"Do you like my cock, Jill?" He continued to stroke it in a slow, rhythmic movement. The head turned a darker purple and the thick veins ribbing the sides pulsed with the flow of blood. His balls hung soft against his thighs.

"Yes." Jill ran her tongue across her lower lip. "Yes. I do."

"Would you like to take it in your mouth? Taste it the way I taste you?"

"Please." Lord, would she.

"I want that too. And in a little while that's exactly what you're going to do. Are you close to coming, darlin'?"

She nodded.

"Stop, then. Right now."

She wanted to cry out with frustration. She was so close. So very close.

Gabe lifted her as if she were nothing but a feather and turned her over, stretching her out. When he moved near her head he held a silk scarf in his hand. "Just a blindfold. Take away one sense and all the others are heightened."

He tightened it so it was secure but not uncomfortable. Jill closed her eyes against the soft fabric, the darkness almost comforting. In a moment his hands circled her wrists. She visualized him locking the padded cuffs from the drawer into place, fastening her hands to the headboard. The pressure on her clamped nipples as she lay on them almost sent her into a climax, but she bit her lip, wanting to hold back. She tugged just a little, knowing she was immobilized.

"Get up on your knees," he told her, trailing kisses down the length of her cheek. "Come on. Let me see that sweet ass."

Balancing herself as best she could, she got to her knees, her head lowered, her buttocks lifted, waiting while Gabe slid the bed pillows beneath her. When he tugged on the nipple jewelry, pinpoints of sensation stabbed at the engorged buds. "Your nipples are so swollen, sweet Jill. I could play with them all night." He stood up. "All right. One more thing and we'll be set."

Manacles encircled each ankle, soft as the ones on her wrists. When Gabe eased her legs apart she knew he was fastening them to the tiny knobs on the bedposts at the foot of the bed. She was helpless and exposed to him, her body available for whatever he chose to do. A dark thrill chased through her.

"Okay, Jill?"

"Yes." She swallowed, heat flushing through every vein as anticipation rode through her.

"Good." He placed a kiss on each cheek of her buttocks. "We're all set then."

In the next moment a hand came down on her flank in a stinging slap. She flinched then forced herself to relax. Mike had introduced her to the stimulation of spanking and the intense heat it brought to her body until he'd taken her to the point where she craved it.

She waited for the feel of his hand again but nothing happened. *Where is he? Has he left the room?*

"Gabe?"

Then she heard a soft chuckle.

"Ah, Jill. I hoped you'd want more." His laugh was a low rumble. "I'm going to make that ass so red you'll feel the heat in every inch of your cunt."

She thought of the flogger. Did she dare ask him to use it so soon?

As if reading her thoughts, he said, "No flogger tonight, sweet thing. We have to save something for the next time."

Now his hand came down again and again. More. Heat streaking from the contact. There was no steady rhythm, as if his goal was to keep her off-balance. She tried to arch into it, shaking her buttocks with need, but Gabe had his own ideas.

Slap! Nothing. Then three slaps in a row. Nothing again. And so it went, until she lost count of the times his hand met her flesh. Her ass and thighs were warmed by the spanking and she could smell the scent of her musk. *More,* she wanted to scream. *Fill me. Fuck me. Suck me. Do anything to me.* But she gritted her teeth, praying that his next move would ease the ache building inside her.

When his hands separated the cheeks of her buttocks, she almost came just from the thought of what he might be doing.

"God, you have a magnificent ass," he breathed. "I can't wait to feel it tight around my cock, squeezing me in that hot, dark channel."

Her heart skipped and stuttered when his mouth pressed kisses to her inflamed skin. Soft kisses, gentle and soothing, that drew the pain and left the pleasure. His breath was sweet as he moved over her in slow motion.

"Sweet," he murmured. "So sweet. Like a treat from heaven."

When he stopped, there was more movement and something drizzled into the cleft between her cheeks.

Oil! She could tell by the feel of it.

Oh, God!

She knew all too well what that oil could do. *Drive me crazy, that's what.* Turn her so wanton she could lose her mind with unrelenting need. The first time Mike had used it on her she'd gone crazy, her climax stretching out so long she'd thought she'd have a heart attack. But he'd always been careful, letting her go just so far, bringing her back at the last possible moment. *Does he know what a powerful stimulus this is?*

Again he seemed to read her mind. "Don't worry. I know all about this oil and what it can do. And exactly how to use it. I'd never do anything to hurt you, Jill. Ever. I want you to believe that."

She forced herself to relax. Then one finger slid into her rear, spreading the oil inside, rubbing it into the so-tender tissues. With tantalizing slowness he slid his finger in and out of her ass, a gentle motion that drove her wild. Her pussy spasmed, clutching on empty air. She pushed back against the invading finger but her movements were too limited.

Her clamped nipples throbbed and ached. Every time they brushed against the pillowcase beneath her, streaks of sensation shot through her. She wanted Gabe's mouth on them again, now that they were so swollen and sensitive. Then his other hand crept between her legs to rub the oil on her naked sex. At once every muscle in her body quivered and every nerve fired.

She was desperate to thrust her hips, to push down on his hands, anything as the oil seeped into her tissues, raising the intensity of her arousal until every part of her throbbed and pulsed with demanding need. *Please,* she wanted to beg. *Please fuck me. I can't stand it.*

And the oil kept working its sensual magic, turning her body into a mass of craving flesh.

Suddenly he stopped and she wanted to scream.

"Gabe?"

She sensed him moving around on the bed until he was in front of her, his sac resting in her cuffed hands. He touched her lips, brushing over them, just a light touch.

"Open up, darlin'. I've got something special for you here. Open wide and I'll make you feel really good."

She opened her mouth as wide as possible, waiting. In a moment his cock was pushing its way past her lips, onto her tongue and toward the back of her throat.

He cupped her chin in the palm of one hand. "I know it's a lot, but you've got me so damn hot tonight. That's what you do to me." A light stroke across one cheek. "Just breathe through your nose and let it slip in a little at a time. That's it. Good girl. Oh God, Jill. Holy sweet Jesus!"

The position she was in made it difficult to do what he wanted, especially with her hands unavailable. Still, she managed to take most of him into her mouth. She caressed his length with her tongue, licking the silken skin over the hard shaft as she moved her head back and forth. Gabe threaded his fingers through her hair, guiding her, showing her how he liked it. Before long she established a rhythm, moving her mouth as he rocked his hips back and forth.

He leaned over her then, separated the cheeks of her ass, dripped more of the oil onto her tight opening and inserted first one then two fingers inside her. The new application drove her close to insane. Her senses were on overload, her pussy quivering and throbbing, her clit begging for Gabe's touch, every inch of her body crying for the release of an orgasm.

She eased forward onto his cock, backward onto his thrusting fingers, her pace increasing as her body became more aroused, her need more intense. He filled her mouth, the silken head of his cock bumping the back of her throat, the soft skin covering his balls tickling her chin each time he thrust forward.

Suddenly he jerked his shaft out of her mouth.

"No," she wailed, bereft, wanting to wrap her lips around him again.

"I don't want to come in your mouth," he rasped. "Not tonight. Not when that sweet little cunt and that hot ass are just begging for my cock."

He moved around behind her again and in a moment he drove his fingers into both her ass and her pussy. She went crazy, the effect of the oil driving her beyond any semblance of control. She jerked her hips, riding his hands and his fingers inside her were driving her to the edge. She was ready to beg for release when bang! There it was. Without warning the orgasm raged over her, sweeping over her body, shaking her, rocketing her into space. Colors exploded behind the blindfold and she struggled to catch her breath. Just as she thought she'd reached the end, Gabe increased the pressure in her ass, squeezed her clit and she was thrown into the whirlwind again.

It went on and on, gripping her, pulling everything from her. She yanked at the headboard, trying to free her hands, and clenched the muscles in her thighs, trying to close them, but she was so restrained with such effectiveness she had almost no opportunity for movement. She could do nothing but lie there shuddering and shaking, Gabe's fingers stroking her without mercy as one orgasm ended and another began.

Ohgodohgodohgod.

She heard someone sobbing and realized it was her.

At the very moment, she was sure she couldn't stand it another instant, she felt a vibrator slide into her aching sex, heard the snap of latex and Gabe's thick shaft pushed into her ass. She screamed at the double intrusion, pushing against them as much as she tried to pull away, and another climax overtook her.

She had no idea how long the spasms went on, driving her from one edge to another. Gabe never varied his motion, stroking her from one release to the next, taking her higher every time until she thought the next one would kill her. And each time her body slowed, he reached under her and tugged on the clamps, pinching nipples now distended to twice their size, cream flooding around the vibrator just from the touch of his fingers on them.

When Gabe's climax roared through him, he shouted her name, over and over, his hot seed burning her through the latex sheath.

She didn't know how much time had passed until he released her wrists and ankles. Then with gentle hands he turned her over and removed the nipple rings, soothing the tortured buds with tiny licks of his tongue. He pulled her into his arms and rocked her, his thundering heart beating against hers.

"Jill, Jill, Jill," he crooned. "How the hell did I ever live without you all these years?" He sprinkled kisses on her forehead. "God! This is like having every dream in my life come true all at the same time."

She curled against him, so exhausted she wasn't sure she could move if she had to. Gabe continued to feather soft kisses on her while he stroked her arms and her back. Then he rolled off the bed and picked her up in his arms.

"Where are you taking me?" She only wanted to lay her head down and go to sleep.

"Shower. No," he said, when she started to protest. "You need hot water on those sore muscles and if I don't get rid of that oil, you'll be in pain tomorrow."

She knew he was right, so she let him prop her up in the shower, adjust the showerhead so hot streams pounded down on her, rub soapy lather into every inch of her, inside and out, bathing her as if she was a baby. When he'd patted her dry, he carried her back to the bed and placed her on her stomach. Then he pulled a bottle of lotion from his satchel, poured some into his hands and warmed it with his palms.

As he kneaded and rubbed each area of her body, he followed the path of his hands with kisses. When he worked the lotion into her buttocks, he traced the creases between buttock and thigh with the tip of his tongue. The warmth that flowed from the intimate touch was not meant to arouse as much as to provide comfort, to signify tenderness and affection.

A soft sigh escaped her and she was convinced just a single sponge could mop up what was left of her.

Gabe's strong hands turned her over, her body now limp and pliable, and followed the same process on her front. When he rubbed the lotion into her swollen, aching nipples, she moaned in pure bliss. Even when he eased apart the bare lips of her sex with slow tenderness and attended to every inch of it, she felt no tingle of sexual awareness, only soft pleasure. She had never felt so well cared for.

The last thing he did was climb into bed next to her, spoon her against him and pull the covers over both of them. Her brain was so numb, her body so depleted, she couldn't be one hundred percent sure but she thought she heard him say, "I love you."

Chapter Six

I'm making a big mistake.

Jill looked at her face in the bathroom mirror, lips still swollen from Gabe's kisses, eyes heavy-lidded with the after-effects of unbelievable sex, even after sleeping eight hours. What the hell was wrong with her that within what seemed like minutes of the time she'd gotten inside the limits of Bluebonnet Falls when she'd fallen into bed with the man who'd dumped her and rolled into a pit of erotic sensuality with him?

Ask me if I care.

Okay, so I should, but...

She remembered Gabe slipping out of bed just before seven, pulling on his jeans and shirt and placing a soft kiss on the lips. "I need to get home and change for an appointment at my office. Darlin', you are spectacular."

"Mm," she'd hummed. "You too." She'd snuggled deeper into her covers, clinging to the comfort of her dream.

"Out doing more research this morning?"

She'd nodded, her eyelids drooping again.

"Come by the office about one," he'd told her, "and I'll buy you lunch."

She'd smiled. "I don't know if I can take another lunch like yesterday. Especially after last night."

He'd chuckled. "Maybe I'll think of something different this time."

She'd nodded, asleep before he even left the room.

When she'd woken again, he'd gone and sunlight streamed through the window. She'd rolled over and pulled the pillow Gabe had slept on against her face, inhaling his special scent, rubbing her cheek against the place where his head had left an indentation. Lying there, wrapped in the sheets still musky with the aroma of sex, she'd relived in vivid detail every moment of the previous night.

What a shock to discover that Gabe Carter's sexual preferences had grown in the same direction as hers. She'd thought about everything that had happened since she had driven into Bluebonnet Falls. He had never asked her about her tastes, just moved forward, figuring she'd tell him if anything was too outrageous or turned her off. What were the damn chances, anyway, that their desire would mesh so perfectly?

Just thinking about it had made her shiver with delight.

Of course, they hadn't discussed anything beyond a sexual relationship since the bombshell he'd dropped about Robin. Maybe this was all he wanted. Maybe whatever emotion he'd felt had long since disappeared.

Her body ached but with a pleasant feeling, much better than it might have been, she was sure, if not for Gabe's magic massage. She could still feel his fingers moving over her with tenderness, rubbing and kneading, until she was reduced to the limpest of noodles. But, more than that, she remembered the heated spanking that had made her ache and cry, the oil that had almost driven her into a frenzy, the nipple clamps and Gabe's cock, even more magnificent after all these years.

Had she just imagined what he'd said as she drifted off to sleep? The entire night, although he'd been loving as well as demanding, he'd said nothing to indicate his real feelings. Had it just been wishful thinking that planted those words — 'I love you' — in her head?

She'd sighed and rolled out of bed. *One day at a time.* And she had too many things to do to lie around in bed like a lovesick teenager.

A hot shower took care of the residual soreness from last night and found herself humming as she dressed in slacks and a poppy-red shirt and pulled her hair back with a red-and-gold clip. Gold hoops at her ears and red lipstick and she was ready.

Although she'd bought some things at the market to have for breakfast, Jill decided what she really wanted was a gooey nut and cinnamon roll from the Harvest Moon Bakery. Nancy Wettersein baked them freshly each day and Jill had never found any place that could duplicate them.

Of course that meant the usual ten minutes with Nancy, recapping her life for the woman as she ordered the roll and a cup of cappuccino. She was getting her story down pretty pat.

"Bluebonnet Falls is really growing since you left," Nancy told her.

"Oh? In what way?"

"For one thing, you ought to take a look out at Limestone Hills," Nancy told her, handing over the food and drink. "See what all's going on out there. Might fit into your article."

Jill raised an eyebrow. "In what way?"

"New community being built just outside town. Big houses, park area, office building." She narrowed her eyes at Jill. "Gabe Carter represents one of the investors."

"Oh? How nice." Did she have a sign plastered on her face that people automatically assumed she'd be interested if it involved Gabe? Or were their memories long enough to stretch back to that disastrous summer? "I'll check it out."

Everything else aside, that seemed like a good idea. If she was writing about the old in Bluebonnet Falls, she should also include the new.

Nancy gestured toward a small table. "That's him right there."

Jill glanced at where Nancy pointed. "Him?"

Nancy nodded. "That's him. I hear he's none too happy about the way things are going."

Jill's reporter's antennae sprang to life at that. She loved travel writing but like every good reporter she was always on the hunt for a great story. When she sat down, she took the opportunity to study the man. Medium height, wearing a suit and tie, and she guessed his age at late fifties. When she caught him studying her, she looked away at once. Could she approach him and ask him about Limestone Hills? Would Gabe be upset if she spoke to his client?

She was halfway through the mouthwatering pastry when he stood and approached her table, carrying his coffee.

"May I?" He gestured at the chair opposite her.

"Yes, of course."

"Since I've come to identify the majority of people around here in the last few months and you're a new face, can I safely assume you're Jill Danvers? The magazine writer?"

Jill smiled. "I didn't realize my fame had spread so far."

He laughed. "Everyone in town's been talking about you. Anyway, Nancy's greeting was hard to miss."

Jill's smile widened. "No secrets in this town, that's for sure. What can I do for you, Mr…"

"Armstrong, Gary Armstrong." He reached across the table to shake hands.

"Nice to meet you. Are you a new resident here?"

He shook his head. "Not exactly, although as much time as I've been spending here, I might as well be. Did I understand from what Nancy said you're a friend of Gabriel Carter's?"

"Yes. Gabe and I…" *What?* "Grew up together."

"I see. Well, he's handling a legal matter for me here. Have you heard of the new community, Limestone Hills, proposed for the north end of town?"

"Proposed?" Jill put her coffee down and gave him her full attention. Her antennae were sending her messages. Maybe this would be her chance to break out of travel magazines, as nice as they were, and into hard news.

Hard news in Bluebonnet Falls? Come on!

But you never know.

"I thought it was a done deal." She tried to be as casual about it as possible. If this was just some disgruntled investor with no real ax to grind, she didn't want to give the impression she was writing a tell-all. But if it wasn't, she wanted to get every scrap of information.

"Me, too." Armstrong nodded. "But things seem to be dragging along at an unusually slow pace. I wondered if you were going to include anything about it in your article."

"Funny you should mention that." She popped a piece of roll in her mouth and chewed for a moment. "I was just thinking it would make a nice contrast between the old and the new."

And give her a chance to poke around and see what was what. She'd have to get directions, but how far could it be? Then her table mate solved the problem for her.

"Then perhaps I can convince you to take a ride with me to look at it," Armstrong said. "I'm sure you've seen a lot of these things in various stages. I'd like to get your objective opinion. You're a reporter, after all."

"Magazine writer," she corrected.

He shrugged. "Whatever. You could still have the resources to do some digging around if you were interested, right?"

Jill shifted in her chair. She was a little uneasy at interacting with one of Gabe's clients but determined to discover what he was so worried about. Would he approve or tell her to keep her nose out of it? And out of what? "I don't know if Gabe—"

"I think Gabe would be pleased that I was looking at it with someone who doesn't have a vested interest." He drained his coffee. "What do you say?"

"All right." She finished her own coffee. "How about if I follow you out there?"

"I'd be happy to drive you."

She patted her mouth with her napkin and picked up her purse. "Thank you anyway. I always like to have my car with me."

And just because Gary Armstrong was a client of Gabe's didn't mean he was trustworthy.

It doesn't mean that Gabe is, either.

She dumped the thought as soon as it popped up. Gabe could never be anything but honest. *Could he?*

Following Gary Armstrong to Limestone Hills was easy enough. Bluebonnet Falls wasn't really big enough to get lost in and heading north out of town, there wasn't much except ranch and farmland. About a mile down the highway, Jill saw the first sign for the development, another a half mile on at the turn-in and the third at the site itself. A huge billboard proclaimed the ultimate in Texas living.

She got out of the car, grateful she'd worn low-heeled shoes as she trudged across the dust to where Gary Armstrong stood.

"Well, damn." He said the words in a soft voice.

"What's the problem?"

He indicated the chain link fence that ran left and right as far as she could see. "This is brand-new. Investors and inspectors are supposed to be able to come out and walk the property at any time."

Jill frowned and, shading her eyes from the sun, she turned and looked in every direction, searching for something that just wasn't there.

"But there's nothing in there to see."

Armstrong snorted. "No kidding."

"So what are they protecting?" She stood next to him at the fence, staring off at nothing but empty land. "How long has it been since the plans were announced and the signs put up?"

"Well over a year."

She glanced sideways at him to see him studying her. "A year," she repeated.

Long enough to have more than this square mile of cleared dirt and nothing beyond but waving prairie grass and clusters of trees. Nothing. Not even a sales trailer or a construction shack. And no earthmoving equipment whatsoever. Jill had the funny tingle in the pit of her stomach she always got when a story popped up out of nowhere. She had interviewed several times with news magazines and two online news services, but they hadn't seemed too interested in a travel writer. Why had she ever thought it didn't matter where she got her creds as long as she was published? Now she couldn't get a news organization to take her seriously. And while *Life in America* was held in high regard, she wanted to break out of that mold. Maybe this trip to Bluebonnet Falls would impact her life in more ways than one.

"Well, I'm just a hack writer, so I guess there's a lot I don't know about getting a big project like this started." She shrugged, not knowing what else to say. "It probably takes a lot more preparation that I can even imagine."

"This isn't the first time I've done this," Armstrong told her. "That's why I'm a little concerned. And the excuses the developer keeps giving me don't appear to hold water."

"You mind if I ask you some questions?" she queried.

"No. Go ahead."

Jill took out her cell and pressed the Record feature.

"How about telling me what first interested you in this project. How you got involved?"

For the next ten minutes, she listened to him tell her how Dolman had sought him out as someone who invested in developments like this, sold him a bill of goods, then…nothing.

"No progress, not even a bulldozer sitting out here. Nothing."

"I understand you've spoken to Gabe Carter about this."

He nodded. "He said he's going to put an investigator on it." He sighed. "I tell you, it was hard finding someone who wasn't hooked into this thing."

His words made Jill feel a little better, but she still wondered if Gabe was tied into this in any way. He was an important attorney in the area and could...

Could what? She needed to put it out of her mind and start following the trail her feet were on.

She went to the car and retrieved her little digital camera.

"I'll take some pictures. I can probably use them in the article if I can find out any more about what's happening." She snapped a dozen shots before shutting the camera off and putting it back into her purse. "I'll tell you what I can do, though. Reed Jamison covers business for *Life in America*. He's pretty savvy. I can call him and ask him to see what he can find about Dolman Development if you'd like. Although I'm sure Gabe's already gone that route."

Armstrong nodded. "He has. On the surface, everything looks great. But sometimes writers and reporters can find things hiding beneath the surface. And I've got an itch about this that just needs scratching."

Jill laughed. "I know what you mean. Well, if I find out anything I'll let Gabe know."

"Thanks. I appreciate it."

She didn't plan to stop at Reed, either. Research was one of her natural talents and she knew how to dig. But she didn't want to say anything to Gary Armstrong until she had something solid. And to be fair, she should probably take it to Gabe first.

As long as I'm convinced he'd not involved.

She banished the thought as soon as it popped up. Still…

As they walked back to their cars, a large four-door pickup came down the dirt road fast enough to kick up clouds of dust. A man Jill guessed to be in his forties, in jeans and a plaid shirt, hopped out and came over to them. His face was anything but friendly.

"Something I can do for your folks?"

Jill squinted at him. "No, thank you. We were just looking at the site here. I might be in the market for a new home, depending on when this gets built."

The man stared at her, suspicion sharp in his eyes. "Mr. Dolman has the schedule on that. I'm just supposed to keep people away from here until they get started."

"Oh." Jill made her voice bright. "And when will that be?"

"I told you." His own voice was cold. "When Mr. Dolman says so. At the moment this is private property, so you'll have to leave."

Jill looked over at Gary Armstrong, whose face was a deliberate blank. "That's all right. We were just leaving."

The stranger, whoever he was, stood between her and her car. "One minute."

Jill looked him over from head to toe, trying to see if he had a gun anywhere, but there were no significant bulges. "I think you're in my way."

"Did I see you taking pictures? If so, I'll need the camera."

Inhaling a deep breath, Jill shoved past him. Before he could realize what she was doing, she was in her car with the door locked.

"Get out of the way before I run you over," she shouted.

Armstrong was in his car by now, too, gunning the motor, and the man between them looked from one to the other, then shrugged, accepting the fact he was getting nowhere. Jill saw him in her rearview mirror, standing with the door to his truck open as she and Armstrong drove onto the highway. Her last glimpse of him was him still watching them, a cell phone clapped to his ear.

Once back in the Falls proper, she parked in a space on Winter Street and Armstrong pulled in next to her. He came around to lean into her open window.

"I'll call Gabe and tell him about this. You might mention it also, if you see him before I do." He rubbed his jaw. "I'd say the smell of fish is getting worse."

"I agree. I'm heading to his office right now, as a matter of fact."

"All right. Tell him to be looking out for my call. And let me know what your friend finds out."

By the time Jill slid into the space in front of Gabe's building, she had managed to convince herself she and Gary Armstrong had blown the whole thing out of proportion. Almost. But who on earth would be nervous about a housing development?

Still, that didn't mean she was giving up on researching Dolman Development.

During the elevator ride to the third floor, she checked her hair and makeup and brushed away any residual dust from her clothes. She checked her watch.

Nearly one o'clock. *Good.* She wouldn't be making Gabe wait.

As scenes from yesterday's lunch played in her mind, her panties dampened and her nipples peaked. She wondered what Gabe had planned as an encore. Although, after last night, she needed more than a few more hours to recover. And thinking about tonight made her even more aroused.

The outer office was empty but the door to Gabe's office stood partway open and she heard voices in conversation.

They must be in there working.

She pushed open the door, ready with a cheerful greeting and stopped, immobilized. Every drop of her blood turned to ice and her lungs wouldn't release any air.

Standing in the middle of the office was Gabe, with Robin Fletcher draped over him like a fancy shawl, her arms around his neck and his hands on her shoulders. From the lipstick on his mouth, it wasn't hard to guess what they'd been doing.

Gabe looked up as the door opened wider and every bit of color drained from his face. "Jill…"

"Well, hi there." She gave silent thanks her voice remained so steady. "Sorry to intrude. Christy wasn't out here and I just dropped by to ask some more questions about the celebration. I can see this isn't a good time. Nice to see you, Robin."

"Nice to see you, too, Jill." Venom dripped from every word. "I guess we should have closed and locked the door." She tightened her grip around Gabe's neck.

"Apparently so." Jill turned on her heel. "I'll call you later," she tossed over her shoulder.

I will not cry. I will not cry. I will not let him see how upset I am.

She marched down the hall and toward the elevator with her back ramrod stiff, her steps purposeful, forcing herself not to look back. She had just reached the elevator and pushed the Call button when a hand grabbed her arm with a rough movement and pulled her back.

"Where the hell do you think you're going?" Gabe's voice was harsh, his grip bruising.

"Three's a crowd, haven't you heard? I thought I'd give you and Robin—you know, the woman you hardly ever see—some privacy." The elevator dinged its arrival and the door slid open. Jill yanked her arm away and almost leaped inside.

Gabe tried to follow her, but she pushed him back with all her strength.

"Jill. Wait." His voice had an anguished note to it.

"Get away from me. I won't let you do this to me again." If only she could erase the last two nights, from her brain and her life.

He reached for her but the doors were already closing.

Jill clenched her fists as the elevator descended at its usual snail's pace. *Come on. Come on.* She would not let herself fall apart until she got home, safe within her own walls. How could she have been so stupid as to believe him?

'Do you see Robin?'

'Oh, every once in a great while.'

Yeah, right.

Thank God she hadn't let loose of her heart altogether. But how on earth was she going to stay in this town for another week and do her job with Robin on Gabe's arm every time she saw him?

Her eyes blurred as she fished in her purse for her keys and her finger slipped as she tried to punch the door release. She finally hit it on the third try, but before she could get the door open, she was grabbed from behind and whirled around. She looked up at Gabe, backing her up against the car, anger etched in his face.

"You are not leaving here until we straighten this out." His teeth were clenched so tight his jaw was rigid.

"There's nothing to straighten out. My vision was pretty clear in there."

"It's not what you think at all. Damn it, Jill." His fingers were digging into her upper arms.

"Please let me go, Gabe. It's all right. We had…fun…last night. Let's just chalk it up to that."

"Gabe, honey?"

They both looked up. Robin stood on the sidewalk, one eyebrow cocked.

Jill wanted to rake her claws down that perfect makeup on her face.

"Jill, listen."

"There's nothing to listen to." She slid under Gabe's arms and managed to get her car door open and edge inside.

Robin was tugging at Gabe as Jill drove away, blinking away the tears she'd vowed not to shed.

The moment she hit the house, she immersed herself in a frenzy of activity. The first thing she did after changing into shorts and T-shirt was strip everything from the bed—sheets, comforter, even the mattress and pillow covers. Next, she grabbed the towels from the bathroom. She wanted nothing left in her house with Gabe's scent on it.

She piled as much as she could get into the washer, leaving the rest of it on the laundry room floor. While the machine was filling, she opened both windows in her bedroom in spite of having the air conditioning on, then took a can of polish and began wiping down every surface of every piece of furniture. As she worked, she uttered vicious curses, using anger to keep the tears at bay.

She had just started to spray the bathroom with disinfectant when Gabe walked in.

Of course. The back door.

She should have thought of it.

"Wiping away all traces of the evil demon?" His voice was hard and edgy.

He took the spray can and paper towels from her hand, set them on the counter, picked her up and carried her, kicking and swearing, into the living room.

"I expected this, so I am prepared."

Dumping her onto the couch on her stomach, he placed one knee in the middle of her back to stop her squirming. Then he took the set of handcuffs from last night out of his pocket, pulled her hands behind her back and snapped the locks into place.

"Good thing I still had my satchel in the car. Little did I know I'd need these things in the middle of the day."

"Damn it, Gabriel, let me up." She tried to heave up against him, her legs drumming on his buttocks. "Just get away from me."

"No talking until I have my say."

Before she realized what he was doing, he'd eased her mouth open with his fingers, slid a ball gag onto her tongue and buckled it behind her head. Then he turned her over and propped her in one corner of the couch.

"Now." He glared at her. "You're doing the same damned thing again you did last time." His eyes were cold with rage and his voice sounded like honed steel. "You ran away once without even talking to me. I won't let you do it again. And I certainly don't intend for you not to hear what I have to say. So you either sit there and listen to me or I'll turn you over my knee and the spanking you'll get won't be the kind that turns you on. Are we clear?"

She glared at him, furious, tugging at the handcuffs.

"I said, are we clear, Jillian?"

That stopped her. He only called her Jillian when his anger reached epic proportions. She took as deep a breath as she could and nodded once.

"Good. Then listen to me." He shoved his hands in the pockets of his slacks and started pacing. "I had no idea Robin planned to drop in today. None. Not one inkling. Got it so far?"

She nodded again.

"First of all, don't misconstrue that kiss. Robin's going through a rough patch right now and her emotions are a little…out of control. When I told you I only see her every now and then, I wasn't lying to you. Whenever she's in town to visit her folks we usually have lunch or dinner. I mean, Jesus, Jill, we made a baby together. We were married. She lost the baby and the marriage was a disaster, but you can't just wipe something like that away. We're still friends and right now she needs that friendship."

Jill thrashed wildly on the couch, indistinct sounds coming from her restricted mouth. "Mm-mph-mmm."

He stopped pacing and stood in front of her. "No, I'm not taking that out of your mouth until I say everything I came to say to you." A heavy sigh escaped his lips.

"Robin's in town for the celebration. I guess I should have figured she'd be here. Anyway, she just dropped into my office without warning. For Christ's sake, I hurt you badly enough once, Jill. I'd never do that to you again." He raked his fingers through his hair. "Darlin', please don't do this. Don't misinterpret something and shut yourself away from me again."

She kept her eyes on him but the anger slowly drained from her. Was he telling the truth? Could she trust her heart to him yet again? A heart that had taken ten years to heal yet cracked open again like the thinnest of eggshells at the slightest suspicion of betrayal?

"I told you I won't lie to you and I mean it. I promised to have dinner with her tonight. As a friend," he stressed. "I plan to tell her about us, so there are no misconceptions. But Jill? If I wanted Robin I wouldn't be over here begging you not to run away again, to turn your back on what I believe we started to rebuild."

Jill glared at him but stopped struggling and sat still in the corner of the couch. She wanted so much to believe everything Gabe said.

"Are we okay? Can I take the gag out of your mouth and uncuff you?" She nodded. "Okay, then."

He removed the ball gag first, easing his thumbs over her lips. When he removed the handcuffs, he rubbed her wrists then placed a soft kiss on each one and on her mouth. He stood barely a foot away from her, looking down at her. Jill tried to push farther into the couch, away from his consuming presence.

"I made a lot of mistakes ten years ago and you never gave me the chance to rectify the situation. Or even tell you what my situation was now. This time I'm doing things differently."

Jill couldn't help the tinge of bitterness in her voice. "And what about Robin? I'm sorry, Gabe, but she doesn't look like a woman who's ready to let go of you, even after all this time. And where's her husband? Why isn't he here with her?"

Gabe looked at a spot over her shoulder and when he spoke his voice was toneless and uninflected. "She's filed for divorce."

"And now she's after you again, and again I'm in the way." The words were out of her mouth before Jill could stop them.

When Gabe turned back to her, the rage was back in his eyes. "You must really have a low opinion of me to think that. If I wanted Robin, I wouldn't have divorced her. I could have had her back any time these past years and I know it. But I have no intention of going down that road again."

Jill wanted to believe him so much she ached, but the remnants of the hurt she'd carried for ten years still pricked at her. Along with her heart and her virginity, he'd stolen her easy ability to trust. Now she was struggling to accept what he was saying. And he still hadn't said one word about his real feelings toward her.

"I don't have a low opinion of you, Gabe. If I did I'd never have...had sex with you last night. But that's really what it is between us, isn't it? Some very hot night music? We've discovered after all these years we like the same kind of sex and here's a great opportunity to indulge in it while I'm in town." She got up off the couch and pushed past him, heading for the kitchen. "As outstanding as it was, I guess if that's all you're offering, I'd be a fool not to take it, right?"

She filled a glass with water and stood at the sink, drinking it, waiting. When Gabe said nothing she turned to face him, startled by the stunned look on his face.

"Jill, I..." He stopped, swallowed and started again. "I seem to make one mistake after another with you." He exhaled, a slow release of breath. "All right. Here's what we're going to do. Ten years ago, we really sort of fell into our relationship and it took us over. Now you come back here and I'm like a rutting bull with you. No finesse. So I'm going to change that."

She raised her eyebrows, an indication of the skepticism she felt. "You are?"

He nodded. "Yes." He exhaled a long, slow breath "I think it's time to stop avoiding things—like you did, Jill—and take a good look at what we mean to each other." He was standing in front of her now, gripping her shoulders. He dropped his voice as he pulled her against him. "But don't think that means the sex is out. I think it means it will be a lot better. And a lot more goes with it."

He kissed her with such intensity that her limbs grew weak and she leaned into him. The sweetness and tenderness in his touch it undid her completely. His teeth nibbled at her lip and his tongue lapped at the bites. He pressed against the seam of her lips until she opened and he took possession. He licked and tasted every inch of the inside of her mouth, sucking on her tongue as if to capture and keep it. He savored soft tissue, hard teeth, the inside of her lips, everything his tongue could reach.

When he lifted his head, Jill was stunned at the strength of the passion blazing in his eyes and the tension making the planes of his face stand out in sharp relief.

"Be prepared, darlin'. Just…be prepared."

"And Robin?" She couldn't help herself. She had to ask.

"I told you. Robin is nothing anymore but an old friend. What we shared disappeared a long time ago." He sighed. "I can't turn my back on her when she needs someone, like now with her divorce. I guess it's a messy one. Tonight, at dinner, I'll listen to her problems, make the appropriate sympathetic noises and tell her about us. And that'll be that."

Oh, Gabe, you haven't learned much about women, have you? I saw the lipstick all over your mouth and the look on Robin's face. She wants a lot more than that. Will you be able to walk away from it a second time? Given your history with her?

Jill leaned against Gabe, taking courage from his strength. After all, he had raced over here to make sure she didn't misunderstand things. At least the way he saw them.

"You don't have to say anything," he told her. "Just let me show you. But promise me, no matter what happens, you won't shut me out again like you did before. Promise if you have questions you'll let me explain."

"All right," she said finally. "But—"

"No buts, Jill." He lifted her in his arms and carried her to her bedroom, where he set her down on the freshly made bed. "I swore I'd keep my hands to myself when I came over here to talk to you. Convince you that you misread what you saw today. But darlin', all I have to do is get near you and I'm so hard it hurts."

Chapter Seven

Gabe stared down at Jill for a long moment before he began removing her clothes. As each piece of fabric disappeared, he kissed the soft exposed skin, a bare touch of his lips followed by the tip of his tongue. God, he didn't think he'd ever get enough of her taste. He wished somehow he could put all of her in his mouth at one time.

As he drew away her bra and her breasts sprang free, he closed his lips over one already stiff and swollen nipple. Taking it into his mouth, he circled it with his tongue, flicking it, then grazing it with his teeth. With his free hand, he palmed her other breast, squeezing it with a soft touch, brushing the nipple with the tip of one finger.

Jill's breathing quickened and her body tensed. When he raised his eyes to hers, he could see the glaze of arousal and feel the soft, quick breaths escaping her mouth.

Slow, you asshole. Show her it doesn't have to be hard and rough every time, even if it's what you both want. Don't fuck up again.

When he moved his hand from her breast, sliding down her stomach to the slick pussy he'd shaved just the night before, she widened her legs for him. His fingertips touched the hot folds of her sex, already slick with desire, and the hard nub of her clitoris. When he pressed his hand against her Jill moaned, opening and closing her legs, thrusting her pelvis up to his touch.

"Slow there." He barely recognized his own voice, clogged as it was with lust and need. "Let me worship your body and give you pleasure. Let me make love to you."

Yes, you horny bastard. Show her that you have class, even though all you really want to do is tie her up and fuck her brains out.

Her eyes closed. He caressed her naked sex, loving the smooth feel of the skin. Just touching her made his cock so hard he was sure it would burst through the zipper of his slacks. He moved one finger along her slit until he reached the opening of her sex. One swift move and his finger was in her to the last knuckle.

God, she was wet and hot. Her cream was already coating his skin and he'd barely touched her. Desperate to see her, he shifted position and pulled off her shorts and panties, tossing them to the floor. When he bent her knees and pushed her thighs apart, there it was, her pulsating sex, deep pink and glistening, beckoning to him. He spread her outer lips, giving him a glimpse into her slick channel, and he was sure he would come just from looking at her.

The liquid of her arousal was running from her body down into the cleft of her buttocks. The more he exposed her to his eyes, the more she gushed. Kneeling between her legs, he bent his head and lapped at her cream. He tasted her from top to bottom, teasing at her clit with the tip of his tongue before running it all the way down her slit again, even to the sensitive skin between her vaginal opening and her anus. The more he tasted her, the more her juices ran. Gabe was sure he could spend the rest of his life eating her cunt if only his erection wasn't demanding so much attention.

Jill was twisting from side to side, little moans underscoring her movements. He gripped her hips firmly, holding her for his plundering mouth. When the walls of her slick channel rippled around his tongue, he used the thumb and forefinger of one hand to pull back the hood of her clit and scraped his thumbnail across it.

As angry as he'd been before, he was that tender and gentle now. Her skin was silken to his touch and he was sure he could spend hours just running his fingers over it. And she was so damn responsive, clenching and moaning at every touch. He licked her flesh, thrusting his tongue inside. Nearly drunk from her taste.

She exploded in his mouth, fucking his tongue as if it was his cock, her moans morphing into one long sound of ecstasy. Her hips jerked and her hands gripped the covers as the orgasm ripped through her. He held her in his grip as spasm after spasm shook her.

Even as he sensed the last aftershock ripple through her, she reached for his cock, bumping its hot swollen length with the back of her hand, brushing the soft sac of his balls. He drew in his breath in a sharp hiss as she anchored herself by clasping her fingers around his shaft and pumping slowly.

"Jesus Christ, Jill." The words were a hoarse utterance. "All right, all right."

He couldn't stand it anymore. Releasing her for only seconds, he yanked off his slacks and boxers and positioned himself between her thighs, barely remembering to roll on a condom. He nudged her opening with the now-engorged head of his penis. He slid into her in slow motion. Her legs came up to grasp him around the waist, her heels pressing into the small of his back, pulling him inside her tighter and deeper.

"Please." The plea escaped her lips.

"Ssh," he soothed. "Just feel. Can you feel my cock all the way inside you? Sliding in and out of you? That's me giving myself to you, darlin'. It's better than words."

He whispered against her lips, not erotic words but phases of caring and tenderness and affection. He kept up a steady stream as he thrust very slowly in and out of her, her muscles stretching to accept him.

He wanted to make it last and ignored the urgent motion of her hips to touch harder, reach deeper. Despite her silent urging, he set the pace and all the pleas in the world wouldn't make him increase his speed. Sweat popped out on his forehead as he fought for restraint. But the muscles in her pussy were grasping him so tightly, milking him so hard, his control fractured.

"Please," she begged again.

"Please what, Jill?"

"Please fuck me hard."

"Oh hell, yes."

Quick, hard thrusts brought him to the edge and when Jill leaned her head up and bit one of his nipples, he fell over that edge into a whirling void. His body shook as the spasms gripped him and all he could think about was how right this felt, how they matched perfectly.

His climax lasted a long time, the aftershocks endless. When he could move, he rolled to his side, taking Jill with him.

When he'd seated himself in her with one long thrust, Jill thought the world had cracked in front of her eyes. The rollercoaster she was on climbed higher and higher until it finally plunged her over the steepest drop.

His skin smelled of forest and rain and Gabe, an exotic blend of aftershave and man. She wanted to drink him in, swallow him whole, blend them together into one person.

Gabe, Gabe, Gabe.

She chanted his name in her head while she listened to his labored breathing and felt his heartbeat hammer against her breasts. When the explosion came, it shattered her. She clung to him, sobbing his name until after a long time their bodies quieted and her muscles relaxed.

The sex last night had been so unbelievable and she wanted it again. And again. But this! *This* had been worshiping. Tender. Caring. *This* was much more emotional than physical. It had been Gabe's way of telling her how much she meant to him.

But could she really believe it? And why wouldn't—or couldn't—he say the words?

She sighed, leaning against his big body. She'd just have to force herself to take things on faith. If only Robin hadn't chosen that moment to 'drop in'. And who knew how long she was planning to stay? The little smirk on her face as she'd stood on the sidewalk watching Gabe and Jill didn't bode well for anything.

But somewhere, somehow, Jill knew she had to take a leap of faith. With the way he'd just made love to her, Gabe was asking her to do it now.

She leaned into the hard wall of his chest, feeling the strong beat of his heart against her and wished life weren't so complicated.

"Darlin?" Gabe's deep voice rumbled in her ear.

"Mmmh?" She was hoping he wasn't going to make her move.

"I hate to say this, but I have to go back to the office. I have clients coming in."

Jill pushed herself up to look at him. "Speaking of clients, I met your Mr. Armstrong this morning."

She watched his face as she waited for him to comment.

Gabe raised an eyebrow. "You did? Where?"

"The Harvest Moon Bakery. He heard my name and apparently knows about the article I'm doing."

"What did he want?"

Was that suspicion in his voice or was she imagining it? *Is the situation with Robin coloring my ability to believe in him?*

"He wanted to show me the development he's invested money in." Jill pushed her hair off her face and pulled the sheet up to her waist. "Quite a lot, I gathered. Thought maybe I could include it in the article."

Gabe maneuvered himself off the bed. In the bathroom he disposed of the condom, cleaned himself up and came back in to put his clothes on.

"So did you? Go with him?"

"Yes." She frowned. "And a very interesting thing happened. He told me about his reservations regarding the progress—or lack of it—and I took some pictures with the little digital camera I carry with me. Then some man came driving in like the watchdog of the world and told us we were on private property and to get off. What's that all about?"

Gabe was in the process of buttoning his shirt, but at her words he stopped, not a muscle moving. Then, not looking at her, he tucked the shirt into his slacks.

"I can't really go into details, Jill, but since Gary gave you some of the information, I can tell you there's something strange going on with that project. Very strange. And I'm having the damndest time trying to get a handle on it."

Is he? Or is this just an attempt to throw me off the track? Again she wondered how much of what she was feeling was colored by the Robin situation.

"I suggested I could ask Reed Jamison to dig up something on the Dolman Corporation and he said that might help." She shrugged. "They seem to be aboveboard, but reporters can often sniff out what's beneath the surface. And Reed and I have a great relationship so I don't mind asking for a favor."

Gabe's face tightened with obvious jealousy and she stifled a laugh. Reed Jamison was twenty years older than her, married with three children and the last person to step out on his wife.

"He's our business editor at *Life in America*. He's been around a long time. If there's anything to find, Reed can turn it up."

"I guess I can use any help I can get. Just pass anything you get to me and I'll see Gary gets the information." He sat down on the bed next to her. "I have to go, Jill. I'll call you later, all right?"

"After your dinner with Robin?" She couldn't keep the edge out of her voice. "Isn't that liable to run quite late?"

Gabe took her face in his hands and kissed her, a long, tender kiss that made her want to pull him back into bed with her.

"No longer than it needs to. That's a promise."

"All right. I may go to talk to Ernie again and some of the special events chairmen. Otherwise, I'll be here and I'll have my cell phone on."

"I'll definitely be calling you later." He kissed her again and he was gone.

Jill lay in bed, wishing she could be a fly on the wall at tonight's dinner. For the moment, she was going to shove away all the pesky thoughts that were making her uncertain and daydream about Gabe. At last she got up, showered and changed and sat down at her desk. She booted up her computer and uploaded all the pictures she'd taken at the building site. Then, as an added safety measure, she emailed them to herself at her cloud account. Finally, she pulled out the list of events with the name of each chairperson on it. She was here to do a job. She'd better get to it.

Jill took up her cell phone and dialed Reed Jamison's direct line.

Chapter Eight

"How's everything back in the old hometown?" Reed asked when she got him on the phone.

"The same but different." She paused. "I have a — uh — situation here, Reed, that I could use a little help on."

He chuckled. "Too many events for one reporter?"

"No." She blew out a breath. "I want to ask you about a development that's supposed to be going up here and how to find out why it's not."

"Oh?" Now there was a real edge of interest to his voice. "Okay, let's have it."

"Don't tell me you're getting into investigative reporting," he joked when she told him what she wanted.

"No. Oh, well, maybe. I'd just like to do a favor for an old…friend." She just hoped she really was doing him a favor and not opening a can of worms that he was right in the middle of. "Anyway, can you help me out here?"

"No problem. I know about Dolman Development. It's pretty big. I shouldn't have trouble getting the info. Meanwhile, you can do a public search on your laptop that will give you background and maybe even mention some people who have invested with him before. You could contact them and see if they'll talk to you."

"I want what's not for public consumption," she reminded him.

"Give me a few hours to do some digging. I'll get back to you no later than tomorrow. And Jill?"

"Yes?"

"Tread lightly. This could all be on the up and up, but if it's not, you could find yourself dealing with some really nasty people."

"I'll be careful," she promised and hung up, wondering if she was biting off more than she could chew.

But I want to be a reporter, right? So suck it up.

Buoyed with fresh makeup and filled with determination, she headed for downtown Bluebonnet Falls. The committee for 'The Celebration' had chosen six events in the history of the town and built special activities around them. Market Days on Main Plaza would celebrate the opening of the general store which had made the Falls a functioning town. The rodeo recognized the growth of cattle ranching in the area. And so on. On the final night the schedule included a parade, a pageant at the fairgrounds, a barbecue and a fireworks display — a multifaceted event that the entire committee would work on.

Meeting with that particular chairman was not something Jill looked forward to, considering who it was. Standing in front of Unicorn Gifts, she drew a deep breath, opened the door and walked in to confront Robin Fletcher's best friend.

The gift shop was a treasure trove of interesting items, many of them Texan in flavor and design. Except for a small section of jewelry, most of the items were arranged on glass and wooden shelves that displayed them to their best advantage. A tourist walking into the shop would be tempted almost by the time they took the second step.

The owner was working near one shelf unit, her back to the door, her long blonde hair catching the sun as its rays poured through the windows. Bright red silk slacks and matching blouse covered a body thin almost to the point of emaciation. Her arms, as she moved them, reminded Jill of two sticks covered with skin.

Well, nothing new there.

She cleared her throat. "Hi, Missy. Long time, huh?"

Melissa Spellman turned so quickly from the shelf display she was arranging that she almost dropped the piece of pottery in her hands. Her clear hazel eyes widened almost as much as her mouth did. "Jill Danvers. My lord, how many years has it been?"

"Ten, as a matter of fact." Jill kept her voice pitched low and even.

"Ten years." Missy shook her head. "Where does all the time go?"

In their nastier moments, Jill and her friends had referred to Missy and Robin as the 'Blonde Barbie Twins', two nearly identical women with hair like golden corn silk, figures too perfect to be real and a popularity quotient off the charts. Jill had never been able to understand how Gabe, attached at the hip to someone as sought-after as Robin, would have wanted anything to do with her. She'd been just an ordinary human rolling along through life. But that summer had happened and, at the time, she'd believed every word he'd said to her.

Now she stood before Missy's scrutinizing gaze, wondering if the woman could see the marks of her recent lovemaking with Gabe. Did her face still have that flush that indicated sexual satisfaction? Did her eyes give away intimate secrets? She'd showered for a long time but still wondered if the scent of sex continued to cling to her.

She stifled an overwhelming urge to shout, *Yes, I've just had the most incredible sex with Gabriel Carter. And it wasn't half what we did last night.* But she clamped her lips together to keep the words from flying out. She was convinced that anything she said to Missy would twist around to find some tiny area of vulnerability. She knew that, despite their similarities, the Barbies had their personality differences. Robin might have been selfish and manipulative, a carbon copy of her wealthy mother, but Missy had always been an out-and-out mean bitch. Jill wasn't about to give her ammunition to load into her gossip gun.

"Well," she said in a breezy tone, "I don't know about you, but for me it's taken me all over the world."

Missy's eyes narrowed and her smile tightened. "Oh, yes. That's right. I forgot. I heard you're working for *Life in America* now and you're here to cover the celebration, right?"

"Yes. Gabe tells me you're chairing the big closing event so I thought maybe we could set aside some time to talk about it. The plans look spectacular and I want to be sure to get all the details right. I'll be getting together with Gabe again, of course, but I wanted the nitty-gritty from you as the actual person in charge of that night."

"That's good. Whatever you want to know. Gabe's chairman of the entire celebration, which doesn't give him much free time." She slid a sly glance at Jill. "And of course Robin's in town, so that will probably take up the rest of his time."

Yes. Robin. Who hasn't been married to him for a long time.

"Yes, I ran into her in Gabe's office today." Jill leaned against the jewelry counter, proud that she hadn't shown the expected reaction. She was sure, somehow, that Missy had ferreted out all the details of that long-ago summer and was warning Jill off. "I guess she's here for the celebration."

Missy turned back to the display shelf. "And of course to see Gabe," she threw over her shoulder.

"Oh?" Jill gritted her teeth. "I wasn't aware they were still seeing each other. I understood she'd remarried."

Missy turned back to the shelf display and moved some pieces around. "That just didn't work out. Gabe was her first love, after all, and you know what they say about first loves." She turned back to face Jill, all pleasantness wiped from her face. "Gabe hasn't remarried in all this time. I guess that says something, don't you think?"

Yes, Missy, it does, but not what you think.

"Well, whatever. I'm wondering when you'd have some time to sit down and share some details with me."

Missy tossed her hair over her shoulder in a long-familiar practiced gesture. "That shouldn't be a problem. Trey's out of town on business." The sly look again. "You did know I married Trey Howard, didn't you?"

Thomas Howard III. Son of the president of Bluebonnet Falls Security Bank. It figures. "Actually, I've been out of the Falls' loop for some time."

"Trey's father retired two years ago." She smirked. "He's president of the bank now."

Big deal. "How nice for you." Jill made a point of looking at her watch. "How about dinner tonight? You can tell me all about your event and I can ask my questions."

"I don't close the shop until six-thirty. Can we meet at seven?"

"That's fine. Any place special?" As soon as she said it, Jill wished the words back. She knew where Missy would want to go.

"How about the Mill? It's still the best place in town."

The Mill at the Falls was an old gristmill that two enterprising men had turned into a popular and profitable restaurant. The barnwood structure sat overlooking the Guadalupe River, shaded by giant oaks and sycamores and offering three tiers of dining. Jill was sure that was where Robin and Gabe would be having dinner, and why Missy wanted to go there.

All right. I can play the game.

"Sure. That'll be fine. See you at seven."

* * * *

Gabe clicked off the voice recognition software on his computer and leaned back in his chair. Ever since Christy had installed it, dictating had become so much easier. He just laid down the audio tracks and she picked them up from the shared server. *Electronics!* They never ceased to amaze him.

He opened a desk drawer and took out a small leather folder he'd kept there since the day he'd come back to the Falls. Jill was sitting on a big rock down at the lake, leaning back on her hands, her head lifted to the sun. They had just finished a picnic lunch and, with not a soul around that day, had made the most unbelievable love lying under a huge sycamore. She hadn't known he was taking the picture and her face was open and relaxed, full of the joy of life.

He ran his thumb over the surface of the photo, as if by doing so he could touch Jill herself. He itched to feel the satiny smoothness of her skin again, to cup her breasts in his palms and tease her nipples with his thumbs until they were plump, ripe buds. To slide his fingers inside her hot, wet channel. Or better yet, fill her with his cock, which at the moment was straining against the fabric of his trousers at all the thoughts running through his head.

He was stunned and amazed to discover how her sexuality had developed since they'd last seen each other. She was so very responsive to the things he'd learned, a fact that excited and aroused him. Oh, he'd taken plenty of women to bed, especially as he'd explored his own expanding tastes. With Jill, however, there was a difference that separated her from all the other women he'd taken to bed—he'd never stopped loving her.

So why hadn't he told her yet? Why hadn't he said a word? He'd certainly taken his fill of her body. He hoped the way they'd made love had sent a message to her. But if he was willing to do that, why not say what he felt? Because he still felt guilty for what had happened ten years ago? Or was he still angry and resentful that she'd cut him out of her life and never given him a chance to make things right?

He closed the folder and slid the drawer shut.

He was not looking forward to dinner with Robin. He resented the intensity of the kiss in his office as well as her attitude afterward. Now he wished he could get out of seeing her tonight. He had an uneasy feeling that she had a lot more in mind than just two old friends having dinner.

He still felt a sadness for what they'd shared, but that was the past. They had both grown well beyond that. He'd make sure Robin understood that, stating it in plain and simple language just in case she harbored any strange ideas.

* * * *

Jill spent what was left of the afternoon driving around the Falls, reliving memories of the years she'd lived there, taking note of how much remained the same in spite of the signs of new growth. She left herself just enough time to stop at the house, shower and change into something not quite so casual for dinner. Even though it was a weeknight, the restaurant would be crowded and she'd be on full display for the first time since she'd arrived. Even more so if Gabe and Robin were there.

She slipped on a pale blue jersey dress that showed off her body without being too revealing and buckled on matching strappy sandals. Tonight she left her hair loose, brushing it until it shone, and fastened on her good luck angel earrings. She had just picked up her purse when the doorbell rang.

The arrangement of roses was so large the man delivering it was almost hidden. All she could see was roses, tan arms and long legs in navy slacks.

"My God!" She took a step back. "Did someone buy out all the roses in the state?"

"Just about," a deep voice answered. "Can I please bring these in? My arms won't hold up much longer."

Jill's eyebrows lifted in astonishment. "Gabe?"

"None other than." He moved forward, peering around one edge of the floral display. "How about a hand here? This vase feels like a concrete boulder."

Jill burst out laughing then took his elbow, led him into the kitchen and helped him set the enormous vase on the counter. "More flowers? You idiot. This must have cost a fortune."

"Last night was a simple bouquet of memories." He took her face between his palms and gave her a gentle kiss. "I wanted something to show you I meant what I said earlier today."

"But my God, so many of them." She was stunned by the gesture.

"I'm making up for lost time." He kissed her again. "I couldn't decide between roses and chocolates so I sort of combined them." He reached into the roses and pulled out a perfect chocolate rose, to hand it to Jill with a bow.

"Gabe." She stared at it. "This is too beautiful to eat. Let me put it in the fridge so it doesn't melt. Can you carry this gigantic arrangement to my bedroom? I'd like to keep it in there so I can see it first thing in the morning and last thing at night."

"No problem." He hefted the huge vase. "Lead on."

She had him set the arrangement on the low table in front of the window where they were visible from any place in the room.

"Jill?"

"Yes?" She turned from fussing with the flowers, eyebrows raised at the strange look on his face.

His arms were around her before she could turn away, his lips pressed to the top of her head. "You smell so good. Like jasmine and vanilla. I almost asked you for your pillowcase today so I could take it home and put it under my head at night." He tilted her chin up and touched his mouth to hers, rubbing his lips gently back and forth, the heat from them warming hers.

He smoothed his tongue lightly over the surface of her lips, sending tiny shivers down her spine. When she opened her mouth on a soft sigh, he thrust deeper, caressing the inside of her cheeks, the shiny enamel of her teeth, the roof of her mouth.

Jill leaned into the strength of his body, feeling his stiff erection behind the fabric of his pants hard against her lower abdomen. She had no willpower where this man was concerned. None. One touch and she was lost.

He eased one hand under her skirt, bunching the fabric up to her waist so he could insinuate his fingers beneath the froth of a bikini thong she wore. When he caressed the bare skin of her buttocks, her blood heated as she anticipated what he could do. Might do. Liquid seeped into the crotch of her thong and her pussy began its familiar throbbing demand.

"I have a present for you," he whispered against her mouth. "I want to give it to you now."

"A present?" She looked at him with unfocused eyes. *Now he wants to talk about presents?*

"Uh-huh."

He continued to stroke her ass, the pads of his fingertips tiny flames as they drifted into the cleft of her buttocks, following the line of her underwear. As one fingertip pressed against that tight opening, her juices flowed and one drop shimmied its way down the inside of her thigh.

She made a supreme effort to pull herself together. "Gabe. We can't... We have to—"

"Ssh." He brushed his mouth over hers again. "It's all right. We will. But first my gift. You have to promise me you'll wear it tonight."

"Wear it?" He pressed his fingertips harder, pushing at that tiny opening.

Her legs suddenly threatened to collapse beneath her.

"Uh-uh." He held her tight to his body with his other arm to keep her from falling. "Will you promise?"

"O-Okay." *Yes. Anything. As long as you keep doing what you're doing.*

He reached into his pocket and pulled out a clear rectangular package which he held up to show her.

Jill's jaw dropped. "A butt plug? But—"

"I know you have some. I saw them in your drawer."

"You *saw!*" Her erotic fantasies had never included images of Gabe and a butt plug. In fact, she was still shocked at the degree to which his sexual tastes had developed. Whenever she'd thought of him, she'd been sure he'd be turned off if he ever found out about her new desires and needs.

"But this one is from me." He licked the edges of her lips. "When I called Robin to say I'd be a little late picking her up, she mentioned Missy Spellman had called to tell her you'd been into the shop. Told her the two of you were having dinner at the Mill. I'd hate to think Robin was yanking my chain, although after today I'm beginning to wonder if I knew her at all. Anyway, Missy will be on the alert tonight to see how you react when you see me with Robin. I want to finesse the situation."

"You want me to wear this tonight? In the restaurant?" Jill shook her head but couldn't take her fascinated eyes off the package. "Are you crazy?"

His touch was getting bolder and she saw by the look in his eyes he had no doubts about what he was doing to her. "Yeah, I am. For you. And when we're sitting with our respective dinner companions, I want us to be sharing this tiny little secret."

"Gabe, I cannot go out to dinner with a butt plug inside me."

"Sure you can." His voice lowered. "You can pretend it's my cock."

Jill tried to swallow, her mouth suddenly dry. *This is unbelievable! I can't do this! I'll just tell him no.*

"A-All right." Apparently her brain was on vacation. "I must be losing my mind, but go ahead."

Gabe kissed her, this time a savaging kiss that seared every inch of her mouth. "You have no idea how hard I'll be just watching you. I'll make sure to sit where we can see each other. God, Jill, if we had time, I'd fuck you right now."

He turned her around and bent her over the bed, spreading her legs as far apart as he could and slipping down the thong. Jill heard the drawer of her nightstand open and in a moment felt the cool smoothness of the lubricant she kept there. Gabe placed a soft kiss on each globe of her buttocks, then with great care spread the lube around her opening and inside. Then came the pressure of the plug and its slow progression as he eased it inside her.

"Am I hurting you?"

"No." She felt breathless. "I'm fine."

He leaned over her and brushed his lips against her ear. "I really do wish this was my cock inside you. But it will be, Jill. Soon. I promise you. Would you like that?"

More wetness seeped from her and a dark ribbon of thrill coiled low in her abdomen.

"Yes," she whispered. "I would."

"Good." He pulled her thong back to place and smoothed down her skirt, helped her to stand up again then kissed the tip of her nose. "That's as much of a kiss as I can allow myself or we'll never leave this house. Come on, we don't want to be later than we already are."

* * * *

Jill was sure everyone would look at her and know. *Know!*

She walked carefully, conscious of the greased toy inside her. Not that this was the first time she'd used one. Mike had introduced her to the pleasures of it early in their relationship, but she'd never worn one out in public before and the thought of it had her so stimulated she was surprised she didn't climax just from the images in her mind.

'Soon this will be my cock inside you.'

Gabe's voice echoed over and over in her head. She wished she could believe this was more than just explosive sex that would burn itself out. The long-ago summer had been the stuff of dreams, but looking back on it, had it been real only in *her* mind? Yes, they'd passed almost all their time together. Yes, he'd indicated commitment to her. But they'd spent so much time alone that hardly anyone knew about it, so when he'd married Robin, whatever the reason, no one had given Jill a thought.

What did he want from her now? Could she believe him when he said he wanted to rebuild their relationship or did he just want to fuck her brains out while she was in town?

Stop it! You're making yourself crazy!

Missy waved at her from a table by the window.

"Sorry I'm late," Jill apologized, lowering herself in the chair. "Something unexpected came up." She almost laughed out loud at that.

"No problem." Missy brushed her words away. "I've just been enjoying my cocktail and the view. Let me get the waiter so you can order a drink."

Jill shook her head at Missy's appletini and ordered a wine spritzer. She needed to keep her wits about her tonight, no doubt about that.

"So tell me all about your fabulous job." Missy leaned back in her chair, the stemmed cocktail glass held in her long, tapered, graceful fingers. "I guess you're quite the celebrity."

"I don't know about that, but I am very good at what I do." Jill's voice was firm. She wasn't going to boast but neither was she about to let Missy Spellman wave her off as some little nobody. "I earned my credentials the hard way and it's paying off. That's why my editor has me doing these articles. Speaking of which…" She fished in her purse and took out the small tablet she carried. "Why don't I start with a few basic questions and you can fill in the details?"

"Oh, why don't we just relax a little first?" Missy's patented fake laugh drifted in the air and she leaned closer in an artificial air of intimacy. "We haven't seen each other in so long. Let's have some good old-fashioned gossip."

Gossip. Okay. Shall I tell you about the plug in my ass, which I can feel sitting here in the chair? Would that be enough gossip for you?

She took a deliberate sip of her wine. "Actually, Missy, I'm not much of a one for gossip. Never have been. And I really want to get working on this story, so if I could just ask you some questions?" She took out her stylus and flipped open the leather cover of the tablet. "Let's start with the timetable for the evening."

If the situation hadn't been so annoying, Jill would have laughed out loud. For the next twenty minutes she plied Missy with questions while the woman finished one drink, ordered another and tried not to look like she was peering toward the front door. As the minutes crawled by Jill, too, wondered to herself where Gabe and Robin were. He'd had plenty of time when he'd left her house to pick up his 'date' and get to the restaurant. He should have been there by now.

Don't make yourself crazy. Gabe may not think Robin's up to tricks, but just between us alligators, we know differently.

She knew at once by the change of expression on Missy's face when the couple arrived. The woman's eyes took on an avaricious gleam and she curved her lips in a spiteful smile. "Well, look who else is having dinner here." She waved her hands like a maniac and raised her voice so the whole restaurant could hear her. "Hey, Robin. Gabe."

Jill turned and at once her eyes locked with Gabe's. Her blood pulsing through her veins seemed to turn to a fiery liquid and her sex clenched. She could feel Missy's eyes boring into her. As Gabe and Robin made their way to the table, she noticed the fixed smile on Robin's face and the tightening of her grip on Gabe's arm.

Just friends, my ass!

As they approached the table, Jill was sure everyone in the restaurant could see the shimmer of electricity between her and Gabe. Robin's hold became more possessive and her jaw tensed visibly.

Gabe eased his arm from her grip. "Hello, Jill." His voice was low and soft. "And Missy." Now there was a touch of mockery. "What a surprise finding you here."

Missy flashed her practiced smile at him. "You know this is the best place around. Jill hasn't been back in forever, so I didn't want to take her to some tacky diner."

"Of course." A mischievous grin flirted with the corners of Gabe's mouth. "Since we're all here, why don't we join you?"

"Oh, Gabe." Robin's artificial laugh floated on the air as she tried to tug him away. "I think they have business to discuss. Don't you, Jill?"

What is it they said about a death stare?

"Yes, we do." She was more than ever aware of the lubricated toy inside her and shifted just a bit in her seat. She could never sit across from Gabriel Carter through an entire meal with that shared knowledge between them.

Gabe's look was heated and the knowledge of what he was doing to her was obvious in his eyes. "Too bad. Well, enjoy your meal, ladies."

And there it was again, that spark she was so sure was visible to everyone. The plug suddenly felt enormous and arousal trickled down her thigh. She bit her lip and forced herself to take slow, even breaths.

Robin gripped Gabe's arm again, digging her nails into his muscles. "Let's sit on the lower level, can we?"

"But I asked for this table by the window. The view downstairs isn't as good and I know how you used to love sitting there." Gabe looked over his shoulder and winked as he moved away.

He did this deliberately, damn him!

Jill could not have repeated one word of the evening's conversation or told anyone what she'd eaten if someone had held a knife to her throat. She knew her mouth moved and words came out, her pen wrote on the little notepad and she cut food and chewed it. But she didn't seem to be inhabiting her own body. She was only aware of Gabe sitting fifty feet away from her, gorgeous in charcoal slacks and a pale blue button-down shirt, consuming his own meal.

He'd placed Robin with her back to Jill, a back that became ramrod stiff as Gabe casually shook off the hand she kept reaching out to him and her efforts to entwine their fingers. Although he engaged in conversation with her, he flicked his gaze to Jill far too often for anyone's comfort.

Teasing. He's teasing me.

By the time the check arrived, she was sure the slightest touch of Gabe's hand on her skin would bring on an orgasm of epic proportions. After arranging to meet Missy again to do a walk-through of the closing night's program, she left the restaurant, proud that she could keep herself together. It took all her willpower to keep from looking at Gabe one last time.

* * * *

Jill let herself into the house with a sigh of relief. The evening had been draining. Missy Spellman had been a constant irritant, her remarks as pointed as a sharp stake. Watching Gabe and Robin eating and drinking scant feet away from her, with Robin reaching across to touch Gabe's arm, his hand, his long, tapered fingers ever few minutes, had been an exercise in self-control. The hot, knowing looks Gabe had kept directing at her didn't help, either. By the time she and Missy had finished with dinner, her thong had been so damp she was surprised she hadn't slid off the chair. She was more than ever aware than ever of the plug Gabe had placed inside her.

In her bedroom, she tossed her purse aside and stood a moment in front of the huge display of roses, admiring their lush beauty. As she bent over them to inhale the fragrance, she thought, *what an utterly romantic gesture.* She rubbed one of the petals between her thumb and forefinger, enjoying the satiny feel and thinking about Gabe.

He was right about one thing. Nothing could erase the fact that he and Robin had a long history, not the least of which was their brief, disastrous marriage and the loss of their unborn child. But if he thought all Robin Fletcher had on her mind was dinner with an old friend, he was either stupid or blind. Robin was getting ready to take the invisible thread that still connected them — one Gabe seemed reluctant to let go of — weave her spider's web around him and suck him in.

I'd love to know the details of that miscarriage.

The thought hit her out of nowhere but wouldn't let go. *What's to find out?* The woman had gotten pregnant and lost the baby. But knowing Robin, Jill had a feeling there was more to the story than that. *What if there wasn't a pregnancy at all?* She made a mental note to see what she could find out.

Now you're just being a jealous witch.

Well, okay, but as long as she was playing detective, she might as well check everything out. At least she'd be satisfied.

She took great care removing the plug and cleaned it, then stood under the hot pounding spray of the shower for a long time. But later, lying in bed, she was still wound up tighter than a drum, sleep eluding her. She could think of nothing but Gabe — his hands on her, his thick cock inside her, his mouth touching hers, first tender then bruising. Questions danced through her mind. She couldn't stop thinking about whatever was really going on between them and about Gabe's true feelings. He had yet to say what she wanted more than anything to hear and a finger of unease kept prodding her into wakefulness.

The LED readout on her watch showed eleven-thirty when she finally threw back the covers and padded into the kitchen. When she opened the door to the fridge, the chocolate rose lay in solitary splendor on the middle shelf. *Too bad life can't be that perfect.* She shrugged and took an open bottle of wine and a paper cup back to her bedroom, where she settled herself against the pillows, filled the cup and drank half of it without stopping. Maybe she could get herself drunk enough to sleep and with any luck avoid having any dreams.

The shrill beep of her cell phone made her hand jerk, sloshing wine onto her thighs.

"Are you in bed?" Gabe's voice was low and warm.

"Yes, as a matter of fact." She cleared her throat. "And you?" *And are you alone?*

He laughed. "In bed, you mean? I sure am, darlin'. Just not with you, unfortunately." Silence. "Every time I looked at you in the restaurant tonight I thought about that plug in your ass. I was so hard I was afraid to get up from the table."

Jill laughed. "That would have been an interesting sight."

"How did it make you feel?" His voice hummed with excitement. "With everyone sitting around us, feeling that thing stretching you and just the two of us knowing exactly what was happening?"

Her voice caught. "Hot. It made me hot."

"Did your cunt get wet?" His laugh was low and rich. "I'll bet it was dripping."

"Yes, damn you." *I should just hang up the phone.*

"I wanted to come over to see you."

"Why didn't you?"

"Because I have a breakfast meeting at six-thirty and I'd be in no shape to function if I saw you tonight. Hell, I'd be lucky if I even made it on time. Anyway, I have something else in mind."

She frowned. "Something else?"

"Uh-huh. What are you wearing?"

"What?"

"I said, what are you wearing to bed?"

"Oh." She looked down at the ancient but comfortable sleep shirt. "Just an old thing I've had forever. Why?"

"Take it off."

She nearly choked on the wine. "Take it off?"

"Yes. Right now," he ordered. "I want to picture you naked lying on that bed."

"A-All right. Hold on." She put down the phone and the wine, pulled the sleep shirt free and tossed it to the foot of the bed. She refilled the cup, picked up the phone and leaned back. "Okay. It's off."

"Good. I'm closing my eyes and imagining you. What are you doing while you're lying there?"

"Drinking wine. Why?" *Where is all this going?*

"Put the wine down, spread your legs and touch your pussy. I want to know how it feels to you when you touch it with no hair on it."

Jill's heartbeat kicked up a notch and her hand trembled as she set the wine down. She could refuse him, of course. Even hang up the phone. But neither of those seemed to be an option for her.

"Tell me when you're doing it," he commanded.

Jill slid her free hand down over her stomach, opening her thighs as she did so, and rested her fingers on her very bare mound. Tiny ribbons of thrill danced through her. Already she could feel small flutters inside her sheath.

"I-I'm touching myself." Phone sex was not something she'd done before, but somehow with Gabe it seemed the natural thing to do. She closed her eyes and tried to imagine him lying on his bed, naked, his cock hardening as he listened to her.

"How does it feel?" His voice rumbled through the phone.

"It feels...good. Yes, good." She resisted the urge to stroke herself, just lay there waiting for his next instructions.

"Are your legs spread wide apart?"

"Yes. Yes, they are."

"Good." A husky tone crept into his voice. "Now bend your knees and put your feet flat on the bed, your legs as wide as you can get them. Pretend I'm kneeling between them and my hands are pushing them apart. When you've done that, tell me."

The pulse throbbing in her womb picked up in intensity and a tiny trickle of fluid seeped out of her opening, running down into the cleft of her buttocks.

"All right," she said softly. "I did it."

"Now touch yourself. Slip your fingers down into that soft flesh between your lips and tell me if you're wet. I know you are."

She moved her fingers as he'd ordered her to and felt the slickness of the moisture on her skin. "Yes. I am."

"God, I'm getting hard just thinking about this. My cock is throbbing so badly it feels like it's going to break. It needs your mouth on it, darlin'. Isn't that right?"

The thought of his thick cock pushing past her lips into the warmth of her mouth, the broad flat head resting on her tongue, made her gush onto her probing fingers. "I-I'd like that," she whispered.

"Would you?" His breathing wasn't quite as steady. "Would you like to suck me dry? Feel my cum hit the back of your throat and slide into your body?"

Oh, God, what is he doing to me? A thick coil of need was building inside her, driving her crazy. She licked her lips. "Yes. I want to suck you."

"Jesus, Jill." She could hear the rasp of his breath. "Slide your fingers inside yourself for me. Tell me how it feels."

She had no trouble inserting two fingers, as slippery and wet as she was, and with very strokes moved them in and out. "Wet," she whispered. "I'm very wet."

"Can you feel your pussy ripple? Do your fingers feel good inside you? Do you wish they were mine?"

"Yes." She nearly shouted it this time. "Yes, yes, yes." Her hips moved against the rhythm of her hand and she longed for the heavy feel of Gabe's body pressing down on her.

"You're fucking yourself with your fingers, aren't you?" he demanded, his tone thick with lust.

"Yes." Still barely above a whisper.

"Okay. Reach into your nightstand drawer and take out one of those vibrators I saw in there." He gave a low chuckle. "I'll let you choose which one."

Jill put the telephone down, opened and the drawer and, with fingers sticky with her own juices, plucked a flexible red dildo from her collection. She loved the silky feel of it inside her. "I have it," she said, picking up the phone again.

"All right, darlin'. I want you to ease that thing inside you and while you're doing it, pretend that it's me. That my cock is entering that tight little hole. Can you do that?" His voice had dropped even lower.

"Yes." She was struggling to breathe. "I'm doing it right now." She didn't even have to wet it with her mouth first as she often did. She was so wet that the toy slid into her body with no problem and her pulse accelerated at the sensation.

"Is it in?" The strain in his voice was evident.

"Yes," she gasped. "All the way."

"Now turn it on."

Jill reached for the bottom of the dildo, turned the wheel and at once vibrations shook her, radiating out to every part of her body. "It's on." She could hardly get the words out.

"Okay, sugar. I'm taking my cock in my hand. Jesus, it's so hot it burns my skin. I'm pretending it's your hand, your fingers wrapped around me, stroking me, pumping up and down. Your thumb rubbing the fluid over the swollen head."

His words were arousing her, stimulating her senses. She closed her eyes and images of him lying on his bed masturbating danced inside her eyelids. She wanted him here where she could stroke him herself and feel the thickening of his shaft and the throbbing of the vein that ridged it.

"All right now. Take your forefinger and start rubbing your clit, back and forth but not too fast. I want us to get there at the same time."

Obeying his order, she stroked herself, the action at once sending streaks of lightning through her. The vibrator was doing its work, drawing her up the tight spiral of need, pulling at her, every muscle in her sex clamping down on it. She increased the speed of her finger, her breath escaping from her in uneven spurts.

"Take your other hand, Jill." Gabe's voice was close to breaking. "Pinch your nipple and tug on it. Do it, darlin'. And while you're pinching your nipple and massaging your clit and that vibrator is shaking that sweet little cunt, think of me fucking you, of my cock driving into you, my mouth sucking on your nipple."

"Yes, yes, yes," she chanted. Her senses were on overload. She ground her hips into the bed, her skin suddenly too tight for her. God, she wanted him here with her, the crisp hairs on his chest rubbing her breasts and his hips rolling in that movement that sent the tip of his cock right to the sweet spot. Her heart hammered against her ribs.

"Almost there, darlin'." He was panting harder now, the heavy rasp of his breath filling her ears.

"Me, too." Every nerve in her body was firing, pushing her toward fulfillment.

"Drag your nail across your clit, Jill. Right now."

She scraped her nail over the swollen bud, her body convulsed and just like that the orgasm stormed through her. She writhed and twisted, her inner muscles dragging hard on the vibrator, her fingers pinching her nipple. The spasms racked her from head to toe, shaking her body.

"Gabe!" she screamed.

"Jesus Christ. I'm coming, Jill. Now. Aaah, God. Jill, Jill, Jill."

Their cries mingled over the phone connection, voices harsh with the force of their twin releases.

At the point when Jill thought her body would surely have shaken itself apart, with one final shudder the tremors subsided. At last, with great effort, she reached between her legs, turned off the vibrator and pulled it free, letting it fall to the covers. Her skin was slick with sweat and she wasn't sure she'd ever be able to breathe again.

At the other end of the phone, Gabe drew in huge lungfuls of air, his breath wheezing.

She had no idea how much time passed before either of them spoke.

It was Gabe who finally broke the silence. "Jill? You there, darlin'?"

She had to swallow twice before she could make her mouth form words. "I'm here, Gabe."

"That was…incredible."

"Incredible. Yes." Such an inadequate word for what had happened. Jill was sure she'd have to lie there until someone found her body, as drained as she was. She wasn't sure any of her muscles would ever move again. "Gabe?"

"Yeah, darlin'?" Gabe was having his own trouble speaking.

"I've never done…that before with anyone. H-Have you?"

"No." In the silence she could hear his still uneven breathing. "No one."

"I wish you were here to hold me."

"Me too." A pause. "Jill?"

"Mmm?"

"I…"

She waited but he didn't finish his sentence. "What is it?"

"I'll catch up with you tomorrow. I have a pretty tight schedule, but I'll call you on your cell. I want to see you tomorrow night."

"Me too."

"Night."

"Good night, Gabe."

She managed to disconnect the call and put her cell phone back onto the nightstand. With her last remaining energy, she pulled up the covers and dropped into a dreamless sleep.

Chapter Nine

When she woke in the morning Jill felt as if she'd been thrown under a steamroller — twice — then tossed into a rototiller. She and Gabe had enjoyed far more sexual excesses two nights ago, but somehow last night's episode had plucked at every muscle and nerve in her body. It had been one of the most erotic experiences she'd ever had and had created a new sense of intimacy.

She just wished she could wipe Robin Fletcher from her mind. As innocuous and innocent as Gabe seemed to think their relationship was, Robin sent a different set of signals. Was Gabe deliberately misreading them, hoping they'd go away? Or did he have something else in mind?

Jill shook herself. If she kept mentally debating the issue she'd go crazy. She had more than enough to do without falling into that destructive process.

She was heading for the bathroom when her cell phone beeped.

"You do run into some interesting stuff, don't you?" Reed Jamison's voice held a hint of laughter.

Jill sat down on the bed, holding the phone to her ear. "Not always by choice. Got something for me?"

"Maybe even something for me," he told her. "This looks like a story I can sink my teeth into."

"Don't keep me in suspense," she prodded. "Give."

"First of all, I was a little curious as to why a company like Dolman would be pouring big bucks into a development in Bluebonnet Falls. Forgive me, Jill, but it isn't exactly the hot spot of the world. Or even the state. And not Dolman's usual cup of tea."

Jill nibbled on a fingernail. Had Gabe somehow been the one to attract him here? Did he play a role no one knew about yet?

That's stupid. Idiotic.

But the thought just would not disappear.

"I realize that, Reed, but there is a lot of growth going on here."

"Just not enough to warrant a commitment like this." Papers rustled across the connection. "Okay. My sources tell me the Dolman Company has, shall we say, overextended itself a little. They're developing two very large communities in the Northwest and apparently presales there are slumping. His investors in those projects aren't as patient as he'd like them to be and they're making noises about pulling out."

A tiny feather of unease ran through her. Did Gabe know all that? Had he told Gary Armstrong or was he keeping secrets?

Jesus. I'm going to drive myself nuts. This is Gabe I'm talking about.

She tapped her finger on her thigh. "You think he's using the money from the development here to pay off the others?"

"I don't know, but I'm damn sure going to find out."

"Because he could be doing the same thing here," Jill guessed. "Whatever that thing is."

"You could do some digging around in Bluebonnet Falls," Reed pointed out. "Maybe interview the banker about the newest huge project in the community and what it will mean to everyone. And the mayor. One of them is either involved under the table or has suspicions and they're more likely to open up to you than me."

"You think they will? Open up?"

"Don't know, but if you've got the makings of a news reporter you'll figure out how and what to ask them."

She snorted a laugh. "You have a lot of faith in me, Reed Jamison."

"I do. And I also know you want to move into hard news. Here's your chance to find out if it works for you."

"You're right." She chewed her bottom lip. *Gabe's client isn't going to be very happy about this.*

"Better to find out now than later," he told her. "And you'd better tell your old friend about this, also sooner rather than later."

"I hear you. As soon as you get anything, let me know."

"I will. You do the same. Oh, and here's something else. There has to be a local connection somewhere. Like I said, this isn't exactly Dolman's cup of tea, so I'd say there's more going on under the surface than anyone knows. In that case, locals have to be involved.

Tell your friend he might want to check into that." He paused. "Unless of course he, uh, is the one involved."

And there was the sticking point. The Gabe she knew would never be involved in something like this. But how well did she know him after all these years? The thought she might have misjudged him made her ill.

It's not him.

"Jill? You still there?'

"Sorry. Yes, I am."

"Okay. Let's talk again soon."

Too many unpleasant thoughts were running through her mind after she hung up. The Falls had always been a warm, friendly place to live. Hardly any crime. A little conflict over the mayor's race but not much else. Now, at the exact moment the town was preparing for the biggest celebration in its history, dirty business was likely to erupt. *Not the best timing in the world.*

She wanted to pass along Reed's information to Gabe, but after yesterday's disastrous episode she decided calling was better than stopping by. Besides, she really needed to see his reaction when she gave him the news. If he was in with a client, she'd just ask Christy to have him get back to her.

"You just missed him," Christy told her. "He said he'd be gone until after lunch. Can I give him a message?"

"Just ask him to call me, please. I'll have my cell with me."

"No problem."

That was all she could do for the moment. Meanwhile, as she went about gathering information for her article, she could do some snooping into what was what in Bluebonnet Falls. Showered and dressed at last, she decided to treat herself and stop at the Oakwood Café for a late breakfast. Then she'd tackle another member of the celebration committee. While she ate, she could study the folder Gabe had given her. She'd only glanced through it and wanted to figure out who should be next on her list. Seated in a booth with a cup of coffee in front of her along with the menu, she was startled to realize someone was standing next to her.

"Mind if I join you?" Robin Fletcher's practiced drawl scraped her nerves.

Jill looked up, stunned that Robin would choose to sit down with her and irritated because she knew this would not be a pleasant confrontation.

"Oh, don't worry." Robin slid in across from her without waiting for an answer. "I don't actually plan to eat. I just thought we could have a little chat. You know, girl talk."

Girl talk. With Robin Fletcher. Sure.

The woman looked almost the same as she had years ago. Straight blonde hair in a shoulder-length cut that swung as she moved her head. Skin tanned to a golden hue. Nails long and polished with a bright red color. But if Jill had thought Missy was thin, Robin made the other woman look positively fat. Jill wondered if she ever ate. The lines on her face were too deep for makeup to conceal and the shadows under her eyes gave her a haunted look. Life had not been kind to Robin Fletcher and Jill had to force back the feeling of sympathy that welled up.

She picked up her coffee cup and eyed Robin over the rim. "So what would you like to talk about, Robin? How is life in Atlanta?"

"I think we both know Atlanta isn't the subject on the table." She leaned forward. "I made a mistake letting Gabe Carter get away ten years ago. I won't do it again, so stay away from him."

Jill set her cup down with careful precision. What she wanted to do more than anything was throw it in Robin's face. "Don't you think in all these years if Gabe wanted you back, he'd have done something about it?"

"Listen, Jill." The polite smile was gone from her face. "I made a lot of mistakes where Gabe was concerned, not the least of which was leaving him alone that summer so you could get your hooks into him. But Gabe and I have history and I'll use it to whatever advantage I can. So write your stupid little story and get the hell out of town." She stood up, the phony smile back in place. "Enjoy your breakfast."

Jill stared after her as Robin walked to the front of the restaurant and out of the door.

Get the hell out of town? What is this, a catfight? Are we teenagers?

With great effort she shook off the anger climbing through her. She had to believe what she'd told Robin—if Gabe wanted her, he'd already have her. He'd had plenty of chances. But if he thought all there was between the two of them was a lingering friendship, he was in for an abrupt shock.

She found it impossible to block out her feelings for him. And there was no way what he felt for her was casual. Her faint hope was that Robin wouldn't find some way to destroy it again.

Her breakfast sat in her stomach like a lump of lead as she opened the folder and pulled out the committee list. George and Sarah Wolfe were hosting a reenactment of a minor skirmish in the Mexican-

American War that had been fought just outside
Bluebonnet Falls and were following it with a chuck
wagon barbecue. A visit to their ranch might be just
what she needed to clear her head.

* * * *

Gabe's breakfast meeting ran much longer than he
expected and when he arrived back at his office, it was
to find his next appointment already waiting for him,
and none too patient. His calendar was stacked for the
day without much room to breathe and what he hadn't
needed was Robin's phone call.

Dinner again. Only this time she'd offered to cook it
for him at his house. Discouraging her without an
argument had been no easy task. She'd made it obvious
at dinner last night that the celebration was just an
excuse for her to spend time in town and rekindle the
flame between them. Only there was no flame.
Whatever had been there had died out long ago and
Gabe was searching for a way to tell her without
causing her too much pain.

He was no fool. Sidestepping Robin's obvious
innuendos all these years had taken some fancy
footwork, but he was unwilling to hurt her by pulling
away from her. Just like he'd told Jill, he and Robin had
history and she was still lodged in a small corner of his
heart. Not with any sense of love — that had long since
disappeared — but with an affection for what they'd
had and a shared sadness over the child they'd lost.

His hope was that with time she'd get the message
and stop clutching the past to her so tightly. Only as
each of her marriages had failed, he could feel her
grasping at him with more and more desperation. Yes,

that was the word for it. Robin was desperate. She'd made a lot of bad choices in life and they had taken an obvious toll.

But he wasn't her fallback. His renewed relationship with Jill was still too fragile to allow anything to damage it. And he knew that would be Robin's first point of attack. Of all the things good and bad between them, the summer she'd been gone and he'd fallen in love with Jill festered in her the most.

Thinking about last night brought back the memory of the erotic phone conversation with Jill and a stab of lust shot through him. His cock leaped to involuntary attention as his mind called up the images they'd created for each other. *Jesus!* With all the sophisticated sexual practices he'd learned and enjoyed, last night's episode had been a first for him. Maybe because it had been somehow more intimate than anything else, somehow more connected on a primal level. With Jill he wanted to explore everything, push both of them to their limits.

Lying in bed, listening to her describe what she was doing to herself, hearing her full-throated cry when she reached her climax had undone him. He could still feel his hand clamped around his cock, his hot cum spilling over his fingers as spasms racked his body. Right this minute, just thinking about it, he wanted her naked and under him, her legs wrapped around his hips, his erection seated to the hilt in her hot, wet depths, her pussy clenching hard.

He was so afraid of pushing her yet unable to keep himself from doing it. Would she laugh if she had any idea how unsure of himself with her he was after all these years? He'd promised her the moon then created a situation that had taken it all away. No wonder she'd refused all his calls. Now he had another chance and he still had no idea what her real feelings were. He wanted to lay his heart on the table for her but he was too afraid of getting it destroyed. Did she feel that way too?

He wanted to be with her every night, take her every way possible, show her with his body how much he cared. Plunge himself into her. Lap at her slick, quivering flesh as he teased and tormented her.

God!

He leaned back in his chair and raked his fingers through his hair. He had to get himself under control before his next appointment. He'd rushed his lunch meeting to get back to the office and prepare and all he'd been doing since he'd returned was nearly imagining himself into a wet dream. *Great.*

He punched the button on the intercom.

"Christy, when Avery Hodges gets here, can you hold him off for five minutes? I'm still getting his stuff together."

Liar!

"Sure. And Jill asked that you call her on her cell. Do you have that number?"

"Yes. When did she call?"

"This morning. I told her you'd be out until after lunch."

"Okay. Thanks."

He'd better check himself before he called her back or his painful erection would only get worse, an unfortunate circumstance with a client due any minute.

"Hello?"

The soft sound of her voice sent heat rushing through his body, straight to his groin. Well, so much for composing himself.

"Hi! How are you today?" He banged his fist on his forehead. *Am I eighteen years old? Is that all I can say? How do I think she is after last night's intense episode?*

"I'm fine, Gabe." She paused. "How are you?"

"Horny as hell, if you want to know the truth," he blurted out.

She laughed, a tinkling sound like crystals in water. "That's good to know. I think maybe we can do something about that."

"Hold that thought until tonight. How about if I pick you up at seven?"

"That would be fine. Where are we going?"

"Someplace special."

She laughed again. "Great. I love special."

"And dress comfortably. Meanwhile we need to discuss something else or I'll embarrass myself when my client gets here."

"I think the information I have for you will be equal to a small pail of cold water." She repeated everything Reed Jamison had told her, especially the part about some possible local help. "That doesn't sound too good."

Gabe frowned. "No kidding. I hate to think anyone in this town is pulling some crooked shit. And this sure won't make very pleasant listening for Gary." He leaned back in his chair. "I think I'll hold off on the local angle until I have something more concrete to tell him, but I'm considering hiring a private detective."

"I'm like you," Jill said, her voice sober. "I don't want to think someone I know may be one step away from prison." She paused. "Can you think of who that might be?"

"Are you kidding?" He didn't know whether he should laugh at the absurdity or be angry that she asked him. "Why would I know anything?"

"Okay. Then why don't you wait until I talk to Reed again tomorrow before hiring anyone? He may sniff out a lead or two. He's very good at what he does."

"I guess I can wait that long. I just hate to have things hanging fire with the celebration starting in three days."

Jill swallowed, feeling a tiny sense of relief. If Gabe was involved, he wouldn't be hiring an investigator, right? How could she even suspect him, anyway, if she felt about him the way she did?

Because the reporter hiding inside me doesn't trust anyone, and I hate it.

"By the way, don't you have meetings to go to or something? I don't want to keep you from your responsibilities. This event is the biggest thing to ever hit the Falls."

"Don't you worry. I've got it all under control. See you tonight."

And exactly what did 'under control' mean?

He hung up before she could ask him anything else. So far his anticipation for the evening was the only bright spot in his day.

* * * *

Cottonwood, the ranch owned by George and Sarah Wolfe, was just as beautiful as Jill remembered, a jewel nestled in a hollow of the rising elevations of the Hill Country. The long caliche drive from the road wound around to the big two-story limestone ranch house, the pristine barns stretching beyond it to the acres of pasture. In a white fence corral, half a dozen horses played and pranced, showing off for the hands just riding in from tending to cattle. The Wolfes ran ten thousand head of cattle and bred some of the finest Santa Gertrudis around. When George had paid a king's ransom for a blue-ribbon bull from the famed King Ranch, everyone had thought he was crazy for spending so much money. He'd made it back a hundred times over. Now people were coming to him for breeding stock.

"I am just so glad to see you, Jill." Sarah Wolfe enfolded her in a warm hug. "I sure do miss your folks. What a devastating loss for you."

Jill accepted the older woman's affection with gratitude. The Wolfes and her parents had been good friends.

"It's good to see you, too," Jill told her, following Sarah through the house to the back patio.

"I thought we'd have iced tea out here," Sarah told her. "It's still cool enough before the summer heat and we always get a nice breeze in the back." She filled two glasses and handed one to Jill. "So tell me all about this article you're writing? We're just so proud of you being a featured writer for *Life in America*. And covering our celebration! How much better could it get?"

"I'm really enjoying myself." Jill leaned back in her chair and pulled her tablet out of her purse. "Let me explain how I plan to frame the article. Then I want to ask you some questions about the reenactment and the barbecue. Oh, and I'll want to get pictures, of course."

When Jill finally sat back, she was startled to realize three hours had gone by. "I'm sorry, I didn't realize how much of your time I'd taken up." She pointed to the little tablet. "But you gave me some great stuff for the article. I can't wait to see this. I'll be bringing a photographer, too."

"Oh, honey, don't worry about taking up my time. I love sitting here with you after all these years. This is great. But I'll bet you're starved. I didn't even offer to feed you."

Jill shook her head. "Don't worry. I ate a late breakfast." She took a sip of her iced tea. "I see there's a new community going up outside town. Limestone Hills."

Sarah nodded. "Supposed to be huge homes on lots of acreage." She grinned. "For folks who want to pretend they're ranchers but aren't, I think."

"There doesn't seem to be much activity, though. I thought I'd include it in the article, but I drove out to look at it yesterday."

Sarah frowned. "That's true. We've wondered about that. The developers came to see George, wanted him to invest in it, but he told him the cattle have first call on our money." She shrugged. "I guess it's just as well. George says he doesn't know if the thing will ever get off the ground."

"That's too bad. The idea seems like a good one." She wet her lips. "Gabe hasn't said much but it seems like something he'd want to get involved in. Although I have no idea what his financial situation is."

That much at least was true.

"He's done very well for himself, but I don't think this is his cup of tea. He hasn't had much good to say about the situation. In fact, I think Gary Armstrong hired him to go over the agreements he'd signed and do a little investigating."

Although she'd still keep checking, more than anything Sarah's words convinced Jill Gabe was on the side of the angels.

An awkward silence dropped between them then and Jill saw a strange expression on Sarah's face.

"Sarah? Is something wrong?"

The older woman's eyes were focused on her face. "I don't know if I should say anything, honey. It's really none of my business, but I always felt like you were mine as much as your folks'."

"Please. Say whatever's on your mind." *Oh, Lord, now what?*

"Not too many people knew about you and Gabe that summer before your parents were killed. You were home alone and the two of you kept pretty much to yourselves."

Jill's heart thumped. Whatever was coming couldn't be good. "We…just wanted to be low-key. Robin was gone and Gabe hadn't yet had a chance to tell her it was over."

Sarah nodded. "If George and I hadn't run into you those few times, we might not have known either. You did a good job flying under the radar in a town this size." She picked up her iced tea and finished the last swallow. "Anyway, no one had to paint me a picture when you left here with your aunt and uncle. The Fletchers couldn't really keep Robin's pregnancy a secret, not when the wedding ended up being so rushed. I never saw an unhappier man than Gabriel Carter."

Jill shifted in her chair uncomfortably. "Sarah—"

Sarah held up a hand. "Just let me finish. Please. I think it was a relief to him when the marriage was over, even though the circumstances were so tragic. I think

Gabe's been in love with you every minute since that summer. I don't know what's kept the two of you apart all these years, but Robin's in town for the celebration and, I can tell you, she'll fight to get him back."

"Oh?" Jill didn't know what else to say.

"She's tried marriage twice since then, throwing it in Gabe's face and getting no response. I think she thought if she played the friendship card, she could turn things around with him. But he's not having any of it. I promise you he'll do whatever he has to while you're in town to rebuild the relationship with you. The reason I'm saying all this is because I hear Robin's taken the gloves off now and I don't want you to get hurt."

Jill twirled her empty glass, staring at it. "Pardon me if I'm being rude, Sarah, but how do you know this?"

"The Fletchers were at the same dinner party we attended a week ago and Harriet Fletcher was informing everyone Robin would be coming home for the celebration. She was gushing about how nice it would be for Robin and Gabe to get back together. She didn't say much about Robin's current husband except that he was practically history."

"Well." Jill didn't know how to react. Her gut instinct had told her this had been the case when she'd walked into Gabe's office yesterday, but having it confirmed made her stomach knot and her neck tense. "That's always assuming, of course, that Gabe is willing."

Sarah leaned across the table and put her hand on Jill's arm. "I'm telling you this, my dear, because if Gabe is showing any interest in you at all, don't let him get away. But be warned that Robin will do anything to torpedo it. Over the years she's turned into as big a bitch as her mother and I say that with all sincerity."

Jill burst out laughing. "What on earth would I ever do without you?" She stood and hugged the other woman. "Don't worry. This time if I think there's something there, I won't turn tail and run. And thank you for this."

But driving home, she had to work to push away the doubts crowding in. She was grateful for Sarah's support and knew she had the best intentions in saying what she did. Robin had always been a formidable adversary. She'd be even more so now if she was desperate and saw her prize slipping away from her.

Gabe was being very attentive — not to mention the sex was better than she would have believed — but he still hadn't told her what he wanted from their relationship. Where this was going? Was he waiting for her to speak first?

Her head was pounding by the time she pulled into her driveway. *Aspirin. Shower. Nap. In that order.* By seven she planned to knock Gabe's socks off.

* * * *

As seven o'clock approached Jill had changed clothes five times. Not that she'd brought an extensive wardrobe with her, but enough to carry her through the two weeks of her planned stay. Finally, she settled on a pair of cotton slacks and a soft pink T-shirt with a rounded neck and cap sleeves.

I don't remember being this nervous for a date when I was in high school.

But the desire in Gabe's eyes when she opened the door was worth it — appreciation, heat, lust.

"You look good enough to eat," he grinned. "Maybe I'll change the menu for dinner."

"You didn't say where we were going, just to dress comfortably. I hope this is appropriate."

"The only thing better would be to wear nothing at all. Come on, let's go before I ravish you right here on the floor."

"Wow! Ravish! What a yummy word." She laughed as she followed him to his car.

Gabe drove for about fifteen minutes before Jill realized they were outside the town limits of the Falls. He turned off the highway onto a narrow two-lane road then onto a short driveway that wandered through thick oak trees before ending in a circle before a sprawling brick and stone house.

She turned to Gabe, eyebrows raised. "Is this the special place?"

He nodded. "Chez Carter. I bought it about five years ago. It needed some work so I spend time on it whenever I can. It helps work out the kinks in my brain."

"It's beautiful," she told him and meant every word.

The wood floors gleamed with polish, the crown molding softened the lines and angles and the huge windows let in floods of sunlight. At this time of day, when the sun was just beginning to dip below the horizon, the glow was more rosy than yellow and gave everything a warm, almost surreal appearance.

"We're having dinner here?" she asked as he led her into the kitchen, a masculine room of granite and steel. "Don't tell me you cook."

He turned to face her, his hands on her shoulders, his face a millimeter away. "I have many hidden talents and lots of time for you to discover them."

Then he pressed his mouth to hers, the contact so gentle as he teased the seam of her lips with his tongue, grazing the edges with his teeth. She gripped his shoulders and pulled herself up to her tiptoes, opening her mouth to him. When he thrust his tongue inside, moisture dampened her panties and the familiar pulse in her sex began its steady rhythmic beat.

Gabe moved his head to better adjust his lips to hers, sliding his hands down her arms and around to her breasts. Palming them, he brushed her rigid nipples with his thumbs. Jill pressed against him, feeling the hardness of his erection against the softness of her belly and wanting him inside her with a need she hadn't believed possible.

Moving his hands to cup her face, he eased his mouth from hers. "If we don't stop this right now, we really won't get to dinner tonight. And the manual says the man should dazzle the woman with his culinary talents."

Jill drew in a deep breath and let it out slow and easy, her mouth still swollen, her nipples still tingling. "Okay. I'm ready to be dazzled."

Gabe opened the refrigerator door and took out the makings for fajitas. "I've been marinating the steak since this morning. We can have some wine outside while I wait for the coals to heat and throw the steak on. Can you grab that bottle in the fridge and the glasses and opener from the counter? I'll get the fire started."

It was pleasant sitting outside on the patio, watching the day end and evening roll in. The wine was another Rochelle winery product, a crisp pinot grigio chilled to perfection and so smooth going down Jill had finished her first glass before she realized it. She watched Gabe at the barbecue, loving the play of muscles in his arms and beneath his shirt. No one had ever aroused her more or tantalized her senses more than he did, even when he was doing nothing more than barbecuing a steak. Ten years ago or now, it was still the same.

They made small talk while they ate—about the upcoming celebration, people they both knew, her job and his clients.

"So how am I doing?" Gabe asked with a grin, folding ingredients into a warm tortilla. "Flowers. Chocolates. Cooking dinner."

Jill had to laugh. "Do you have it planned out, like a legal strategy?"

"You bet. I can't leave anything to chance."

"So is this the surprise? Cooking dinner for me?"

He refilled her wineglass. "Partly. I wanted you to see how charmingly domesticated I am." He waved his hand around them. "Hardworking home owner. Accomplished chef."

Jill leaned forward. "And where is all this leading, Gabe? Where is it going?"

He studied her face, his eyes heated. "You tell me."

No. You tell me first. I can't risk my heart again.

She cleared her throat. "I think we'll just have to see, won't we?"

He reached out and trailed his fingers over her cheek, then along the line of her jaw and finally to the pulse beating at the hollow of her throat. "Yes, we will. You can count on that."

At last the dishes were cleared and stacked in the dishwasher and the leftovers put away. They stood in the kitchen, staring at each other. Jill had a fluttering in her belly that was part desire and part nerves. *And why am I nervous?* The first night she'd been worried what Gabe would think about her sexual desires and the things she liked to do. But now there was no question of holding back, because his desires and needs were even more erotic than hers. So what was causing this attack of butterflies?

Gabe picked her up in his arms and stared at her. "Second thoughts?"

She shook her head. "Not even one." She caught her bottom lip between her teeth. "What about you?"

"You're kidding, right? In all the years I've been dreaming about being with you again, if I had any reservation it was what you'd think of *my* needs and desires. The games *I* liked to play. After that first night, Jill, I'm convinced Fate meant for us to be together."

He was right, she told herself. She should just enjoy this and quit worrying about why he hadn't said a word regarding his feelings for her. Maybe he figured when the celebration was over she'd be leaving again, so he wasn't going to put himself out there.

He stared at her for a moment, watching her with a quizzical expression on his face as if to assure himself he wasn't moving too fast. Her pulse beat so hard she was sure he could hear it. No, he wasn't moving too fast. *God!* All he had to do was give the barest hint that were going to have sex and she was ready and hungry.

"Are we good here?" There was just a hint of uncertainty in his voice, but enough to realize she had control over the situation, too.

"We're very good," she assured him.

His bedroom, like the kitchen, was one hundred percent masculine. A striped comforter covered a massive oak king-size bed. A matching dresser and armoire stood against one long wall and nightstands bracketed the bed. The room was impeccable, neat to a fault.

"How long did it take you to clean up before we got here?"

Gabe threw back his head and laughed. "Found me out, did you? I was hoping you'd be impressed with my housekeeping skills and think what a neat person I was."

She pressed a soft kiss to his cheek. "I don't think it's your housekeeping abilities that interest me right now."

"That's good," he said in a soft voice. He set her on her feet and tugged her T-shirt over her head. His eyes went right to her breasts, framed by the satin and lace cups that barely contained them. He ran one fingertip over the swell. "You have such gorgeous breasts, Jill. You always did. I could suck them all day long."

Shivers tickled her spine but she forced herself to stand still under his scrutiny when what she longed to do was grab his hands and place them over breasts begging for his touch.

"I love to watch you come." His voice was soft yet filled with hunger. "Tonight I want to take you higher than you've ever been, again and again, until you beg me to some."

"Y-You are?"

"Uh-huh. I want to see that gorgeous body strain for release even while you force yourself to hold back…until I tell you it's okay to let go."

"Is that what you want?" She searched his eyes, looking for…something. Some reason for this. She had a feeling after tonight there'd never be any going back for them.

"More than anything." He licked her ear. "I want you to know that I can bring you more pleasure than any man you've ever known."

"Why?"

"Why do you think?"

Say it. Please say it.

But maybe it was enough that he wanted to give her this ultimate pleasure.

He moved his hands down her sides to her hips and around to the front of her slacks, unfastening the one button and sliding the zipper down with a faint rasp. He slipped them and her panties down her legs, balancing her while he slipped them off first one foot then the other. His hands were hot against her skin, blazing a trail wherever he touched her.

When she was completely naked, he paused a moment to study her from head to toe, then reached into the drawer of the nightstand and took out a small box. "I'm sure you won't believe this, but I bought these a long time ago when I was in Austin, hoping that one day I'd have a chance to give them to you."

When he removed the top, Jill just stared at the contents, a pair of exquisite nipple clamps.

"Remember the present I gave you the other night?" Gabe asked.

She nodded. Only these had tiny diamonds and pearls on serpentine gold chains.

"I had these designed especially for you. If Fate ever brought us together again and this didn't turn you off, I wanted you to have some with personal meaning." He removed one from the box and took a nipple between his thumb and forefinger, rolling and tugging. When he put his lips on it, drawing it deep into his mouth, her knees weakened and she clutched at Gabe's shoulders to steady herself.

When the bud was so engorged she thought it would burst, he took the clamp—two narrow gold bands with a long thin chain dangling from them — and slipped it into position. He tightened the tiny screw until she sucked in a breath. Then the sharp pain receded, leaving intense pleasure and a throbbing in her breasts that turned her blood to liquid fire.

Gabe released the tension just a fraction then bent and licked the rim of the areola. "It hurts good, doesn't it? You have no idea how many nights I dreamed of doing just this with you. To you. Sometimes I'd take this box out of the drawer and look at these and fantasize about exactly what we're doing now."

He did the same thing to the other nipple until both clamps were in place. The air was rich with the scent of her arousal and she could see from Gabe's eyes he was affected by it. He tore his gaze away, lifted her in his arms again and placed her on the bed, legs spread wide. Then he stroked her naked mound with one hand.

"I'll have to keep this well shaved so I can see every inch of it every time I look at you."

He reached into the drawer for another box, removed its contents and leaned down to press open her lips. In a moment something cold pinched her already pulsing nub.

"What—"

Gabe drew a thin chain from the clamp on her clit to the ones squeezing her nipples and locked them together with a ring he placed on her navel. He gave a tiny pull and her entire body clenched.

"These look gorgeous on you, Jill." Heat blazed in his eyes. "Your nipples are so distended and dark and your clit is already throbbing. It's gonna be hard to have patience tonight."

She watched while he removed his own clothing, tossing it onto a clothes stand next to the dresser. When he turned back to her, she swallowed a gasp at the sight of his swollen, throbbing erection, the broad head a dark purple, the shaft even more enormous if that was possible. A tiny drop of fluid beaded at the slit.

Gabe walked to the side of the bed, kneeled down next to her and took his cock in his hand. "Lick it for me, darlin'. Go ahead."

She flicked her tongue out and swept it over the head, taking the fluid into her mouth. He jerked against the swirl of her tongue and started to pull back but she closed her mouth over him. A shudder rippled through him and his hand gripped the base of his shaft. Jill reached over, brushing his hand away and replacing it with her own. As she moved, the chains tightened and the three clamps exerted pressure as they were meant to. Lightning streaked through her from her nipples to her core of her sex, setting off a series of tiny spasms.

Gabe's knowing eyes registered her reaction and his cock hardened even more in her hand. She took him in as deep as she could, working his length past the gag reflex until almost all of him was enclosed in her delicate wetness. When she slid her lips up and down, stroking him in an even rhythm, he closed his eyes and threw back his head. His breathing grew heavier and the pulse at his throat beat more strongly.

The skin of his shaft was soft as silk, but beneath it was the thickness that filled her and pushed against the back of her throat. He stretched her lips to the utmost, almost more than she could take, but she refused to back off. Then he moved his hips, sliding his shaft back and forth with increasing pressure.

With her other hand Jill reached between his legs to cup his balls, squeezing them gently.

"Jesus." The word slipped from him on a heavy gasp.

He speared his fingers into her hair, grasping her head and holding it, moving her to show her what gave him the greatest pleasure. She curled her tongue over his erection even as she sucked it in deeper, working his balls, squeezing and stroking them. When they tightened and drew up, she knew he was near orgasm and sucked harder, pumping her hand faster.

He came with a roar, grasping her head, the hot stream of his seed splashing against the back of her throat. The muscles in her neck worked as she swallowed each spurt and she continued to milk his shaft with her fingers until she tasted the last drop. She drew back, letting his cock slip from her lips, the chains pulling at her nipples and her clit as she shifted to lie on her back again. She let a knowing smile play at her lips.

"God, Jill." He struggled for control. "Your mouth is like liquid fire. I couldn't help myself, darlin'."

"I wanted that. I like swallowing part of you, taking you deep inside me."

"You did that all right." His breathing evened out and he lay down beside her. When his cock brushed against her thigh it twitched and he laughed. "Damn thing wants to do it again." He shook his head. "But not before we do what I have in mind for you." His voice was low and husky and hunger flashed in his eyes. "Things that will bring you great pleasure and make your orgasm the most shattering you've ever had. I want to do that, Jill. Make you come harder and better than ever before. Do you want that, too?"

For a long moment she couldn't breathe as erotic images flashed in her brain.

"Yes." She struggled to get out the single word.

"Good." He peppered kisses along the line of her jaw even as he tugged on the chains with his free hand. "Because I'm going to fuck you blind."

A thrill raced along her spine and heated her skin.

Holy God!

From the nightstand drawer he removed a set of handcuffs lined like the others he'd used and clasped them around her wrists, first threading the connecting chain through a slat in the headboard. Then he took out a black scarf of soft silk, folded it and used it to cover her eyes.

She lay there while he secured it at the back of her head. When he tugged on the chains, she made a sound halfway between a yelp and a moan as arrows of sensation shot through her.

Gabe ran the tip of a finger the length of her slit, rubbing her juices against the outer lips. Then he placed his mouth close to her ear, his warm breath tickling her skin.

"Jesus, Jill. I want to make this last but you make me so hot."

When the bed dipped between her legs she sensed him kneeling between her outspread thighs. Something soft and pliable yet firm eased into her sex and her stomach muscles tightened in response.

"Game for something else, darlin'? I have another present for you."

She wasn't sure she could survive many more presents if she didn't get to have an orgasm soon.

He pinched the tiny clamp on her clit and placed something on top of it. Then he slid a dildo into her hot, wet channel and in a minute it started to hum gently, vibrations pulsing through her with a slow beat. They resonated through the clamp on her clit on up to her engorged nipples and in a moment her entire body was one long vibration.

Gabe put his mouth on her leg and began kissing his way slowly up the inside of it, taking little bites and sucking at each of them. When he reached the crease of thigh and hip, he drew a long line with the tip of his tongue and began a slow descent along the other leg.

She wished he'd turn the vibrator to a higher setting instead of leaving it where it worked its magic on every nerve in her cunt. The combination of the low vibration and his kisses had her hovering at the edge. But then it stopped—his mouth, the vibrations, everything. She wanted to scream.

"Gabe?" Her voice betrayed the strain she was feeling. It seemed Gabe's one goal for the evening was to drive her as close to orgasm as possible without giving her relief. She wondered how many more ways he'd learned to torment her and drive her crazy. She wondered if it would ever be her turn.

"I know you want to come, but we're not there yet."

He moved between her legs again, tugging the skin just below the vibrator, and used the tip of his tongue to tease that sensitive flesh between both openings. When she tried again to shift, he held her in such a way that movement was impossible. He stroked the skin with his wickedly clever tongue and once again brought her nearly to the brink. Again he stopped.

"More," she moaned. "Please."

"More is what you'll get. Lots more."

The mattress shifted as he moved and in a moment he pressed another toy in the sensitive spot just below her core. *Another vibrator!*

Oh, God!

Every vibration shook her and pushed her more toward release without ever letting her reach that peak. She didn't know how much more of this she could stand. By now she was sobbing and begging, pleading with him to let her come. She had never, ever been so turned on in her life.

Gabe's hands were warm and strong on her, holding her in place, anchoring her or she was sure she'd have disintegrated. It was almost too much for her to bear.

Then it stopped again. Everything.

She lay there panting, waiting for what came next, wondering if this time he'd let her reach that precipice that he held just out of reach. Wanting his touch. Wanting to climax. Wanting something. Anything.

Then his hands again. This time reaching down to separate the globes of her buttocks and spreading something cool on her opening and the skin surrounding it.

"Remember how you loved that plug, Jill?" His voice was low and thick with passion and lust. "This one's even better."

He slipped first one then two fingers into the dark tunnel, spreading the lubricant and stroking her inner tissues. In another moment the cylinder slid inside her, slowly, so as not to cause her pain. When it was fully seated he leaned down to bestow an openmouthed kiss on her skin just above her clit. Then he placed one on each cheek of her ass.

"Hold back, Jill. Hold back as long as you can. It will be worth it, I promise."

The toy buzzed, sending wave after wave of sensation through her nerve endings. Then the one in her sex kicked into life, the extension pressing on the clamp on her clit. Then Gabe positioned his mouth on the inside of her thigh and kissed and licked his way up and down the insides of her legs again. She lost all sense of time and place, thrashing on the bed, her entire body so stimulated it was overloading her senses. She tugged at the handcuffs, tried to thrust her hips and a long low moan escaped her.

Oh God oh God oh God oh God.

She couldn't stand it. It was too much. Tears ran down her cheeks from beneath the blindfold and this time she couldn't hold back. Her body was slick with sweat and harsh sounds ripped from her throat. She fought it as hard as she could but then her thigh and abdomen muscles clenched and the orgasm built and built.

"Please," she sobbed. "Oh, please."

"All right, darlin'." His voice was taut, as if his own control was slipping. "Come now."

The climax roared through her, shaking her from head to toe. On and on it went, every sinew grasping at it and her internal muscles sucking the dildo deeper. Just when she thought everything was slowing down, Gabe increased the speed on both of them and she was thrown out into the void again, convulsions racking her body. She couldn't catch her breath as she rocketed from peak to peak.

At the moment she was sure her entire body would break apart, the vibrations slowed and finally ceased. One at a time Gabe withdrew them from her. When he was finished he removed the clamp from her clit, held his mouth over the sensitive tissue then used long strokes of his tongue to lap all her juices. When he was finished he moved up on the bed and lay down beside her. His warm hand stroked her face and pushed back the hair from her forehead. At last he removed the blindfold and tossed it to the side. When she slid her glance to his face, a soft smile curved his lips.

"Okay, darlin'?"

She released a shuddering sigh. "Yes. I think. Maybe."

Okay? I've just had the most intense orgasm in my entire life, more shattering than I could ever have expected. 'Okay' seems such an inadequate word.

"That was amazing," she managed at last.

"You're amazing." He continued stroking her face. "You are so responsive. And so hot. Making love to you is like making love to a flame. You know it will burn you but you don't care." His cock was hard again, brushing against the soft skin of her thigh. "I want to slide myself into your greedy cunt and fuck your brains out."

She wanted that, too.

He sat up. "But first, let's get you out of all this. I think we've both earned a glass of wine."

Chapter Ten

Gabe released the handcuffs, rubbing her wrists and massaging her arms, then moving them to lie at her sides. When he unscrewed the clamps on her nipples, shards of pain shot through them as blood rushed to the tips. He took each one into his mouth in turn, licking it with his tongue and sucking on it. He did the same to her clit, pressing his lips to it in soft kisses and giving it a gentle tease. Her body ached from head to toe but it was a pleasant ache. She felt well used but in a good sense.

Somehow it didn't seem at all strange to Jill to be sitting opposite Gabe on the bed, cross-legged and nude, so limp she almost couldn't sit up, sipping the delicious white wine. She found herself staring at his cock, erect once more, jutting forward proud and thick from the curls surrounding the base. The vein under the soft layer of skin pulsed and the head was again a deep shade of purple. Without realizing it she ran her tongue over her lips as she remembered how he'd tasted, how the thickness of his rod had more than filled her mouth. How hot and salty-sweet his cum had tasted spurting down her throat.

Gabe saw where her eyes had wandered and laughed. "Oh, yes, darlin', I'd love to feel those warm lips around me again. You can bet on it! But before that I'm going to bury myself inside you so deeply you won't know where one of us ends and the other begins. So deep no one else can ever take my place."

She shivered at the thought and focused on her wineglass, wondering if she should ask Gabe what was uppermost on her mind. "Is that how you'd like it, Gabe? So we're like one person?" That was as close as she could come to asking him outright what his feelings were. She wasn't an insecure person and she needed to stop making herself into one.

He leaned forward and cupped her chin in his hand. "What do you think?" He placed a light kiss on her lips, just a brush of his mouth against hers, and ran his tongue along the edges of her lips.

She searched for an answer that wouldn't be too aggressive and, finding none, instead kept silent.

Gabe took her wineglass and set it with his on the nightstand. "Come on. I think what we both need right now is a hot shower."

The bathroom was outfitted with a large Jacuzzi and a shower that Jill was sure would hold a group of six. The walls were granite and multiple showerheads produced soft jets of water, almost like mist, from every direction. When Gabe was satisfied he had the settings the way he wanted them, he moved Jill so she faced one wall and placed her hands flat against it.

"You'll love this." His voice was low and confident. "I promise you'll feel terrific when we get out of here."

He reached for a plastic bottle sitting on a built-in shelf, poured some on his hands and rubbed it into Jill's shoulders and back. The aroma of jasmine mingled with the mist and formed a scented cloud around them.

"Pretty exotic for a man," she commented as his hands moved over her.

"I bought it for you. It's what you always wore and still do."

She was touched at this attentiveness to detail. Could he be sending her small signals that this was more than just a temporary reunion? And where did Robin figure in all this? Gabe had to know she wanted more than friendship, but Jill understood he felt tied to his former wife by the child they'd conceived and lost.

Out of nowhere a thought popped into her brain. Along with investigating Dolman and his development, she was going to check into Robin's miscarriage. It just seemed too damn convenient for her.

Then she stopped thinking as his strong hands moved over her, flexing at each spot they touched, adding more soap as he moved down the length of her body. When he reached the cheeks of her ass he separated them to soap the cleft before sliding first one then two fingers inside.

Jill was instantly aroused. Her breathing hitched and Gabe gave a soft chuckle.

"Feel good?"

He withdrew his fingers and began massaging the thick liquid into her legs and ankles. When he turned her around to wash the front of her body, she was almost embarrassed at how quickly her nipples sprang to attention. One corner of his mouth turned up in a half-smile before he bent his head to pull a nipple into his mouth. Sensation shot straight to her core and even in the sluicing of the shower water, the proof of her arousal slid down the inside of one thigh.

Gabe closed his teeth around the nipple then flicked it with his tongue. Lifting to look at her, he said, "Maybe some other part of your body needs attention more." He dropped to his knees in front of her, nudged her thighs apart and slipped a finger into her cunt. "Oh, yes. I'd say this needs lots of attention."

Oh, God, she thought. She didn't think she could take one more orgasm.

But then Gabe bent his head again, dragged his tongue the length of her slit and nipped her now-sensitive clit. She shuddered when he closed his lips over it and began to suck, not hard but gentle. At the same time he pushed two then three fingers into her, probing the tender flesh inside, curling to reach that electric spot that sent her into spasms. He moved his hand in cadence with his mouth, sucking and probing, stroking and teasing, using his shoulders to keep her legs wedged far apart. She threw her head back and grappled for him to steady herself.

He took his time, stroking the rough surface of his tongue against her sensitized inner flesh, sending shivers racing through her. His fingers were magic and somehow he always found that that special place that drove her wild.

"More," she moaned, moving her hips in a silent plea. "Faster, Gabe."

He lifted his mouth and withdrew his fingers, licking them with a wicked gleam in his eyes. "You taste so sweet, darlin'. God! I'll never get enough of eating you out."

"Please," she begged. "Don't leave me like this."

"You hold that thought." He brushed his lips against hers, the taste of her still strong on them. "The next time you come, it will be with my cock inside you."

She leaned against him, limp and boneless.

"We're not done here yet, sweet thing." His lips were close to her ear, his deep voice vibrating through her. "It's my turn to be soaped and rinsed."

Really?

I'm not sure I have the strength to even stand up.

But she drew in a deep breath and accepted the bar of soap Gabe handed her. This one had a woodsy fragrance, not flowery like the one he'd used on her. No, this one had a definite male scent to it that made her nerve endings dance.

She worked the lather over his back, feeling the play of muscle beneath the warm layer of skin. Even as she forced her limp body not to sink to the shower floor, desire raged through her.

When she reached his buttocks, she couldn't help herself. She spread a heavy layer of lather on her fingers and probed his opening as he'd done hers, drawing a sharp gasp from him as she penetrated him. His tight inner muscle clutched at her fingers, sending another wave of lust coursing through her. She fucked him slowly with her fingers, mirroring his action to her, bringing forth a heavy groan.

"Jesus, Jill. Have a heart. I don't want to come again yet."

Now it was her turn to whisper in his ear. "One of these nights maybe I'll slip one of those plugs into your ass, turn it on and make you come hotter than you ever have before. Did any of your playmates ever do that before?"

His silence was answer enough. Not that she'd done it, either. She'd thought about it with Mike but had never had the insane urge that she did with Gabe.

Without warning, he turned around, flipped off all the jets and lifted her out of the shower.

"Playtime's over," he growled, drying them both off and carrying her to the bed. "I can't wait any longer. I have to be inside you right now."

On the bed, he kneeled between her legs and lifted them to his shoulders. His eyes were like twin flames as he stared at her sex, his erection so enormous Jill thought for a moment he was too aroused to fit.

"Don't worry," he told her, as if reading her mind. "You're stretched enough from tonight that you'll take me easily. Put your hands on the lips of your cunt and open it wide for me."

That aroused her even more.

He yanked open the nightstand drawer, pulled out a foil packet and rolled the condom on with quick efficiency. Positioning the head of his shaft at her opening, he slowly began to insert himself inside her. Tonight he felt so much larger and thicker that she bit her lip at the pressure, but he never slowed, never stopped.

With one hard thrust of his hips, he was seated to the hilt, his balls brushing her ass, the hair on his groin rubbing against the lips of her sex. With her legs lifted and her hips tilted, he was as deep inside her as he could get and Jill felt him in every inch of her body. He was right—she couldn't tell where one of them ended and the other began.

He eased his finger away, his eyes still locked with hers. "Take your clit, Jill. Let me see you rub it the way you do when you're alone. Come on. Now, Jill. Do it now."

She reached for the tender nub and began the familiar stroking rhythm. As his hips rose and fell, her sheath squeezing him, the spiral of need inside her tightened even more until her whole body was taut with tension. The faster she stroked her swollen bundle of nerves, the more Gabe reacted. Spasms rippled through her body as he pounded into her again and again.

"Faster," he ordered. "Move your hand faster."

His eyes never left her face, reading her, watching for the signs he needed. The strain of control etched deep lines on his own face. Sweat dripped from his forehead and glistened on his magnificent body. She increased her tempo and suddenly there it was, rolling up from deep within her.

"Now," Gabe shouted. "Come now, Jill."

The climax took hold of her, shaking her with its intensity, Gabe's release filling her. His cock throbbed and his balls slapped against her with every thrust. The convulsions seemed to last forever. Jill felt as if she'd been caught up in some big machine and hurled into outer space. Nothing mattered except this intense orgasm and Gabe's cock inside her.

At last they were still, the silence almost louder than the sounds they'd been making. Gabe moved enough to lower her legs, rolled to his side and snuggled her against him, his shaft still nestled inside her. She made a small sound of protest while he padded to the bathroom and disposed of the condom. Then he was back beside her, pulling the covers over them. He tucked Jill's head into his shoulder and wrapped his arms around her.

She didn't even remember falling asleep.

* * * *

"I hate to wake you when you look so beautiful lying there like that."

The deep voice rumbled in her ear, piercing the thick fog of sleep surrounding her. Jill pried her eyes open to see Gabe sitting on the bed beside her, holding a mug of steaming coffee. He was showered and shaved and dressed in a pale grey dress shirt that set off his golden hair and a tie the exact blue of his eyes. He looked so delicious she wanted to lick every inch of him.

He set the mug down on the nightstand. "Time to rise, sunshine."

"Damn." She brushed her hair back from her forehead. "Is it morning already?"

He chuckled. "Unfortunately, yes. And I have to get to the office."

Jill groaned. "Just pull the covers over my head and wake me next year."

He plucked the sheet and blanket from her hands. "I wish I could, but I need to get you home." He leaned down and kissed her, his lips warm against hers, pressing his tongue until she opened for him.

He tasted of coffee and toothpaste and smelled of that wonderful scent of the woods and the outdoors. She wound her arms around him, conscious of her disheveled condition compared to his well-groomed one but not caring about anything except touching him. She accepted his tongue into her mouth with hunger, reveling in the rasp of it against the soft inner tissues. When he leaned his body against hers she could feel the outline of his erection.

"Mmm." She hummed her appreciation.

Smiling, he pulled back. "We'd better quit that or I'll never get to work and you'll never get out of bed."

"Would that be so bad?" she teased.

"No, but I think you need some recovery time." He kissed her cheek. "Just be ready for tonight, darlin'." He stood up. "Come on, now. I have to get a move on."

"Okay, okay." She gazed up at him from lowered eyelids. "But only because I'll see you tonight."

"Count on it."

She pulled the cover back all the way and swung her legs over the side of the bed. "Give me fifteen minutes and I'll be ready. I can shower when I get home."

Jill hummed to herself as she washed in Gabe's bathroom, brushed her teeth with toothpaste on her finger and pulled on last night's clothes. The night had been fantastic. Unbelievable. Impossibly incredible. She still wished Gabe would get around to telling her what his real feelings were for her, but for the moment she'd enjoy what they had. *Maybe he's just as gun-shy as I am?*

As she crossed the front hall to the kitchen, carrying her empty mug, the doorbell rang. She stopped and raised her eyebrows as Gabe moved to open it.

"Shall I go back to your room until whoever it is leaves?"

"No." His voice was firm. "I'm not ashamed of you being here, Jill. So unless it bothers you, don't hide."

The bell rang again, this time longer as if someone was holding it down and a heavy knock sounded.

"I'm coming, I'm coming. Keep your shirt on." Gabe pulled the door open.

Robin Fletcher stepped through it into the hall. "Good morning, darling. Am I in time for breakfast? I brought it with me." She held up a box from Heidi's Pastries.

The open door blocked Robin's view of Jill, but when Gabe closed it, there was no place for her to hide.

"Good morning, Robin." She gestured with her mug. "Gabe, I'll just put this in the dishwasher. Let me know when you're ready."

She bit her bottom lip hard to keep herself together as she walked down the hall on legs not quite steady. If she was glad of anything, it was the fact that she'd taken enough time to make herself presentable and not as if she'd just rolled out of bed.

"You have that slut in your house?" Robin's voice cut the air like a knife. "I can't believe you'd do this to me. Your little fling with her destroyed any chance for our marriage to succeed. Now, when I need you the most, you can't wait to get her into your bed again?"

"Robin." Gabe's voices had the hardness of steel in it. "First of all, if you show up someplace uninvited, you can't object to whatever you find. Secondly, Jill is not responsible for the breakup of a marriage that had no chance of success in the first place. And finally, do not ever, *ever* refer to her in those terms again. Do you hear me?"

Jill leaned against the kitchen counter, glad she was out of sight. Hands trembling, she managed to rinse the mug and put it in the dishwasher without breaking it. At least Gabe hadn't invited Robin here, nor did he look happy to see her. But the woman had a wild look in her eyes that smacked of instability and Jill's stomach clenched as numerous unpleasant possibilities raced through her brain. She wanted to shut out the conversation but Robin was shouting now and impossible to block.

"Damn you, Gabriel. Don't tell me that. We had eight years of history together. We were supposed to get married. I counted on it."

"Robin, we've been over this. By the time we'd reached that point we weren't even the same two people anymore. If it hadn't been for the baby —"

"You belong to me. Don't you turn away from me."

Gabe lowered his voice, making his reply indistinguishable, but Robin's reply left no doubt as to what he'd said.

"Don't give me that 'friends' shit. We're a lot more than that and you know it. I've waited ten years for you to come to your senses and I'm tired of it. I'll be divorced before you can turn around and you'd better be there."

Another low murmur, then the sound of the door closing. Jill counted to twenty before venturing out into the hall. No one was there, not even Gabe. She stood there, uncertain what to do next, when the door opened and Gabe came back in, his face like a thundercloud. He pulled Jill into his arms at once.

"I can't tell you how sorry I am that you had to hear that." He brushed his lips against her temple while he stroked her back.

Jill drew in a shuddering breath. "I'd say Robin has some issues to deal with."

Gabe drew back a little and tipped her face up to look at him. "Do *not* think there is any validity to anything she said." He kissed her forehead then looked at her again. "I guess I've been deluding myself all these years that she was as happy to have our marriage over as I was. And every time she remarried, I'd hope it would stick." He shook his head. "I should have had a clue when she kept marrying lawyers."

"She was probably trying to recreate you in other people?"

"You're probably right, although the thought never occurred to me."

"She's never forgiven you for the divorce," Jill pointed out. "And if the look in her eyes is any indication, there's a little instability there that makes me nervous."

"You let me worry about Robin. I'll make sure to keep her away from you. And let her know how things are with us."

Jill studied his face. "And exactly how are they, Gabe?"

He opened his mouth to answer and at that moment his cell phone buzzed. "Damn." He turned away as he held the phone to his ear. "Carter. Yeah, I know. Okay, I'm on the way."

"We have to go, right?" Jill gave him a tiny smile. "It's all right. I understand. You said you needed to get to the office."

"That was Christy. My client's already there and none too happy about waiting." He grabbed her arms and kissed her mouth, a brief but hard pressure. "We're not done with this discussion, Jill. I may not get to your place until about eight tonight. Is Chinese takeout all right?"

"Why don't I fix us something simple when you get there?"

"You don't mind?" He ran his knuckles lightly along one cheek.

"No. And we'd better leave or your client will throw a fit."

"Yeah, you're right. But tonight we'll pick up where we left off." He winked. "In all areas."

* * * *

Jill held it together until she waved Gabe out of the driveway and made it inside the house. She slammed her purse and keys down on the little table in the hall, shaking from an explosive mixture of tension and anger. Robin's words still echoed in her head.

'You have that slut in your house?'

How dare she? And what made her think she could just drop into Gabe's first thing in the morning and he'd welcome her with open arms — and a waiting bed?

But Jill knew the answer to that one. Robin had always assumed she'd get whatever she wanted. And that was no doubt the main reason she still nurtured such rage at what happened between her and Gabe. If she hadn't been pregnant, would the two of them ever have married? Had she been convinced that even with the miscarriage she could hang on to him?

Whether or not the answer to that was 'yes', what stuck in her mind was the fact Jill Danvers had stolen something Robin considered her property and the woman was not a forgiving person.

She gained some small satisfaction from knowing that Gabe had been irate on her behalf and had hustled Robin out of the house. But what was next for them besides spectacular sex? And since when had she been such a mess of anxiety about anything?

But I loved him and I still do. That's the one thing I never got over.

Maybe he was trying to tell her with his actions, but a lot had marched through their lives since that terrible, terrible day and she needed to hear him say it.

As she heated water for tea, she thought again about Robin and the divorce she apparently hadn't wanted.

Jill just couldn't picture her as a mother. Maybe while she was in her reporter's research mode, she'd find a way to check the details of Robin's miscarriage. Medical records were private, but Reed knew a computer hacker who could find out anything about anyone. Maybe she could pry his name and number loose.

She carried the cup and her cell phone to her bedroom…and was stopped by the elaborate display of roses Gabe had brought. *Was that just two days ago?* Leaning over, she inhaled the fragrance of the blooms, drinking it into her body. The rich scent calmed her and brought back the feel of Gabe's arms around her, his mouth on hers, his cock inside her.

She thought again about the miscarriage that had been the catalyst for a divorce.

I'm driving myself crazy. I need to get to work and think about something else.

As she set her cell phone down on the nightstand, it buzzed.

"I think you handed me a hot story." Reed Jamison's voice swept aside her greeting. "Who'd have realized what really goes on in small-town America?"

"You found out something?" Jill sat down on the bed, phone to her ear. She wasn't sure at that moment she wanted to hear what he had to say.

"I'm still digging, but it seems the word about Dolman's finances is true. He's using the development in the Falls to get himself out of trouble with his other projects. As soon as that's done he'll get the hell out of Dodge. The whole thing's a scam. That's why there's been no action."

"Oh, Reed." Jill felt sick. *How can this happen in a place like this? A place where people trust one another and help one another?*

An unpleasant thought slammed into her. Was Gabe avoiding an emotional commitment to her because he was involved in some kind of scheme? Did he plan to enjoy her body while she was here, knowing she'd leave once her story was finished and she'd be none the wiser about what he was doing?

God. She hated to think of that. She wanted to believe the Gabe she still loved would never involve himself in something shady or worse yet, illegal. But then she reminded herself she hadn't seen him for ten years. Anything could have changed in that time.

"I also heard he's got some silent partners in this," Reed went on, "and they're all looking to score big from the investors and beat it." He cleared his throat. "I don't presume to tell your friend his business, but he needs to check all the paperwork on this — the sale of the land, how they plan to sell lots, who the subcontractors will be. He'll know what to do."

"Yes, he will. But he won't be any too happy when I pass this along to him." She sighed. "Thanks, Reed. I think."

"Anything you've dug up from your end?"

"Not yet, but I'm working on it." Or she would as soon as she quit thinking about Gabe and started talking to some of the people in town.

"Okay. I'll call again when I have more." He chuckled. "Better make this article a good one. I have a feeling the town's going to need all the good publicity it can get."

"By the way." She wet her lip. "Would you be willing to give me the name of your computer guy who can find anything, even in the middle of the ocean?"

There was a long moment of silence.

"Jill, you aren't getting in over your head about this, are you?"

"No. This is another matter entirely. I promises I won't get him or you in trouble, but I don't think I can find out what I want to know without him."

More silence.

"Okay. I know you enough to trust you. Just be careful."

Jill sat on the bed for a long time after disconnecting the call, worrying her bottom lip. She had to be careful how she composed her message to the computer expert but first she wanted to tell Gabe what Reed had found out. Wait. Before that she needed to do some checking on her own. Or maybe she'd give Gabe a call and see what his reaction was. That would give her some kind of clue. Sighing, she punched his number into her phone.

* * * *

Gabe finished with his client and poured himself a cup of fresh coffee from the single serving coffeemaker he kept on a sideboard. He had fifteen minutes before his next appointment and he needed every bit of it to reflect on the morning's episode with Robin.

He'd used a lot of control to subdue his anger at her intrusion this morning, especially at her attitude toward Jill. That he wouldn't stand for and when he'd walked her out to the car, he'd been blunt about it. They were all ten years older, for God's sake, and he thought

Robin had moved on with her life. Maybe he was the only one who thought they'd married for the sake of her child—a child she'd lost. Maybe she'd gotten pregnant on purpose just for that reason.

Shit!

Sipping the hot liquid, he tried to recall the times they'd seen each other since their divorce. He was sure he'd made it plain to her from the beginning that a marriage between them would never work, that he didn't love her the way he should to make that kind of commitment but that he'd always be there for her as a friend.

Maybe that had been his mistake. He'd felt so guilty about everything—Jill, the baby, the divorce—that he'd promised to do penance without even realizing it. And all the years he'd been chasing Jill around the state and around the world, he still had not cut the umbilical cord to Robin.

He'd never slept with her again. It hadn't even been on his agenda. How could he have told her that by the time everything blew up, sex between them had not only lost its luster but its appeal? Besides, even the thought of it had made him feel somehow unfaithful to Jill, an emotion he hadn't experienced with any of the strangers he'd fucked in all the years since then. No, he'd simply tried to cushion the twin blows of the miscarriage and divorce. When her next marriage had fallen apart, he'd been there to lend an ear, take her to dinner, let her cry on his shoulder. When she'd told him she was getting married again, he'd told her he prayed this one would be the answer for her. He thought she'd accepted the situation the way it was. How had he been so stupid he'd missed all the little signs? At some point, he should have found a graceful way to exit from her life before he'd been faced with exactly what was happening now.

Something was different this time, though. Jill was only a part of it. Robin seemed more uptight, edgier — maybe even a little desperate. He'd never met her current husband, nor did he have any real desire to, but there was something wrong here far beyond the normal stresses of a marriage falling apart.

And Jill. *God!* She'd handled herself today with incredible poise. For the first time since she'd walked into his office, he'd wanted to take her in his arms and tell her he loved her, had always loved her and always would. *So what's stopping me? What am I afraid of?* That she'd welcome him into his body but not her heart? That when she was through here, she'd walk away from him as punishment for what she saw as his desertion all those years ago? Was that why he was so afraid to expose his real feelings to her?

As if the thought of her name conjured it up, Christy buzzed him to let him know Jill was on the phone. He smiled as he picked up the receiver.

"Hi, darlin'. Before we say anything, can I apologize again about this morning?"

"No problem." She brushed it aside. "It's over and done with."

"Jill, I promise you this will never happen again. At least as much as I can prevent it."

"Gabe, it's all right," she protested.

He went on as if she hadn't spoken. "I guess I'm not as smart as I like to think I am, because I seem to have compounded my mistakes where Robin is concerned. But I'll straighten it out. Don't worry — "

"Gabriel!" She nearly shouted it over the phone.

Startled, he broke off mid-sentence. "I'm sorry. I just—"

"Forget it. At least for now. I have news for you that won't make your day get any better."

After she repeated Reed's information to him, he was silent for a moment, trying to absorb the implications.

"I'm like you. I hate to think anyone in town could be involved in this. But you just never know. All right. Keep me up to date on what Reed uncovers."

"What about that investigator you were going to use? Have you put him on this yet?"

Why did he have the uncomfortable feeling she was testing him? *What the hell?* Could she possibly think he was involved?

"No, but I'm going to call him now and get him on it. He's discreet and a bloodhound. Whatever's there, he'll sniff it out."

"If he turns up anything I can give to Reed, it would be nice to return his favor."

"Consider it done. So. What are your plans for today?"

"I want to talk to Ernie again then some of the other committee members, like Trey Howard at the bank and Mayor Hofstra. And Marvelous Missy said to come by and she'd give me a copy of the complete folder on the closing event."

"Wear full body armor." Gabe laughed.

"I can handle Missy. I want to get her to walk it through with me tomorrow night. The celebration opens this Monday. That's only a couple of days away."

"Good luck. I'll see you at eight."

Damnation.

He decided to hold off telling Gary Anderson anything until he had more proof. He picked up the phone and flipped through his contacts, looking for the number of the investigator he wanted. *Time to do some serious digging.*

And maybe ask Jill straight out if she really thought he was involved in this. How could he take the next step with her if she thought so little of him?

Chapter Eleven

Jill went down her list in order. Everyone she met with had been more than cooperative, giving her event schedules and details of activities. Any displays and exhibits would be up for the entire week and the committee members were eager to work with her photographer when he arrived.

Ernie Hoffman welcomed her return visit and was as voluble as he'd been the last time, although today he seemed distracted. When Jill asked if he'd rather she came back another time, he was quick to wave that suggestion away and made the effort to concentrate on their conversation. But without a doubt there was something going on here. *Is lovable Ernie involved in Limestone Hills? Is he salting away bribe money?*

Mayor Larry Hofstra did the best tap dance she'd seen in a long time.

"We're just getting all the permits in order," he kept repeating, "Can't turn over that first shovel of dirt until we do."

"But there isn't even a sales office set up," she pointed out. "Or brochures for people to see. Shouldn't Dolman or whoever he appoints be promoting the community already?"

"All in good time." Hofstra gave her a placating smile. "We all want to do this right."

"You?" She cocked an eyebrow. "Are you an investor, too?"

"Well, sort of." He shifted in his chair, his discomfort obvious. "But I'm talking about the money Dolman has in our bank, from his investors. They need to be protected, too."

"From what?" she persisted.

"From any number of things that happen with a major project like this. Now, Jill, don't go reading anything into nothing. I'll keep you up to date on it, even if you're gone from Bluebonnet Falls. We could use the publicity."

Aware that was all she'd get from him today, she left with her bullshit meter at full tilt.

Missy, as anyone could have predicted, was her usual condescending self. Jill would have bet money Robin had run to her with every detail of the morning's confrontation, but the subject never came up. Jill could tell Missy was torn between treating her like the diseased stepchild and wanting to grab as much of the publicity for herself as she could. It was enough to brighten Jill's day, even just a little.

Her last stop was Majors' Market.

Allie Majors was as talkative as ever as she sacked Jill's groceries, babbling away while Jill kept looking at her watch. She wanted to get home, boot up her laptop and start doing her own research. But Allie always had her own agenda and being rushed wasn't part of it.

"This must be old home week in the Falls," she chattered. "Both you and Robin Fletcher. You haven't been back in ages and we only see her now and then." She stared at Jill over a package of sliced roast beef. "I figured y'all must be too addicted to the city by this time."

Heat crept up Jill's cheeks as she caught Allie's meaning. "Not at all. I don't know about Robin, but I had my reasons for not coming back. Especially after my parents' deaths."

Allie's eyes widened. "Oh, of course. Darn my big mouth anyway. I should have remembered. I'm so sorry, Jill."

Jill waved a hand at her. "Don't worry about it."

"So, I hear Robin and Gabe had dinner at the Mill the other night." Her expression was sly as she waited for Jill's answer.

This is as good a reason as any I stay away from this place. No privacy and too much gossip.

"That's true." She pasted on her professional smile. "As a matter of fact, I had dinner with Missy Spellman at the same time they were there."

Allie's mouth formed a perfect O. "Well. What a nice reunion for all of you."

"Yes, it was great." She waited for her total doing her best to control her impatience.

"I hear you've been seeing Gabe, too." Allie glanced sideways at her as she bagged the last of the groceries.

Jill ignored her and handed over her debit card. "If you don't mind I really need to get going."

Now it was Allie's turn to redden. "Oh. Sure. Sorry. I guess I just talk too much."

No kidding.

As she opened the door to her car, another vehicle turned into the parking lot and Robin herself jumped out. When she spotted Jill she marched toward her, rage lining her face.

"Just a minute, slut," she snapped. "I want to talk to you."

"Not today." Jill was proud of her control as she shut her car door and pulled into traffic. But she was shaking so hard with anger she didn't know how she could drive.

* * * *

The episode with Robin had been a bad omen for the rest of the day. The moment Gabe hung up from Jill, he called his investigator and told him to get on this sooner than now. The news about Dolman had turned the contents of his stomach to acid and the investigator's comments didn't make it any better.

"So you've got someone tied up in this mess?" He cleared his throat. "This seems to be getting bigger by the day."

"Do you have others who've hired you, also?" Gabe wanted to know.

"You'll be number three." He gave a short laugh. "At least y'all can split the expenses three ways."

"So there really is something rotten going on?" His stomach knotted.

"Appears to be. And it's just come bubbling to the surface in the last couple of weeks. I think one of his silent partners may be the cause. Personal problems. Needs to get his money out fast."

Gabe huffed a tired sigh. "Just keep on with what you're doing, I guess. And daily reports, okay?"

"You got it. Call you tomorrow."

What a fine mess to present to Gary Armstrong. On the one hand, Gabe wondered how a man that smart could have fallen into a swindle like this. On the other, the Dolman Corporation had built up a solid reputation over the years so no red flags had been flying.

The rest of the day wasn't much better. Clients showed up early and complained he wasn't there, or were late without apology, bumping his schedule way out of whack. He missed lunch altogether, satisfying himself with the packages of crackers Christy kept in her desk for just such occasions.

Now he had his last appointment of the day, a meeting with the celebration committee. At least everything there seemed to be running with smooth efficiency. He was pleased at the feedback on Jill's contacts with them and the excitement generated by it. But now he was ready to bag it, head for Jill's and wrap himself around her body.

This is getting to be a habit. And one I apparently don't want to break. Will she trust me this time and not cut and run? If I tell her how I feel, will she believe me? She hasn't said anything herself but one of us has to say the words first.

Another thought had plagued him all day, too. Did she really suspect him of involvement in whatever Dolman's scheme was? Was that how she really saw him?

Fuck.

Nothing had gone as he'd planned from the moment she'd walked into his office.

But as if God had decided he needed one more sharp nail in his day, when he opened his office door to leave, Robin was standing in the corridor, poised to enter. She'd obviously taken pains with her appearance. She was dressed in a white silk pantsuit with heavy gold earrings and a matching bracelet and her flawless makeup bespoke the time she had spent applying it. But not even painstaking applications could hide the lines of tension around her eyes and mouth or the feral gleam in her eyes.

"Robin." He moved close to her, enough to force her to take a step back, pulling the door shut behind him, listening for the click of the lock.

"Hi, Gabe. I, um, saw your car still in the side lot and thought I'd stop by. Aren't you working awfully late?"

"Yeah, it's been a long day." He started toward the elevator, forcing her to follow along. "I'm glad it's finally over."

She linked an arm through his and leaned closer. "So why don't we go out for a drink to help you relax? Or I have a better idea." She dropped her voice to an intimate tone. "Why not come home with me? Mother and Daddy are in Houston for two days. We've got the house to ourselves and I can really help you work the kinks out."

The elevator had reached their floor and the doors slid open.

"I don't think that's a good idea." Gabe entered the elevator car, disengaging Robin's hold on him.

"Why not?" Her voice was strident. "I'm all but divorced, if you have a thing about married women. There's really no need to wait."

Gabe sighed. "Listen to me, Robin. What we had between us was over years ago. By the time we married we weren't even the same people who'd first become lovers. We aged. Grew up. Became different people."

They were in the lobby now. How lucky that at the moment almost nobody was around. Gabe tried to head for the doors but Robin blocked his way.

"Are you saying you didn't love me? That you don't now?"

He stopped walking and captured her gaze. "I'm saying what we had was a different kind of love. If we'd stayed married, it would have been a destructive relationship. You got on with your life and I'm getting on with mine."

"I'll bet," she snorted.

"I told you I'd always be your friend and that's what I've tried to do." He shook his head. "It's probably my fault if you misunderstood, which is why I think we need to put some distance between us."

"Oh, please." She snorted. "Don't give me that line of horse manure. You're just tied up with that little whore while she's back in town. But she'll be leaving and I can wait."

Gabe dropped his briefcase and gripped Robin by the arms hard enough to make her flinch. "Don't ever, ever say anything like that about Jill ever again. I won't tolerate it."

Her eyes flashed at him and she jerked her arms away. "Well, well, aren't you the protector. You'll be very sorry about this, Gabriel. I could have done a lot to benefit you. Now it just won't happen. You'll just be some small-town fish in a tiny pond slogging away every day of your life."

"I'll manage. Look, why don't you go back to Atlanta and try to patch things up with your husband? You said the other night he isn't a bad guy. Maybe you can work through your problems."

There was wildness in her eyes now. "If I wanted to patch it up I'd be there, not here. We aren't finished, Gabe. *I'm* not finished. Before we're done, you'll be running back to me as fast as you can, begging me to let you back into my life and help you solve your problems."

A warning light flashed in his brain. "What problems?"

"You'll see." The grin on her face before she turned away was malicious. "So long, *darlin'*. You will be seeing me around."

Gabe watched her walk away with an unsettled feeling in his stomach. He didn't believe for a minute that Robin could create major chaos, but he was sure she'd do anything to torpedo his life. He and Jill would both have to be on the alert for that. Right now more than anything he wanted to hold Jill in his arms and assure himself he hadn't been imaging the past few days—and nights.

* * * *

Jill spent two hours after she got home researching Dolman, his other projects and any articles she could find on him. She included her impressions of Larry Hofstra and Trey Howard. Tomorrow she'd put everything together in logical form. Right now she had used up the last bit of her concentration.

She was watching through the living room window when Gabe's car pulled into the driveway. It was well into dusk and the street lamps were on, giving her a clear view of his lean body unfolding from his car. She hurried to the door and pulled it open as he climbed the porch steps. Not even the three glasses of wine she'd drunk had taken the edge off the day she'd had. Only Gabriel could do that for her, could ease the need inside.

"I'm glad to see I'm so welcome," he stated.

Jill grabbed his arm and yanked him inside, slamming the door. She pulled his face down to hers, forcing his mouth open and thrusting her tongue into it. She wanted to taste every inch of him, drink him into herself.

Gabe finally broke the kiss. "Hello to you, too." His voice wasn't quite steady. "To what do I owe all this?"

"I want you."

She took the hem of her long T-shirt, the only thing she'd put on after her shower, pulled it over her head and tossed it to the floor. Then she began unbuttoning Gabe's shirt in feverish haste, rubbing her body against his. His erection was already straining the front of his slacks.

"I want you too, darlin', but can we manage to make it to the bed?"

"Yes. No. I don't know." She unfastened his clothes in frantic haste, tossing them aside. "Maybe. Hurry, hurry, hurry."

He had toed off his shoes and was down to his boxers when he swung her up into his arms and marched down the hall with her. She coiled herself against him, pressing her breasts against the hard wall of his chest, taking little nips along his collarbone. His cock was thick, bobbing against her side through the thin cotton of his boxers and his skin was hot to her touch.

When they reached her bedroom, he managed to get her to the bed, but the minute he tumbled her out of his arms, she grabbed for him and yanked him down on top of her. He reached down between them and probed her sex with a questing finger.

"Whoa, Jill, you are dripping wet and hotter than a spent cartridge. Not that I'm complaining, mind you, but what's got you so aroused?"

"Later." She pushed his hand away so she could reach for his cock and pulled it toward her waiting opening, spreading her legs wide to give him room to thrust. "Right now just fuck me. Shove your cock inside me and fuck my brains out. Hard."

When he stopped abruptly, the head of his shaft barely inside her, she clutched at him.

"What's the matter? What's wrong?" She was desperate to feel him inside her.

He gritted his teeth. "Condom. In my pants in the other room."

"Nightstand drawer." She reached backward and pulled it open, exposing the enormous pile of condoms lying there. Condoms she'd driven to the next town to buy.

Gabe's eyes popped as he looked at them. "You stocking up for the century, darlin'?"

"Just didn't want us to get caught short. Take one. Hurry, damn it, come on, Gabe."

In seconds, he had the foil ripped open, the latex rolled on and he was sliding into her hot, welcoming body.

Jill wound her legs around him and pressed with her feet, pulling him inside her so as deep as she could. The moment her inner muscles clamped around him she moved in the now familiar rhythm, unwilling to wait for him.

Gabe braced himself with his arms on either side of her and drove deep. He held himself still for so long she wanted to scream at him to move. Then he did, faster and faster, increasing the speed with each thrust. Jill felt the thickness of his cock as with every push, he dove harder into her and she slammed her hips forward to meet him.

"Faster," she screamed, feeling her orgasm building inside her. "Harder, harder."

The ride was wild. Jill locked him to her with her legs and heels. She wound her arms around him, pulling him tight against her body. If it had been possible, she would have pulled every bit of him inside her.

They exploded together, Gabe's hips pumping until he'd emptied every bit of himself into her and he collapsed on top of her. For a long moment, the only sound in her room was the rasping of their breath as they tried to suck air into their lungs.

Gabe disposed of the condom in record time. Then he rolled to the side, taking Jill with him and pulling her against his chest. She was limp and boneless, yet inside her body the need was already beginning its slow upward spiral again.

I'm turning into a sex maniac but oh, God, how I needed that.

"Well." Gabe ran the tips of his fingers up and down her arm from elbow to shoulder and back again in a lazy pattern. "Care to tell me what that was all about?"

Jill closed her eyes to pull her thoughts together.

How to present this? How to go about this, without chasing him away?

When she didn't say anything, he pushed himself up on his side and looked down at her. "That wasn't you, so how about letting me in on your secret?"

"This will sound so stupid," she protested.

"Nothing is stupid except keeping things from each other."

All right. No stretching it out.

"I ran into Robin again today. When I stopped at Majors' Market to pick up a few things."

Gabe's body tightened. "I'm guessing it wasn't a pleasant encounter?"

Jill tucked her head into the curve of his arm, not looking at him. If she was the one he was going to be mad at, she didn't want to see it.

"I drove away before we had yet another confrontation. She's on a crusade, Gabe. A war of vengeance."

"God damn it." Gabe sat up, every line of his body rigid.

"Gabe?" Jill scrambled to her knees and leaned into his shoulder. "I'm so sorry. I didn't mean to upset her, if that's what you're worried about."

He turned so fast he almost knocked her back down onto the mattress. The kiss he gave her was more intense than the one she'd greeted him with, so hot it nearly burned her alive. His tongue was a living thing, devouring her, drinking of her. She felt everything — lips, teeth, tongue — every part of that wonderful masculine mouth. When he lifted his head at last she tried to pull him back, but he grabbed both of her hands with one of his, his eyes burning into hers.

"Listen to me, Jill, and listen carefully." He closed his eyes for a moment, then opened them, looking deep into hers. "Robin and I have a history, but it's past history, emphasis on *past*. If anyone's at fault for anything here, it's me. I'm the one who irresponsibly got her pregnant. It disgusts me that I was secretly relieved when she lost the baby. I can't imagine what our household would have been like for him or her to grow up in."

"Oh, Gabe, I—"

He touched her lips with his fingers. "When I met you that summer, I realized just how little there was left between Robin and me and how you and I had something wonderful building."

"But—"

He shook his head. "You use that word too much. I was mistaken when I thought Robin and I could maintain a friendship. Apparently, all these years she's been reading something into it that isn't there and never has been. I was stupid about it and that's why we've come to this situation."

"She said—" Jill began again.

"I can imagine what she said. And telling you to pay no attention to it is like putting a Band-Aid on a gaping wound, but I'll say it anyway." He placed a light kiss on her nose. "And here's something I should have said before but I've been too afraid to do it."

"Afraid?" She wrinkled her forehead. "Of what?"

His eyes closed again. "That when you were through here, you'd pack your bags and leave. Payback for what happened before."

Jill pushed him away from her and sat up, eyes blazing. "Is that what you think of me? That I'd be so vindictive and callous that I'd do that to you?"

He had the good grace to look embarrassed. "You shut me out of your life for ten years, darlin'. I was trying to figure out just where we're going with this."

"And where are we going, Gabe? Because according to Robin—"

"Forget Robin. Damn her to hell. You can bet I'm going to make sure she understands how things are and stays the hell away from me."

Jill snorted a laugh. "Good luck with that."

"Yeah." He raked his fingers through his hair. "But this isn't about her. It's about us." He tightened his arms around her and brushed his lips against the fine hairs at her temple. "You have no idea how many times I've beaten myself up about what happened with us, asking myself if there was anything I could have done differently. When you walked out of my life, I thought I'd never feel whole again."

"Me neither. I couldn't run far enough or fast enough." She snuggled against his hard warmth. "Even Europe didn't seem to be far away. I swore I saw you on every street corner."

"Same here. I actually chased a woman three blocks once because I thought it was you." His lips turned up in a rueful smile. "I guess I'm a coward, because I was waiting for you to say it first. I wanted to be sure it wasn't just the incredible sex that tied us together. The sex will only get better and I don't want to wait any longer." He lay back down and pulled her against him. "I love you, Jill. I have right from the beginning. And I don't think I'll ever stop loving you. I want to make a life with you. Marry you. Have kids with you."

She was shocked to hear the words after all this time, words she never thought he'd say. Tears trickled down her cheeks. "I want that, too. I was afraid, too. Afraid it was just the sex and when I was through here, you'd let me go. I love you, Gabriel Carter. Now and forever."

"Don't cry, darlin'." He lapped her tears away with his tongue. "I'll think you're unhappy."

"Oh God, Gabe." She squeezed him hard. "Never. I think this is the happiest I've been in years. I can hardly believe it. You have no idea how often I wished for this, shoving it out of my mind because I didn't think it would happen."

"Every time I tried to contact you and got turned away I thought, Okay, maybe it just wasn't meant to be. But then I'd remember how good we were together and refuse to just let it lie." He sighed. "And today I could not believe you actually thought I was involved with whatever Dolman's situation is."

"Only because I couldn't figure out why you wouldn't tell me how you feel. I thought you were trying to bide your time until I left and didn't want me to know what was going on."

Anger flashed across his face for a brief second then was gone.

"I'm going to chalk that up to the insanity we've been dealing with," he told her, "so we can get back to what's really important." He tilted her face close to his. "Us. Our future."

This kiss they shared was neither heated nor passionate but tender and full of promise. Everything they'd felt so long ago, had stored away behind walls all these years, spilled out in that intimate contact. Jill was still crying, the tears washing away years of anguish, and Gabe continued to lick them away. For the first time since his appearance at her door with the announcement that Robin was pregnant, the chain around her heart began to loosen.

They lay curled together for a long time, unwilling to break the physical connection. At last she pushed herself up and tugged at Gabe's arm.

"Now we've got that out of the way, it's time to eat. You'll definitely need your strength tonight."

"Is that a fact?" He grinned. "No more than you. Okay." He swatted her on the backside. "Feed me, wench."

Fire flashed in her eyes at the touch and Gabe grinned.

"Such a sexy ass. And so spankable." He caressed her buttocks. "I love making these beautiful globes turn fiery red. Watch the heat streak down to that beautiful pussy of yours and see your cream gush and wet your thighs. I think maybe I'll save that for dessert." He pulled her against him. "I've had sex with other women, Jill, but with you I make love. Just remember that."

After they showered, Jill pulled on another long T-shirt and Gabe knotted a big bath towel around his hips. Dressed in that fashion, they sat at the kitchen table eating roast beef on hot rolls and drinking beer.

Gabe took a long swallow and put down his glass. "I'm sorry again about the scene this morning."

Jill shrugged. "Not your fault. I'm just going to do my best to stay away from her. If that's possible in a town this size." She put down her sandwich and studied his face. "It's odd, you know? I can tell she's obsessed with you, but it seems like something more than that. I think the woman is truly unbalanced."

Anger flashed in Gabe's eyes and the muscles in his jaw tightened. "I never expected this kind of behavior from her, especially after all these years, but maybe I was just fooling myself." He reached across the table and took one of Jill's small hands in his large one. "Somehow I'll figure out a way to put an end to this. I can handle her, but I don't want her bothering you again."

"I'm good as long as things are right between us." She looked down at her plate. "I really wasn't sure if you wanted her after all and this was just, you know, a fling of some kind for you."

"Jill." He forced her to look up at him. "Let's make this formal and official and put any doubts to rest once and for all. Jill Danvers, will you marry me? As soon as possible?"

She smiled even as tears pricked her eyelids again. "Yes, I'll marry you, Gabriel Carter. Just as soon as we can arrange it."

He leaned across the table and kissed her, seal the bargain. "I think we should make the jewelry store our first stop tomorrow. It doesn't get more official than a ring on your finger."

"Are you sure?" she asked, still amazed that this was happening.

"I am. What about you?" A flash of uncertainty crossed his face.

"Oh, Gabe. You couldn't beat me off with a stick now. You're stuck with me."

"Good. I'll hold you to that." He leaned back in his chair. "We do have some logistics to work out, though. We can't be very married and live in two different places. And I won't ask you to give up your job, not one that you worked so hard to get."

"That may not be as difficult as you think." Jill rose and began clearing away the debris from their food. "I don't spend that much time in the office as it is. I can write from anywhere as long as I have my laptop. I'd probably have to go into San Antonio once a month for meetings, but that's about it."

"You're not kidding?" Gabe carried the rest of the dishes to the counter. "It's that easy?"

She turned and found herself bumped up against him. "It's that easy." She smiled.

Gabe put his hands on her shoulders, rubbing his thumbs with a gentle motion against her skin. "I don't have an appointment until almost eleven tomorrow. We can hit the jewelry store as soon as it opens."

"We need to discuss what we've discovered about Dolman, too. Make a list of what we know. I have all my notes from my conversation with Reed Jamison. And I got a little research done today while I was waiting for you, as much as I could concentrate."

"I've got my investigator on it, but you're right, let's see where we are. We can do it over breakfast. How does that sound?"

"Fine by me."

"I love you, Jill." He pulled her into his arms. "We're good together. Really good. We'll have a very, very good life."

She rubbed her cheek against his stubbled one. "Yes, we will. I love you, too, Gabe."

"That being said, how about a shower and early to bed? We have an important date tomorrow."

She raised her eyebrows. "Oh? And what would that be?"

"We're going to make a very special purchase."

Chapter Twelve

They had a laughing disagreement in the jewelry store picking out a ring. Gabe would have bought her something large enough to light up the city while Jill wanted only a modest ring. They finally compromised on a three-carat emerald-cut solitaire on a white gold band. As luck would have it, the ring was a perfect fit.

Gabe slipped the ring onto Jill's finger, happy to put a dent in his platinum American Express card for this particular purchase. Then he pulled her into his arms and kissed her so hard and so deep they forgot about their surroundings until the sound of a throat being cleared penetrated the fog.

Jill stirred in Gabe's arms and looked in the direction of the sound to see Jennie Schroyer standing at the counter next to them, wearing a wide grin.

Shit!

She extricated herself from Gabe, smoothed her hair back and pulled her lips into a smile. "Hi, Jennie. Nice to see you again."

"Well, Gabe, I guess I don't have to ask if there was anything about that dinner you and Robin had the other night." She couldn't keep the avid curiosity from her voice.

Gabe kept one arm around Jill, holding her close. "Robin and I are just…friends. That's it. Jill and I are getting married as soon as we can make arrangements. We've wasted enough time already."

"How nice." Jennie tucked a strand of hair behind her ear. "Jill, won't that make a problem with your, um, career? Your magazine is located in San Antonio, right?"

Jill wanted to smack Jennie's face but instead simply gave her a cold look. "Actually, Jennie, I can write anywhere as long as I have my laptop. And I'm thinking about going freelance anyway. Gives me more flexibility."

Gabe brushed a kiss against her cheek. "We'll do whatever it takes to make sure her work situation is taken care of, Jennie. You can tell that to anyone who's interested."

Jennie blinked, seeming startled. "I'm sorry. I certainly didn't mean to offend either of you. I'm very happy for you."

As if to make a point, Gabe lifted Jill's hand and held it out. "And you can tell everyone I would have bought her the biggest ring in the store if she'd let me."

"Gabe." Jill squirmed with embarrassment.

"The ring is beautiful," Jennie told them, her voice more subdued. "I wish you both happiness."

At that moment the salesman returned with the receipt and credit card. Gabe signed, stuck his copy in his pocket and almost pushed Jill from the store.

"That bitch," he murmured as he opened the car door for Jill. "Once upon a time, I thought she was a nice person. I'll bet she runs Jim Schroyer a merry race."

"It's okay." Jill leaned over and kissed him as he slid into the driver's seat. "But I guarantee you in the next five minutes, everyone in town will know about this."

He squeezed her hand. "Good. I want everyone to know. Maybe it'll put a stop to all the gossip and speculation about Robin and me once and for all."

"I wouldn't count on it," she sighed. "And I can promise you there'll be hell to pay when she finds out."

Gabe insisted they have a late breakfast at the Oakwood Café, despite Jill's anxiety at public reaction. "We can't hide forever, darlin'. We're both way too visible for that."

But her prediction about Jennie was right on the nose. The restaurant was jammed with late-morning customers, all of whom insisted on shaking Gabe's hand and hugging Jill as they made their way to a booth in the back.

"Told you," Jill whispered when at last they were seated.

"Good. The sooner everyone knows the better, as far as I'm concerned."

Cathy Morgan, always referred to by Gabe's father as the oldest living Oakwood waitress, brought them coffee and menus. "Congrats, you two. Fred said to tell you breakfast is on the house this morning, so knock yourselves out."

"Tell Fred thank you." Gabe grinned. "We'll need the energy."

Jill blushed and Cathy laughed as she walked away.

"Gabe, you can't keep doing that."

"Sure I can." He brushed his fingers against her cheek. "Maybe then everyone will settle down and leave us alone."

"Fat chance. But we'll see."

By the time they'd finished breakfast, Jill was sure half the town had found an excuse to stop into the restaurant and seek them out. She was glad when they were done and could make their escape.

"There's still Robin," she reminded Gabe as they pulled out of the parking lot.

"Let me worry about that. What's on your menu today?"

"Last-minute visits with anyone I can find who's available. The big opening ceremony's tomorrow night, Mr. Chairman. How come you aren't all tied up with it?"

"I have a great committee." He grinned. "That's the secret to being a successful chairman. Delegate the work." His face took on a serious look. "I want you with me tomorrow night, Jill. I have to be up on the platform for the opening speeches, but you'll sit at the head table with me for dinner and we'll hit the street dance."

"I don't know," she began.

"Enough." His tone was harsh now. "Robin Fletcher doesn't control our lives. If we're going to live in this town, we can't spend our time hiding."

She let out a long sigh. "You're right. I guess I'm just not looking forward to the confrontation. With her or her friends."

"Changing the subject, that was quite a bit of information your reporter friend dug up. And you did a pretty good job yourself."

"He was adamant that Dolman always had a local who works with him on the scams, but I can't seem to pinpoint who it is here. What about your investigator?"

"I'll check with him when I get to the office, although I'm sure he'd call if he has something." They pulled into Jill's driveway and Gabe put the car in park. "I've got to run, but why don't I pick you up about seven? And pack a bag. I'd much rather we stay at my place." A tiny grin tilted up one corner of his mouth. "Can't get you used to it soon enough."

She laughed. "All right. I'll do that."

"And call one of the realtors today to put your house on the market." He cupped her chin and turned her head toward him. "It's time, you know."

She nibbled her bottom lip. "You're right. It's just, oh, I don't know —"

"Letting go is hard, Jill, but your folks wouldn't want you to hold on to the past forever. Just the good memories."

"Okay." She gave him a quick kiss. "I'll do it. I promise."

"And tonight, we'll talk about the wedding. The sooner we do this, the better."

Jill stood in the driveway, watching until he backed out into the street and drove away from her. Then she headed into the house to make a phone call and pick up her briefcase and laptop.

* * * *

The streetlights in downtown Bluebonnet Falls already sported pennants proclaiming the bicentennial, but today the decorations committee was busy adding Lone Star flags and stringing a long banner across Main

Street. Jill decided to peek in at the community center to see how things were coming for the opening ceremonies.

The first thing she noticed was the huge platform in the street outside the building, at least eight feet high, no doubt meant for the speakers. Rolls of bunting and layers of chairs were stacked to the side. Inside, at least twenty people were busy arranging things. The tables had been set up and wore centerpieces of artificial bluebonnets and miniature Texas flags. The tablecloths alternated red, white and blue with contrasting napkins.

At one end of the room, a platform had been erected similar to the one outside but smaller. This one had the chairs already set up in a row and urns of bluebonnets filled every available inch of space. Two men were on ladders, hanging a banner proclaiming the celebration.

Jill stood in a corner, making herself as unobtrusive as possible and jotting down notes in her little memo book. If she was lucky, she told herself, she could get what she needed and get out of there before anyone noticed. But the voice at her ear banished that prayer.

"Congratulations, honey. I hear you finally snagged Gabe Carter."

Arms enveloped her in a bear hug and she look up to see Corinne Fellowes, a friend of her mother, smiling at her.

"Hi, Corinne." Jill gave her a rueful grin. "I guess the gossip line still beats the newspaper in the Falls."

"Same as always." Corinne grabbed her left hand and held it out to the light. "Glad to see that man had sense enough to buy you a decent-sized rock."

Jill chuckled. "He would have bought one that blinded me, but that's just not my style. So how are you, anyway? And Frank?"

"Just as good as can be. Lord, Jill, your mama would be so proud of you."

Tears pricked at her eyelids and her throat tightened. The ringing of her cell phone gave her a chance to pull herself together. Making an excuse, she walked into the hall and answered the phone.

"Sweetheart, you have just given me a ticket to fame and glory." Reed Jamison's voice was loud with excitement, more than Jill had ever heard.

"There's really something going on? Here in the Falls?"

"Going out is more like it. The Dolman Corporation is about to go belly-up. I got this straight from an attorney who has his finger on the pulse of corporate bankruptcies."

"But then what happens to the project here? My friend's client isn't the only investor. The investigator he hired is working for two more people."

Jill pictured Reed at his desk, bending a paper clip as he talked. "I hate to tell you there are people in your town greedy enough to help this along for what they're getting from it."

"Wait a minute." Jill booted up her tablet and scooched down to prop it on her knee. Gabe would need this information. "How can they make money if nothing is being developed and sold? There isn't even a sales trailer out there."

"Word on the streets is Dolman's salted all the investor money away in off-shore accounts. He just conned some big venture capitalist in Dallas into handing over a hefty piece of change and he's using some of that money to pay off the people who helped him with this. But time's running out for him. He's got to get out before someone decides to sic the IRS and the legal system on him."

"Supposedly he has it all in the local bank here." But the memory of Trey Howard's sense of unease flashed back at her. "Damn." She bit her lip. "I'll pass this along to my friend. His name, by the way, is Gabe Carter. He's an attorney here and I've known him for a long time."

"You sure he's not involved in some way?"

"Positive. For a lot of reasons. So what kind of people here should he have his guy check into?"

"Anyone responsible for granting permits and staying on top of them. Real-estate people. Bankers. Dolman always does business with local banks. You said there's an account in Bluebonnet Falls. Get Carter to hire a forensic accountant and put him on that."

"Thanks, Reed." She closed the notebook and stood. "I think."

"I'll see you in a couple of days. I'm coming out there during your big wingding to snoop around. Any suggestions for lodging?"

"Sure. You can stay at my house. I still have the one I grew up in."

She could feel Reed's smile through the air. "Compromising your virtue for me?"

"You wish. No, I'm staying at Gabe Carter's house."

Silence.

"Wait a minute. Is this the same Gabriel Carter whose phone calls you won't take?"

Jill laughed. "Things have changed a little. We're getting married."

"Well, damn. Let you slip through my fingers again."

"You're good for my ego, Reed. Don't say anything to the boss yet, though. I need to tell him myself. Let me know when you're getting here and I'll meet you with the key."

"Talk at you later."

Jill slipped her phone back into her purse and turned to reenter the big room, only to find her path blocked by an immovable object. Harriet Fletcher. Robin's mother.

Uh-oh.

"Hello, Harriet." She arranged her mouth in the best smile she could manufacture. "How are you?"

The woman didn't move, just stood there with one hand thrust into the pockets of her exquisitely tailored slacks, the other toying with a button on her silk shirt. One strand of silver-frosted hair escaped from her otherwise perfect chignon and rested on her face with its meticulous makeup job. Her expression could have frozen fire.

"You think you've got everyone fooled with that sweetness and light act, missy, but you don't fool me one bit."

Jill stared at her. "I beg your pardon?"

"You ruined Robin's marriage the last time you got your hooks into Gabriel Carter. I won't let you stand in their way this time."

"I think that is most likely Gabe's choice to make. He and I are getting married, so maybe Robin needs to redirect her own life. Anyway, isn't she married to someone else?"

"A mistake. Just like the last one. She's always loved Gabe and this time she's going to have him."

Jill tamped down her simmering anger that threatened to erupt. "Again, I say that's Gabe's

224

decision. If he wanted her, he could have had her any time during the past ten years. Now, if you'll excuse me, I have work to do."

She brushed past Harriet, literally shoving her to one side.

"Oh yes, your big famous job," Harriet called after her. "See how much that gets you. Consider yourself warned."

Jill made it to her car in the parking lot and fell into the seat, shaking with fury. *Damn all the Fletchers, anyway.* She didn't want a fight, but she wasn't about to let them intimidate her either. And over something so stupid. Robin had had her chance with Gabe. It wasn't Jill's fault that things hadn't worked out or that Robin had reached some kind of desperate point in her life.

When she finally had herself under control, she started the car and pulled out of the parking lot. She really needed to get Missy to take her over to the fairground and walk through the closing event with her, but today was not a day to spend face-to-face with Robin's closest friend. She'd check in with Ernie again and maybe talk to him about listing the house at the same time.

* * * *

Gabe hung up the phone from his conversation with Dick Goodrich, his investigator, with a very unsettled feeling in the pit of his stomach. Getting Gary Armstrong's money back wouldn't be easy but at this point, if he got the proper papers in order and filed in time, he could at least prevent Dolman from accessing any assets.

But it was the thought there were people in his hometown whose palms were being greased to help this along that made him feel sick. If Dolman was getting ready to bolt, Gabe had to move fast. *But how to proceed?* This couldn't have come at a worse possible time, what with the celebration set to begin the next night. He had meetings this afternoon and again in the morning. That left only this morning free and tomorrow afternoon before his time was fully committed.

Damn. Damn. Damn.

It didn't help matters when Jill called to report on her conversation with Reed Jamison, although hearing her voice was the best tranquilizer he could imagine. After he hung up, he closed his eyes and leaned back in his chair, remembering the activities of the previous night.

God, fucking her was better than going to heaven. Whenever he sank his cock into her body, he felt as if he was in the best place on earth. Although putting his mouth over her sweet, sweet cunt ran a close second. And her breasts, with nipples like tiny strawberries and their soft yet firm skin.

He'd spent years by himself because he'd let her run away from him and put him off. He should have stormed her office or wherever she lived, carried her off someplace and fucked her senseless. Well, he'd be sure to make up for lost time.

He had no doubt he was in for another confrontation with Robin, who seemed to have a lot of emotional baggage for some reason. But he'd handle that when it came up. He and Jill were finally getting married and nothing was going to screw that up.

Rubbing his eyes and sitting forward, he had Christy get Gary Armstrong on the phone.

"You do whatever you have to in order to get these bastards," he told Gabe. "I'll be in at three like you asked."

The next thing he did was call an attorney he knew in San Antonio to get the name of a good forensic accountant. That taken care of, he spent an hour drafting the pleadings he'd need, then hurried to the courthouse to find Judge Harrison, file the suit against Dolman and ask the judge to freeze company assets. Back in the office, he had Christy fax a cover letter and the injunction to every bank his investigator had uncovered where Dolman had an account.

When Gary came in, Gabe listened to him rant and rave for an hour, realizing it was part of what the man was paying him for. At four, he left the office for the celebration committee meeting and then, thank God, at six o'clock he was done for the day.

In his car he punched in Jill's cell number.

"I'm done early, darlin'. I'm on my way."

"Come on ahead," she laughed. "I have a little surprise for you. I hope it's okay."

"Will I like it?"

"I think so."

"Then it's okay."

But when she opened the door for him and he saw what was in the hallway with her, his jaw dropped.

What the hell?

Jill had waited nervously for Gabe to get there, wondering if she'd made a mistake.

No.

She gave herself a mental shake. They were engaged. Going to be married. It shouldn't matter that she asked him first. When his car pulled into her driveway, she'd opened the front door and was waiting for him. He looked stunned as he took in her luggage and boxes and his jaw tightened.

"Going somewhere?" His voice sounded strange.

"I-I hope so." She twisted her hands. "Maybe I shouldn't have just presumed but, see, Reed's coming to town—"

"Jamison? Your reporter friend?" Gabe hadn't budged from the open doorway.

"Yes. And there's hardly any place to stay in the Falls. Oh damn it. I don't know why I'm making such a big deal out of this. We're getting married, right?"

He still hadn't smiled. "That was my assumption."

"Well, I told Reed he could use this house and I figured I'd just move in with you. Is that okay?"

Gabe stared at her for a long moment then burst into laughter and reached out for her. "Darlin', you just gave me the scare of my life. I thought for a minute there you'd changed your mind and were planning to leave."

"Leave?" She tilted her head back. "Are you out of your mind? I was just afraid you weren't ready yet for me and all my stuff."

He tilted her head back and pressed his mouth to hers, tracing the seam of her lips with the tip of his tongue. When she opened for him, he pulled her into a kiss so deep it made her head spin. She still clung to him, anchoring herself, when he lifted his head.

"Jill, listen to me. That's your home now. If I'd had time after we bought the ring I would have suggested we do this right then." He kissed the tip of her nose. "Come on. Let's load up your stuff and get going. Then I'll tell you about my day over a nice glass of wine."

Jill was amazed at how easy her things fit in with Gabe's. Of course she still had an entire condo to take care of, but even with that she had ideas how they would work things out. By the time they'd put away her things in the master bedroom and bath and Gabe had given her part of his study for her workspace, she had the strange feeling she'd been living there for years.

"We have plenty of time to shop for whatever you want in here," he told her. "This is your home. Whatever you want, it's yours."

He looked at her with such love and possessiveness it made her knees weak.

"What if I tell you I want a naked man in the kitchen to fuck me while I make dinner?" *Oh, God, did I really say that?*

Gabe's eyes heated. "I'd say that can be arranged if the cook is naked too." He unbuttoned her blouse and tugged it from her shorts. When he met bare skin his eyes widened. "No bra? Well, well, well."

Jill went to work on his clothes at the same time. "Keep going. You might find other surprises."

He cocked an eyebrow. "And that might that be?"

She lowered her eyes in a mock demure look. "You'll just have to find out."

He gasped when he unzipped her shorts and bent to slip them down her thighs.

"Why, Miss Danvers, you hussy. No panties. What would the ladies of the Falls say?"

She stood on tiptoe and pulled his head down so she could reach his ear. "They'd say Jill Danvers knows how to keep her man entertained."

Gabe gazed at every inch of her naked body. She wondered if he had any idea just how ready she was for him. The thought of moving into his house today had aroused her so much she had barely been able to wait for evening.

She knew he could tell when he said, "Your scent fills the air."

He kneeled on the carpet before her and nudged her thighs apart. With great care he opened her outer lips and pressed back the tiny hood shielding her clit. When he leaned forward and sucked it into his mouth, it was all she could do to stand upright.

"You're dripping, darlin'," he told her, sliding two fingers inside her. "I think we'll have to take care of this right now."

He swung her up in his arms and moved away from the living room but not toward the stairs.

"Where are we going?"

"I'm going to fuck the cook, even before she fixes dinner." His eyes darkened. "So I hope the dinner is damn good."

She gave him a wicked smile. "I promise you'll enjoy it."

The big granite table in the kitchen was cold, but it felt good against her heated skin. Gabe yanked off her clothing and tossed it over a chair. With firm hands, he separated her thighs as wide as he could, then pulled her legs over his shoulders. There was something so erotic about being spread out on the kitchen table stark naked, her pussy and her ass exposed like this, while Gabe stood before her, shirt open but still fully dressed.

Tiny quakes fluttered through her vagina and her womb as he just stood there, looking at her, his clever fingers stroking every inch of her pussy and rubbing the cream that was trickling down into the cleft of her buttocks and around her anus. His eyes were like twin lasers pinning her in place.

"I can't decide what I want to do to you first." His voice was thick with lust. "I want to fuck you with my fingers and my tongue, lap up all that sweet, sweet juice in your pussy. I want my cock inside you so badly it hurts. But at the same time fucking that gorgeous ass is pure heaven." He rubbed her slit again. He stared at her, his eyes devouring her. "What a dilemma."

He pressed one arm across her thighs to hold her in place, the long fingers of his hand finding her clit and pushing back its tiny hood to fully expose it. With her cream coating the fingers of his other hand, he reached down and slid two of them into her ass. He shoved hard and fast, sending spikes of pleasure through her body. When he bent his head and stabbed his tongue as deep as he could get it into her vaginal sheath, a small orgasm rippled through her body and her low wail filled the air.

Gabe lifted his head, his mouth slick with her juices.

"Hold your breasts, darlin'," he rasped. "Pinch your nipples for me. Hard."

Unable to think, to make her brain work, she did as he asked and the little bite of pain warmed her body with pleasure.

"Don't stop," he told her. "Keep pinching and pulling them."

His fingers in her ass had never stopped moving, finding that hot spot and rubbing it over and over. Her clit was on fire, burning like an exposed nerve. When he took possession of her pussy again with his tongue, a hungry need raced through her body. As the walls of her sex pulsed and the muscles of her belly and thighs clenched, Gabe slid a third finger into her and the wail became a scream.

Her hips moved as she arched up to him and her buttocks slapped the polished surface of the table. Gabe fucked her harder and harder with his mouth and his fingers, the one arm like a steel bar limiting her movement.

Almost there. Almost there. Almost there.

Then it crashed over her like a thunderstorm, her entire body shaking and shuddering as spasm after spasm racked her. He was merciless, not letting her come down until the very last drop of fluid had poured from her sex and every tremor had subsided.

At last he removed his hands and trailed kisses along the insides of her thighs. He washed his hands at the sink then came back to help her sit up, cradling her in his arms against his bare chest.

"I guess we christened the kitchen," she managed when her heart rate had slowed enough to permit speech.

"And in a most spectacular fashion." He took off his shirt and handed it to her, stopping to give her a brief, tender kiss. "Put this on. I won't make you cook dinner, but I think we've earned some wine."

"But you didn't…"

"Jill." His expression was both serious and loving. "When two people love each other the way you and I do, at least half of the time for the man it's as much about giving pleasure as receiving it. Making you come like that, watching you respond the way you do, is satisfaction enough." He winked. "For now."

He carried the bottle and two glasses out to the deck at the back of the house. When they were comfortable on the padded loungers and each held a full goblet of wine, Gabe told her what he'd learned from his investigator.

"Do you think the court can act fast enough to freeze the Dolman accounts?" Jill asked.

"I hope so. I faxed everything to the Feds as soon as the judge signed off on the order. If Dolman tries to touch the money, he'll be in for a rude surprise. But that's only part of the problem."

Jill nodded. "We need to find out who his mysterious 'silent partner' is and who in the Falls is involved." She stared into her wineglass. "I just hate the thought of someone I know being a part of a scheme like this."

"Thank God they didn't open a sales office or anything. We'd have another mess on our hands, not to mention a bunch of lawsuits clogging the court."

Jill twirled her glass, thinking of all she'd learned. "Reed said a local real-estate person had to be in on it because of the land deal."

"He's right." Gabe drained part of his drink in two swallows. "Someone who factored the sale knowing nothing would ever be built. And someone who could put the zoning commission and the city council in his or her pocket."

"You know, I hate to say this." She ran a finger around the edge of the glass. "I went to see Ernie Hoffman today, about tomorrow's opening ceremonies and also to talk to him about listing my house. When I started asking him question about Limestone Hills, he acted very strangely."

"Yeah?" Gabe lifted an eyebrow. "In what way?"

"He shifted a lot in his seat, the way someone does when they don't like the questions you're asking. And he told me too many times he doesn't know anything about anything. And he wouldn't look me straight in the eye either."

Gabe sighed. "I'd hate to think Ernie's involved in this, but he's the perfect person to pull the local strings. Damn."

"Well, there's not much more we can do today. I think—"

But what she thought was interrupted by a loud voice behind them.

"You shouldn't leave your gate unlocked, Gabe. So. You brought your little slut home with you. How cute."

Robin Fletcher strode across the lawn to the deck, anger in every step she took.

Chapter Thirteen

"Damn it, Robin." Gabe set his wineglass down and stood up. "You can't come barging in here just like this."

"How else am I supposed to see you?" Her eyes blazed with an unholy light. "You avoid me at every turn."

"That should indicate something to you. And by the way, if you ever insult my future wife again, you won't like the consequences."

"Oh yes." She laughed, a bitter sound. "I heard all about that. Half the town hunted me down to tell me."

"I'm not kidding, Robin." Every muscle in his body was taut with rage.

"You know." She was in his face now. "This is probably a good thing. I wouldn't want you after fucking this piece of trash. Taking you back the first time was bad enough. I couldn't do it twice."

A muscle clenched in Gabe's jaw. "You've got that a little backward. You didn't 'take me back' to begin with. If not for the baby, we'd never have married. And this time there wasn't even a glimmer of a chance."

Robin crossed her arms in a belligerent gesture. "You'd never have divorced me even after I lost the baby if you hadn't been as sick as a calf over her."

Gabe clenched his fists at his sides. "Not true, Robin. We were done long before that. We just didn't realize it."

"Well, you won't have to worry about me anymore," she spat at him. "I found out a few secrets of my own. I'll be wallowing in money before long and I can kiss you and this backwater town goodbye forever."

"Planning to soak your husband in the divorce settlement? That suits your style. Rich daddy. Rich husband. When is it enough for you?"

Robin lifted a hand as if to slap him, but Gabe grabbed her wrist, his fingers tight around her flesh. "Best you don't try that, little girl. I'm usually pretty low-key but being slapped could easily change that." He dropped her wrist. "Now get the hell out of here and don't come back. Or my office, either."

Robin glared at him, rubbing her fist where he'd held her. "Good riddance. You know, I could have made you a very rich man, Gabriel Carter. Now instead of laughing all the way to the bank, you'll be crying along with the rest of the fools."

She ran to the gate and was gone, the metal clanging behind her.

Gabe lifted his glass, drained the rest of the wine and poured a refill. "It's hard for me to figure out what I ever saw in her. Damn bitch."

Jill sat forward. With a great effort she had kept silent through the entire episode, even though she'd wanted to rip Robin's eyes out. "Gabe, I don't ever think I've heard you curse a woman. And she's not worth having you break a habit for."

"I know, I know." He took another swallow of wine then leaned over and kissed Jill, a ferocious kiss that said *You're mine and the rest of the world can go to hell*. With a sigh, he dropped back onto his lounge chair. "But I won't take it back."

"Did you see her eyes? I have a sneaking feeling Robin Fletcher, or whatever her name is now, might be on drugs of some kind."

And she might have another secret if that computer hacker is really as good as Reed says he is.

"God, I'd hate to think so." He shoved his fingers through his hair. "I wouldn't wish that on anyone, no matter who they are."

"Well, something's driving her. She just doesn't look or act right. And what do you suppose she meant about money? Her father settled a trust on her when she turned twenty- one, a very hefty one according to town rumors. And she's had two rich husbands since you. Isn't she ever satisfied?"

"I had the same thought. I'd say she's planning to take Number Three for the ride of his life." He shook his head, unfolded himself from his chair and held out a hand to Jill. "Let's go inside, darlin'. I need to get the taste of Robin out of my mouth."

"I know you said not to cook," she told him in the kitchen. "Not that I know what you have anyway. Why don't I just see what's in your fridge and maybe make us some sandwiches or omelets?"

"Later?" He folded her into his arms, his hands caressing her back, his head resting on her chin. "I need to lose myself in you, right now. I need to bury myself so deep inside you we can't tell where one of us ends and the other begins."

"That sounds like just what's needed right now. Come on."

She took his hand and led him into the bedroom. With fingers shaking only a little she helped him remove his clothes. Then they were lying together on the bed, skin to skin, hands roaming bodies, legs tangled together.

"My turn," she told him and pushed him onto his back.

As he'd done to her so many times, she trailed kisses over his body, starting at his jaw and working her way down to his neck, then to the hollow of his throat where his pulse beat strong and steady. She traced a line across his chest, pausing to nip at each dusky nipple and drag her teeth through the crisp, curly chest hairs. She could tell he was forcing himself to lie still and let her work her magic, even though the male in him wanted to take charge.

When she swirled the tip of her tongue in his navel, he jerked then fisted his hands to control himself. But when she wrapped one hand around his swollen erection and swept her tongue against the broad, flat head, he couldn't stifle the moan or keep from reaching for her.

She raised her head, a devilish smile on her face. "Let me work my magic, Gabe."

And so he gave himself over to her, letting her work her 'magic' on his body. She teased his cock with easy strokes, reaching between his legs to cup his testicles and brush her fingers against their tender surface. He jerked at her light touches and sweet moans of pleasure burst from his throat. But when she bent and took him fully into her mouth, he yanked her head up and rolled her to her back, pinning her with his body.

"Enough with the torture." His voice was a ragged whisper. "Time to get serious."

He nestled in the cradle of her hips and she pressed upward against him.

With a groan, he tore himself away long enough to sheath himself then slid his shaft inside her with one stroke.

"Look at me, Jill," he commanded. He braced himself on his elbows and held her head tenderly in his hands. "Let me see your eyes. Let me look into your soul."

When he locked his gaze with hers, what she saw that told her he was right. She couldn't tell one of them from the other.

Time stretched on forever as he continued the steady rhythm. His gaze was still locked with hers and she couldn't have looked away if she'd tried. Her body began to tremble and she felt the same quivering in Gabe's muscles, but still he stroked, his movements slow and steady. Then it began, the deep-seated clenching, the spasms that rolled through her. And his shaft pulsing inside her as he found his own release.

"Gabe?" she whispered.

"Ssh. I know. Just be still and let it happen."

They lay there, her walls convulsing around him. It was the most erotic climax she had ever had in her life. Their bodies were slick with sweat, skin adhering to skin and their hearts bumped against each other as pulses raced and lungs struggled for air. At some point Gabe rolled to the side and pulled her against him.

"I love you," she murmured. "I've always loved you."

"Me too, darlin'."

"I'm sorry I kept you out of my life for so many years. I was stupid. Look at all the time we've lost."

He ran his fingers through her dampened curls. "That's behind us. Now we need to look at what's ahead of us. Nothing but a good life together."

When he returned from disposing of the condom, she sat up.

"We should probably eat something."

Gabe chuckled and cupped her sex with a warm palm. "I can think of something mighty tasty."

She slapped weakly at his hand. "Okay, but maybe we'll try a sandwich for the moment."

"Come on." He pulled her to her feet. "I make a mean omelet. Let's shower and eat. Then I think we should try for some sleep. We have four busy days ahead of us."

* * * *

Busy didn't begin to describe it. The town was filled with tourists, each day bringing more, claiming the meager supply of local accommodations. Business was booming in all the shops and restaurants. Harvest Moon Bakery couldn't turn out their famous scones fast enough, Buddy's Bar B Q had their pits running twenty-four-seven and tables were scarce everywhere.

Jill was happy to see the economic infusion, but she scanned the face of every stranger she saw, wondering if Dolman's people were there, blending in with the crowd.

Gabe's time was consumed with overseeing the celebration and following through on the lawsuit against Dolman. The federal government had acted quickly to freeze the offshore accounts his forensic accountant had identified. Then he'd used a friend from the law firm where he used to work to file in the Dallas courts, ensuring the suit proceeded in both places, and with luck covering all Dolman's opportunities to escape the system.

Reed arrived in town and Jill met him at the house to give him the key and show him where everything was.

"Not much food, I'm afraid, but there are enough places to eat if you hit them off- hours. You can grab some stuff at Majors' Market a few blocks away, but wear earplugs. Allie never shuts up."

"Not to worry. If I cooked for myself I'd die of poisoning. I'll be fine." He hooked the key onto his key ring. "I really appreciate this, Jill. Not just for the bed, but staying here will give me some privacy to work from too."

She filled him in on what Gabe had learned from the investigator and what had happened since they'd last talked. "He said he could spare you about a half hour in the morning if you have any questions for him. And of course he can't discuss the lawsuit."

Reed nodded. "No problem. I'll appreciate whatever he can give me. By the way..." He gave her such a serious look her stomach muscles knotted.

"What? Is there some problem I don't know about it?"

"Maybe. Possibly. I don't know yet for sure. But Dolman's silent partner could be someone right in this town. If I'm right, they've been doing business together for years."

Jill swallowed against a tightness in her throat. "What do you mean? I thought this was something that just came up. Has he been pulling crooked deals all along? How could it possibly be someone here? Everyone knows everyone else's business."

Reed barked a short laugh. "Don't kid yourself. When people want to hide things, they can. I'm just telling you in case my lead pans out, so you'll be prepared."

"Thanks for the heads-up. I think."

She left him making calls on his cell phone and headed to the Community Hall. The opening ceremony would start in an hour and she had to meet the photographer the magazine had sent.

She wasn't sure how she got through the evening's program. It took every bit of discipline she had to smile and chat with people. On the one hand, she was very much on display as Gabe's fiancée, nervous as she anticipated people's reactions. But aside from Missy Spellman, the Fletchers and a few of their friends, everyone's happiness at the news seemed genuine. On the other hand, she kept searching every face, wondering whose name Reed was going to pull out of a hat. However this came out, the Falls would be a long time getting over it.

By the time the street party was winding down, Gabe managed to extricate himself from people and share a dance with her. It gave her a chance to pass along what Reed had told her.

"I hate to think someone in this town has accumulated wealth by stealing from other people," he told her. "But the sad fact of life is, it happens too often for comfort. I just never thought it would happen here."

"Who do you think it is? I look at every person I see as if I expect them to confess any minute."

Gabe shrugged. "There are a lot of people with accumulated wealth in the Falls. It would take a team of accountants to check everyone's financial history and find out where their money came from."

Jill leaned her head against his shoulder. "I'll just be glad when this is all over."

"Me too. My friend who filed the papers in Dallas said there are ten investors who each forked over half a million now screaming for blood. And these are supposed to be smart businessmen."

"According to Reed, Dolman's created enough success with each of his projects to establish a good track record for himself. And I wonder how often he's 'teased' his financial statements to entice investors."

"Okay." Gabe kissed her forehead as the music stopped. "Enough about business for tonight. I'm beat and I'm sure you are. Let's go home and try to get some sleep."

She looked up at him. "Try?"

"Darlin', any time I get near a bed with you sleep is the last thing on my mind."

She laughed and followed him to the parking lot.

* * * *

The next three days whipped by so fast Jill wondered if they'd even happened. She and Gabe did little more than pass each other except at night. Then they fell into bed, made brief but passionate love and caught whatever sleep they could.

Of all the events, Jill liked the one at the Wolfe ranch the best. The reenactment gave the photographer some excellent subjects to shoot and Jill took time to relax while eating barbecue and chatting with people she hadn't seen for so long. Her engagement ring came in for its share of admiration and the people who hadn't expressed their happiness before hugged her now and wished her well. She was beginning at last to feel that living in the Falls again would be all right. Only Robin and her tight little circle seemed to be resentful. Jill was sure she'd find a way to ignore them in light of everyone else's support.

She also had a nugget of information for Gabe but she wanted to wait until everything was finished before sharing it. She knew for sure it would send him into a rage.

No one was happier than Jill when the last night of the celebration arrived. She and Gabe met at home so they could change into comfortable clothes. Using what time they had, they caught each other up on what was happening. They were stripping off their clothes in the bedroom when Gabe's cell rang.

"Yeah? Uh-huh. Uh-huh. Okay. I'll see what I can do."

Jill wrinkled her forehead. "What?"

"That was my investigator. He says something's going down tonight. One of Dolman's men — someone who hasn't yet shown his face around here — flew out of Dallas to Austin today and rented a car. Sources say he's headed here for some kind of showdown." He headed into the bathroom to turn on the shower.

Jill was right on his heels but stopped to answer her own phone. "What? Are you sure?" She was aware of Gabe pausing naked in front of her, waiting for her to finish. "All right. Gabe just got a call with similar information, although why the hell anyone would try this with everyone in town out and about, I don't know. Uh-uh. Okay. See you at the parade."

"Camouflage." Gabe's tone was sharp.

"What?"

"Hiding in plain sight. If Dolman's partners want their money and the money's frozen, they're bound to make a stink. But right now, anyone leaving in the middle of this celebration would send up a red flag."

Jill tossed her phone to the bed. "Makes sense. Lord, Gabe. I don't even want to think about the possibilities."

"I know, darlin'. Me either. We've known these people all our lives."

"Damn it all, anyway."

* * * *

The sidewalks were jammed with parade-goers, many waving tiny Bluebonnet Falls pennants. Businesses from as far away as Austin and San Antonio had sent expensive floats and marching bands from high schools in the four surrounding counties high-stepped to their music.

The judges' stand, draped in large banners, was set up in front of the county courthouse. Jill had requested a copy of the announcer's script to make notes on and follow the order of the parade. Gabe rode in the lead car, a convertible, with the mayor and the county court-at-law judge. They were driven by a very nervous high-school honor student who had competed for the honor in an essay contest about the celebration. Jill giggled to herself, hoping the kid didn't crash the car before the finish line.

The parade ended without a hitch, after which everyone headed for the fairgrounds. The pageant committee was already in place, racking costumes and checking scenery. As Jill entered the pavilion, she had the bad fortune to bump into Missy Spellman.

"Well." Juggling a shopping bag and folders, Missy blocked her path as Jill tried to move toward the stage.

"Don't think you'll get to rub everyone's nose in this without paying the price. The whole town knows what you did to poor Robin."

Physically and mentally exhausted, Jill was glad tonight was the last night of the celebration. She'd slept little and she'd had to work hard to focus on her article with everything else going on in her life. The last thing in the world she wanted at the moment was a confrontation with an aging Barbie doll born with a nasty disposition. The thin control she'd managed for four days snapped like a weak rubber band.

"There's nothing poor about Robin. Whatever's happened to her, she did it herself. Maybe she expected to marry Gabe a long time ago, but if he really loved her, he didn't have to divorce her. I'm sick to death of you and the Fletchers acting like I'm some kind of homewrecker. They didn't even have a home for me to wreck."

"Listen, you little bitch —"

"No, you listen. I plan to live here as Mrs. Gabriel Carter and most of the people in this town seem very happy about it. Robin needs to get on with her life. Now get the hell out of my way and let me do my job."

She pushed past the woman and marched toward the stage, giving thanks when she spotted her photographer standing to one side.

"A little hometown stew?" He grinned.

"Nothing to worry about. Come on. Let's see what you'll want pictures of."

Like the parade, the pageant was a huge success, executed without even the tiniest flaw as it depicted special moments in the history of Bluebonnet Falls. The magazine's photographer had a field day snapping shots of everything.

"I could maybe use these if you decide to do something on the history of the state as a whole," he told Jill. "This is great stuff. And these people are incredible."

"Yes, they are." She pushed her hair back from her face, wondering why she hadn't just tugged it into a ponytail. "I'm pretty proud of them."

"By the way, Reed tells me congratulations are in order." He cocked an eyebrow. "Told the big brass about it yet?"

"No." She shook her head. "I thought I'd wait until this was all over and I was in the office. Besides, I want to see if I can talk them into letting me work freelance. And I'd like to tackle some news stories for a change."

He stuffed his camera into the huge bag hanging from his shoulder and pulled out a small digital one. "They'll do it. They don't want to lose you as a writer."

"From your lips to their ears," she told him. "Have you seen Reed around? I spotted him dodging here and there the last couple of days but not tonight."

"He said he's onto something hot and he might need me later."

"Oh? Well, I hope he makes sure I'm in on whatever it is."

"I'll tell him if I see him."

Every folding chair in the pavilion was filled and people stood two and three deep against the walls. Jill watched the entire pageant, from a place wedged into the end of a row. She gave Missy a grudging but silent hand for doing an excellent job. So far a complicated evening was going off without any snags.

Jill and Gabe somehow managed a moment alone to enjoy some barbecue, hiding away in a corner of the fairground out of the limelight.

"I've been keeping an eye out for anything unusual," she told him, "but either whoever we're looking for is damn good or your source and mine are both wrong. And I'm watching for Reed. My photographer said he expected something to go down tonight."

"I can't imagine what could happen in this crowd, though," Gabe told her around a mouthful of pinto beans.

"But like you said, hide in plain sight. Maybe they figure there's so many strangers here for the event no one will notice one or two more." She licked her fingers. "When are you through with your official duties?"

"After I do my last walk around and thank-yous." He took his napkin and wiped a smear of barbecue sauce from Jill's cheek. "As soon as the fireworks start, I'm finished."

"Good. Can we sneak off someplace by ourselves to watch the fireworks?"

"Absolutely." He squeezed her hand then began gathering up their debris. "Then we can go home and have our own big show."

She laughed, a full, throaty sound. "Do you ever think of anything but sex?"

"When you're around it's hard to think of anything else." He winked at her.

"Well, I'm going to run to the ladies' room, such as it is, and wash off the rest of this sticky stuff."

"Okay. I'll find you when I'm released from bondage."

In the restroom she washed with tepid water and blotted her face with paper towels.

"You look like trash," she told her reflection in the mirror. She dug into her purse until she found a bedraggled scrunchie and pulled her hair back into a ponytail the way she wished she'd done earlier. A quick touch of lipstick and she was done. "It's dark," she told the mirror. "No one will see how I really look."

Outside, she mingled for a while, speaking to people she knew and accepting yet more congratulations. Then she decided to head away from the crowd and the food area and followed the path toward the rear of the pavilion. She didn't think she had any small talk left and she wanted some time to herself. So much had happened in such a short time. Two weeks ago Gabriel Carter had had no part in her life. Now they were about to be married.

Gabe was pushing for a quick wedding and she wondered, *Why not? What reason do I have for putting things off?* Aunt Karen would knock herself out to pull a Class-A wedding together and it would be nice to be married here in the Falls, which was once again her home.

Dreaming about wedding gowns and honeymoons, she stumbled over the exposed root of a giant oak behind the pavilion. She caught herself before she fell, balancing against the side of a building and voices drifted to her on the clear evening air.

"I told you not to push me." The low voice was harsh and angry.

"I want my money now. I can't wait any longer." The whisper was so soft Jill couldn't identify who it was, despite a hint of familiarity.

"I told you we have a little problem. That bastard Carter has had the Feds freeze all the bank accounts."

"I don't understand." A little louder. "How did they find them?"

"I don't know and Dolman's pissed. Look, I came all the way out here to bring you what I could. I couldn't risk running it through the bank anymore. That will have to do for now."

Jill edged closer to the corner, trying to see around the side of the building to identify the speakers. The moon was nearly full in a clear sky, but whoever the people were, they were shrouded in shadow. She took a step closer, fearful of betraying herself.

"I need to close up shop with you. It might be time to think about retirement."

Jill started to move forward again when a body pressed against her back and a hand closed over her mouth. She struggled, trying to kick backward until Gabe's voice whispered in her ear.

"Ssh. It's me. I went to find you and saw you moving back here." He moved his hand from her mouth.

"Did you hear...?" she mouthed, looking at him.

He nodded. "I know who that is." His voice, even in a whisper, was tight with anger. "Be quiet until they finish."

"Fine," the stranger was saying. "Dolman's taking a hike anyway before he's arrested. "If that cash is frozen, you're leaving my daughter in a terrible position financially."

Jill's eyes popped. "Brian Fletcher?" she mouthed.

Gabe nodded and pressed his finger to her lips, signaling her to be quiet.

"He earned plenty doing all Dolman's backdoor legal work," came the voice again.

Fletcher's voice rose. "She still gets her percentage for bringing him to the table."

"Are you serious? He couldn't jump in fast enough," the voice replied.

Next to her Gabe tensed, anger pulling at every line of his body. Jill could barely deal with the shock running through her. *What a nasty mess and the Fletchers right in the middle of it.*

Gabe's mouth was right next to her ear. "We have to get out of here. Come on." He tugged her hand.

"You're just going to leave them here like this?"

"Let's get away from here and I'll explain."

They moved as silently as they could until they were back in the picnic area. Jill was shaking so hard she collapsed on the first bench they came to. Anger darkened Gabe's eyes and his body was rigid. A muscle jumped in his cheek.

Jill had to swallow twice before her voice worked. "What now?"

Gabe clenched his fists and shoved them into his pockets. His own breathing was none too even. "We have to do this right or we'll end up with nothing. Tomorrow I'll get a warrant to search Brian Fletcher's bank records. And Robin's husband too." He kicked at the brace on the table. "Might as well include Robin in the party. Damn, damn and damn. Robin. How the hell did she get herself into this mess?"

"Maybe through her father?" Jill suggested.

"Yeah." Gabe's voice was bitter. "The pillar of the community. I'd say he brought his commercial real-estate license to the table. That's probably how he's made his money all these years. I can't believe he's mixed up in something like this."

"I know everyone in town has been all excited about what the development could do for economic growth. They expected a big influx of people with money to buy those high-priced homes."

"I'll bet." Gabe dropped onto the bench next to Jill. "It's bad enough to do it to strangers but to scam your friends is unforgivable."

Jill wrinkled her forehead. "I don't understand the intricacies of how all this works. You'll have to explain it to me. And what happens after you get the bank records?"

"I'll give them to the same forensic accountant who traced the offshore accounts. He'll put it all together." He gritted his teeth. "That means calling in the Feds again. This is in their bailiwick."

"Gabe, I'm so sorry." Jill tugged one of his hands from his pocket and fit hers into it. "I know how hard it is to accept this about people you know."

"And that's not the end of it," he pointed out. "We have to find out who else was paid off here. They had to keep up the appearance that a project the council approved was actually going forward and only the locals could do that."

"I know you're upset about Robin," she said in a soft voice.

"Only because I didn't see this in her before. I should have cut this rope a long time ago. I told you. Robin and I as a couple are ancient history. I was stupid enough to think we had remained friends." He lifted her left hand and rubbed his finger across the ring. "You're my future, Jill. Let's go home and plan a wedding."

Chapter Fourteen

Jill stretched and leaned into the warm body spooned against her. "What time is it?"

"Six o'clock," Gabe said against her ear.

"No," she groaned, turning her face into the pillow.

As tired as they'd been, they'd talked a long time after coming home the night before. For Gabe, talking was the path to solving a puzzle and so they'd gone over every scrap and bit of information they'd collected. He'd had Jill draw diagrams on a pad of legal paper, trying one then another to see which flow worked better. Finally, with exhaustion claiming them both, they'd fallen into bed.

And now his body was next to hers, nothing separating them but skin, and already she wanted him. He skimmed his hand over her body as he spoke.

"I have to get to the office early to draft the warrants and make my calls," he told her. "But I'm not leaving without my morning wake-up."

He pressed his hard erection against her buttocks, a drop of wetness from the broad head marking her skin. When he tightened the arm holding her, she wiggled back against him, feeling him harden even more.

"Tease," he chided and pinched a nipple.

"Brute," she countered with a laugh and snaked her arm under his to reach back and find his shaft with her hand.

"Uh-uh." He pulled her hand away. "I'm in charge this morning."

"You don't think I'd have something to say about that?"

"Sure." His voice thickened. "Go ahead. Say something about this." He lifted her leg over his thigh, reached under it and drove two fingers deep into her pussy. "Wet. I guess that says it all."

And she was. Dripping. It seemed he only had to touch her or give her a certain look and she was ready for him. Would they ever get enough of each other? She hoped not.

He stroked in and out of her sheath with his fingers while he pressed his cock against the cleft of her ass. When he suddenly took his hand away, she cried out at the emptiness it left.

"Be still," he told her. "There's more."

With a deft and gentle touch, he probed her backside, his fingers slick with her juices that eased his way inside her. He scissored them, stretching her tissues, licking her ear, nipping her shoulder. Breathing hot words, love words, sex words into her ear, he pushed into her, slow and steady. When every bit of his cock was inside her, his balls brushing against the backs of her thighs, her inner muscles contracted and more liquid trickled from her down her thighs. That fast she was aroused and hot.

"I love fucking your ass." His mouth pressed against her temple and his tongue traced a lazy circle on her skin. "I swear I could come the minute I'm inside you."

He reached back under her thigh to find her slit and traced a line up and down with his fingertips, every stroke firing the nerves in her swollen lips. Tiny shivers raced through her and she tried to push down on his hand, but he laughed.

"No rush, darlin'." His voice surged through her like heated cognac. "That's why I woke you up early."

He knew just how to torment her and did it seemingly with great delight, murmuring words that suffused her body with heat. He stroked her with the barest of touches, a whisper of a caress that made her pussy walls ripple and the pulse deep inside her beat harder. He pinched her clit with his thumb and forefinger, just enough to fire the nerves and tease her into wanting more. And all the while he moved his shaft in and out of her ass in a steady rhythm.

"Pinch your nipples for me," he whispered in her ear. "Hard."

The familiar bite of pleasure-pain shot through her and more liquid seeped from her. Oh God, she wanted — no, needed — something to fill her greedy cunt. The way she felt even his whole hand might not be enough. She moved her hips, trying to ride herself on his hard, muscled thigh, but he held her just far enough away to deny her any relief.

"Keep doing it and I'll fuck you with my fingers," he told her in a voice hoarse with need.

She moaned, pulled and tugged on the ripening buds, pinching them as hard as she could. At once he thrust three fingers into her, rasping them along the walls of her sex, his thumb now pressing hard on her clit.

"Faster," she urged, breathless, but he matched the rhythm of his fingers to that of his cock in her ass.

He drove her at a steady pace, holding completion just out of reach until she broke down and begged and pleaded. The only sound in the room was their harsh breathing and the slap of skin against skin.

Jill tried to match her movements to his but he had her trapped between his fingers and his cock as he maintained his slow, steady tempo. Nothing existed except the two of them and the dark ribbon of pleasure unwinding inside her.

"I could stay inside you forever," he murmured, his voice strained. "You're like a cool drink of water at the end of a hot day. An ice-cream cone in summer. Sanctuary in the midst of chaos." He continued to rock both his hips and his hand. "I will never forgive myself for letting all those years go to waste. I can be hellfire in court. I should have used the same tactics on you."

"My fault as much as yours." Her words were breathless, all her air trapped in her lungs. "But we're together now."

"And I'm planning to keep it that way."

He increased the pace, thrusting his hips, working his fingers harder. She felt invaded, full, some part of him touching every nerve and muscle of her body. He was relentless, steadily taking her up that dark spiral until she reached the crest, then pushing her over it. Then the ribbon snapped and her orgasm roared through her.

Her mind was wrapped in fog, only her body functioning as she came and came and came. When she was sure she would die from the pleasure, the roaring subsided to quiet aftershocks and eventual stillness.

She was drenched in sweat, her heart pounding like a jackhammer. Gabe's own heart thumped its erratic beat against her back as he held her tight to him.

When they could both breathe again, he slipped from her ass and eased his fingers from her pussy, licking the cream from them. He bent to kiss her, sharing her taste with her, then rolling out of bed and lifting her in his arms.

"I wonder how many years it will take before I finally get enough of you?" he asked with a grin.

"I hope never." She rested her head on his shoulder.

He gave a reluctant sigh and headed for the bathroom, still holding her. "Meanwhile, we both have work, so shower, coffee and clothes."

But the shower took a little longer than planned. Gabe insisted on soaping her, which led to an orgasm that left her boneless. Then, at last, they were both dressed and ready to go.

"You left your car at the fairgrounds," he reminded her. "I'll drop you off there. Call me later so we can touch base."

She was about to answer him when her cell rang and a familiar voice boomed in her ear.

"I'll share information if you will," Reed Jamison told her.

A frisson of excitement skittered through her. "What have you got?"

"Uh-uh-uh." He chuckled. "We meet and exchange. You and me and that sharp fiancé of yours."

Jill held the phone to her chest to muffle her voice and repeated to Gabe what the reporter wanted.

He thought for a moment. "All right. Both of you meet me at my office in an hour and a half. That will give me time to get the paperwork done for the warrants and get them signed before people can clean things up. Then we can pool what we know."

Jill made the arrangements and broke the connection. "He'll be there." She worried her lower lip. "This is going to be nasty, isn't it?"

Gabe nodded, his face serious. "Unfortunately, yes. I'm not looking forward to either a session at the bank or a meeting with Brian Fletcher. The first I can't avoid and the second will find me, I'm sure."

Jill moved next to him and wound her arms around his neck. "This too shall pass and we can put it all behind us."

He kissed her with such a combination of need and tenderness she had to blink away tears.

"And that's what I'm hanging on to." He gave her a quick squeeze. "Okay, let's get out of here. I guess I'm as ready as I'll ever be to face the day."

After she picked up her car, Jill hunted down her photographer, who was taking a few last-minute shots of the area. Over coffee at the Harvest Moon they outlined how she would put the article together and what shots they'd be looking for to best carry the flavor. Just as he was on his way, her cell rang again. This time it was the super hacker who confirmed what he'd told her before. *How in God's name am I going to tell Gabe?*

She was staring into her empty coffee cup when a warm voice broke into her thoughts.

"I'm so glad I ran into you." Sarah Wolfe stood beside her holding coffee and a scone. She nodded at the booth. "Mind if I join you?"

"Oh, please. Are you kidding? I'd love it."

Sarah set her cup and plate on the table and reached for Jill's left hand. "I didn't get to admire your ring properly at the ranch the other night. It's beautiful."

She gave Jill a warm smile. "I'm so happy for you. Both of you. You should have been married for years by now."

"Yes, well..." Jill turned her gaze to the window. "Things happened back in those days."

"Will you be married here in the Falls?"

Jill nodded. "I'd like to be. And I know it would please Gabe."

"You know half the town will want to be there," Sarah pointed out. "At least."

"Yes." She laughed. "We thought about Gabe's house, but it would get crowded much too fast."

"If you wouldn't think we'd be interfering, George and I would love you to have the wedding at the ranch."

Jill's jaw dropped. "You're kidding, right?"

Sarah held up a hand. "If it doesn't suit, I'll understand. We just wanted to offer it as an option. And I'd love to help you and your aunt with the arrangements."

Jill couldn't help the tears that leaked from her eyes. "I don't know how to thank you for your generosity. I'll have to clear it with Gabe, but I know he'll say yes."

"Good." Sarah popped the last crumb of the pastry in her mouth and swallowed the last sip of coffee. "Call me when you've talked to him. The two of you can come out to the ranch for dinner and we'll make plans."

Of all the things — bad and good — that had happened since she'd set foot back in the Falls, this one touched her the most, and softened the harshness of so much else that had taken place.

"By the way," Sarah said, as they left the restaurant, "there's suddenly a lot of chatter that Limestone Hills isn't on the up-and-up and that some Falls residents might even be involved."

Jill bit her lip. She didn't know how much she could say at the moment. "I think there may be some news forthcoming," she finally got out.

Sarah grinned. "The soul of discretion. You'll make a good wife for Gabe. Well, maybe by the time we have dinner, you'll be able to tell me more. Talk to you later."

Jill stood on the sidewalk letting the late morning sun wash over her. She'd be feeling a lot better about things if Sarah hadn't dropped that little nugget in her lap. She hoped it didn't turn out to be something that screwed up the wedding. They were already dealing with enough challenges.

She was just about to set off when her cell rang. She looked at the number. Reed's super hacker. Maybe he had confirmed what he'd suspected.

She was halfway to Gabe's office when her phone rang again.

"How about a little drama with your coffee this morning?" Gabe asked.

"Excuse me?"

"Can you be at the bank in fifteen minutes?"

"I can be there in ten." *Is it really coming together like this?*

"See you there."

Gabe was waiting in the lobby of the bank when she got there, along with Reed Jamison and a man who introduced himself as Cliff Markbright, an assistant county prosecuting attorney. Two other men in suits stood behind him, along with county Sheriff Daniel Britton and one of his deputies.

He shook hands with Jill. "Your fiancé thought you might like to be in on this since you helped get the ball rolling."

She looked from Gabe to Reed and back, frowning. "What's going on?"

Gabe smiled. "Just follow along and watch."

Trey Howard's secretary gave them a hard time about just walking into Trey's office until the prosecutor flashed his credentials. Jill was sure she'd never forget the way Trey's face turned paper white when he was served with the warrant for not only his personal bank account but also for Brian Fletcher's, Larry Hofstra's, two other leading citizens and Dolman Development.

Within fifteen minutes the bank was closed for the day and the two men with Markbright began going through the accounts. But Trey Howard had called Brian Fletcher and in what seemed like seconds Fletcher was pounding on the door of the bank. The deputy, with a nod from Britton, let him in and he headed right for Trey Howard.

"What's this about someone wanting to freeze my account?" He looked from Gabe to Markbright and back to Gabe. "I suppose this is your doing, Carter. Is this your revenge because my daughter won't give you house room?"

Gabe barked a laugh. "I think you've got that twisted around, Fletcher. And if I were you, instead of throwing my weight around, I'd be hiring the best lawyer I could get."

"And who are you?" He glared at Markbright.

"An assistant county prosecutor. But I'm just the placeholder. Federal agents will be here this afternoon to go over every account in this bank with a fine-tooth comb."

"Why you – " He grabbed Howard by the front of his jacket and delivered a hard right to the man's jaw.

Howard hit back.

But it seemed the prosecutor had known what he was doing when he'd brought the sheriff along. In moments both men were in handcuffs and being marched out to squad cars.

"I'll have your badge," Trey Howard yelled at the sheriff.

Britton gave a rough laugh. "Yeah, you'll be able to do it all from jail, right?"

Gabe and Jill left them to it after Markbright promised to give Gabe a full report. Taking Reed with them, they headed back to Gabe's office.

"Howard was sure sweating bullets," Reed commented.

Gabe leaned back in his chair. "No shit. As well he should. This thing has more tentacles than an octopus, which turned up thanks to both my investigator and the forensic accountant I hired. It seems Fletcher's been washing drug money for Dolman for years, using the real-estate deals to disguise it. Every development or project they did, Dolman also invests under a phony name. They set up dummy companies to funnel money back to themselves and the investors get a smaller return on their money. He was getting rich from two sources."

"Greed will do you in every time," Gabe pointed out.

"And Trey?" Jill asked.

"Set up Fletcher's accounts just as his father had done and conveniently forgot to report deposits of more than ten thousand. Robin Fletcher met Dolman at a party when she was between husbands and picked up a bad habit." He slid his gaze to Jill. "You were right. She's been using drugs for a long time now."

"Oh, Gabe." She saw the pain flash across his face. Whatever else had happened, he and Robin had enjoyed a special relationship at one time. "I'm so sorry, sweetheart."

He shrugged. "Means nothing to me. Not now. Except sadness at what she's done to herself. My feelings for her disappeared a long time ago." He sat back in his chair. "To flesh this out a little, they needed an attorney to set up their deals when the one they were using unexpectedly dropped dead of a heart attack. It was just fate taking a hand when Robin ran into Dolman at a party her folks gave. She smelled opportunity, dug around for what was going on and brought in her current husband. A real piece of work, I might say."

Reed picked up the thread. "One thing had led to another, with Robin now demanding a cut, too. Dolman had a feeling the DEA was closing in on his drug operation and he'd milked the real-estate scam for as much as he could. He decided to go for one last score and get out."

"And what about poor Gary Armstrong?" Jill asked.

"We had our ducks in a better row than most people involved in this. We may eventually get all his money back." He leaned back in his chair, eyes sad. "But we've got some local officials involved in the land scam so this thing hasn't stopped wielding its black brush."

Reed's mouth curved in a lopsided smile. "One positive note. I do get to write a great story, which the magazine wants me to send out to the wire services first. Then I'll do an in-depth piece for *Life in America*. I told our editor Jill gets listed in the credits for it. I couldn't have found all this out without her. And you."

"So what happens now?" she asked.

Gabe kissed her fingers then released her hand and sat back in his chair. "The FBI will be here later today. My guess is the sheriff had to let Trey and Brian go since we're still pulling our evidence together. Right now it's still an investigation. But the Feds will be here later with their own warrants and the sheriff's got a couple of deputies watching the two men so they don't disappear."

"Dolman too?"

"No. He's already in custody. There was plenty of evidence against him once they knew where to look." He sighed. "They're still following paper trails to see who else in town was involved."

"And what happens to Robin?"

"Depends if they have enough to charge her on. But she's got worse problems than that."

Jill raised an eyebrow. "Worse than going to jail?"

"When she first met Dolman, she got involved with drugs." He scrubbed his hand across his face. "Just a little at first, but apparently lately it's escalated. I found out Brian had sent her to rehab twice. She was even clean for three years before she got married this time."

Jill's heart cracked at the look of distress on his face. "Gabe, it's not your fault. You have to remember that."

He shrugged. "Maybe if I'd done things differently —"

She slapped her hand on the desktop. "Do not play the blame game. Robin's an adult. She made her own decisions."

"Maybe." Gabe stood up, signaling they were finished, and held out his hand to the other man. "I wish I could say it's been a pleasure, but maybe next time."

"Sure thing." Reed turned to Jill. "When are you coming into the office to break the news?"

"News?" She raised an eyebrow.

Reed burst out laughing. "Come on, Jill. I see that big rock on your hand. I know for damn sure you aren't going to be living in San Antonio while Gabe is here."

"Oh." Her mouth lifted in a gentle grin. "I think tomorrow. I'll have a lot of loose ends to tie up in the city. I'm hoping I can talk Gabe into coming with me for a couple of days."

Gabe walked around the desk and looped his arm around her shoulders. "Believe it. You aren't going anywhere without me. So yes, we'll be going together."

When they were alone again Jill turned back to Gabe. "About Robin."

"I can't help feeling sorry for her."

"Well, you can stop right now, and I've got the cure."

He frowned. "What do you mean?"

"I want you to know I only did this because I was getting some strange vibes from Robin about you, your marriage, the whole situation. Now I'm glad I followed my instincts."

"Jill, what's going on? What did you find out? Let's have it."

Jill fiddled with her skirt, pleating it with nervous gestures.

"Reed Jamison has a hacker he uses sometimes who can find out anything, including whatever secrets the president has. I hope you don't mind, but I had him look into Robin's miscarriage."

Beside her Gabe tensed. "Why? What about it?"

"You were out of town when it happened, right?"

He nodded. "I had to fly to New York for a client. I had the feeling she never forgave me for it." Sadness washed over his face. "I would have done my best to be a good parent to that child."

"Well, you wouldn't have to work too hard, because there wasn't a baby. At all. Ever."

"What?" Gabe jumped up from the sofa and stared down at her, rage drawing lines in his face. "What the hell are you talking about?"

"She went to a private clinic rather than the hospital, right?" Jill asked.

Gabe nodded. "That's where her doctor was and where she would have gone for delivery." He snorted. "It caters to the very, very wealthy."

"Which is why her father could give them a hefty contribution to fake both the pregnancy and the miscarriage."

Every bit of color drained from Gabe's face. He had to make two tries before he could get any words out.

"Are you fucking kidding me?"

"I wish." She swallowed. "According to some — people — I was able to contact, she heard about us while she was away that summer. It seems not everyone can keep their mouth shut." She smoothed down her skirt over and over. "She wanted you and didn't know how else to get you. So when you went to New York, she headed for the clinic and her daddy paid them off to say she'd lost the baby."

For a moment she thought Gabe would pass out.

"I'm so sorry," she cried. "I probably shouldn't have done it, but she just made me so mad, and she wouldn't leave us alone — "

"No." He shouted the word, then pulled in a deep, calming breath. "No. I'm glad you did. It takes care of any vestige of sympathy I might have for her. Fuck. She really is a bitch."

Jill rose and walked over to him. She put her arms around him in a tentative gesture and let out a sigh of relief when he wrapped his own around her and pressed her tight to his body. In a moment he caressed her hair, his fingers sifting through the strands, and he placed gentle kisses on her forehead.

"I know it's early in the day but can we please go home? I need some R&R." He came around to the front of the desk and pulled her into his arms. "I need to go home and get naked with my future wife and blot out all this garbage."

Heat suffused her skin. "Okay. I can get with that program." She stood on tiptoe and brushed her lips against his. "I think I have a great idea to make you relax."

Chapter Fifteen

They were lucky they made it through the front door before Gabe had her skirt up, her panties off and his fly unzipped. He fumbled as he fished a condom from his wallet and slid it on. Pressing her back against the wall, he lifted her hips with his broad hands and plunged his throbbing erection into her with one thrust.

"Sorry, sorry, sorry," he groaned as he rolled his hips. "I just need you — need this — so much right now."

"It's okay," she told him, her voice shaky. "Anyway, I'm right there with you."

And she was, so hot from the energy of his excitement that when she felt the first splash of semen inside the condom she climaxed. The orgasm was brief but intense and left them both gasping.

He eased her legs down and she stood.

"But before the next round I could use a shower and some wine. How about you?"

He pressed a light kiss on her lips. "One shower and one bottle of wine coming right up."

She had just pulled on a short robe from the closet and was tying the sash when she heard the ringing of a cell phone. She checked, discovered it wasn't hers and figured it was Gabe's. She found him in the kitchen, rigid with anger.

"No. You tell that bitch I'm not hiring a lawyer for her, giving her money for a lawyer or even coming to see her. She's getting exactly what she deserves."

His disconnected the call and tossed the phone on the counter.

"What was that about?"

"Can you believe the nerve of that bitch?"

"I assume we're talking about Robin."

"The one and only." He raked his hands through his hair. "The Feds picked her up too, on drug charges and money laundering. Since all their funds are frozen, she doesn't even have money for a lawyer so she had someone call me and ask if I could help her."

Jill couldn't help herself. She burst out laughing. "Well, she certainly runs true to form."

"God damn it."

She walked over to him, looped her hands around his rigid body and stood on tiptoe to kiss him.

"She's out of our lives for good now and we don't need to waste another minute even thinking about her. Come with me. Dr. Danvers has just the cure for this."

She took his hand and tugged him into the bedroom, where she proceeded to undress him one item at a time, kissing every inch of him as she did so. By the time he was naked, he had begun to relax and nature had taken over. When she pushed him with her fingertips, he fell backward on the bed, offering no resistance. Jill tossed her robe to the side and went to work on him, with her mouth, her hand, her tongue.

"Fuck, Jill," he groaned, when his cock stood at rigid attention. "I need to be inside you. Now."

"I think you were not so long ago," she giggled.

"You think once is enough? Think again, little girl."

Before she could realize what was happening he had grabbed her, flipped them both over and was pressing her into the bed.

"Don't use a condom," she told him, her voice steady.

He raised his eyebrows. "What if you get pregnant?"

"Then we'll have a baby. Isn't that the way it works?"

"But—"

"Hush. I want a family with you, Gabe. It's not too soon to start."

"Look at me," he commanded. "I want to see your eyes. I want to be sure you're not just doing this because—"

"I'm doing it because it's what I want, so shut up and let's get down to business." She held his gaze with hers, never wavering, hoping that everything she felt for him shone from them. "I love you. Bury yourself in me."

The feel of him with nothing separating them was more erotic than she could have ever imagined. When he sucked in a breath she knew he felt the same way.

"Jesus!"

"Take me, Jill. Take me now." He pushed harder and faster.

At once he stiffened, threw back his head and an undulating sound wailed from his mouth. He spurted into her, filling her with the essence of who he was. Jill held him against her body until he stopped pulsating inside her. With a whoosh of breath he collapsed on her, his body pressing her into the mattress, and rubbed his face against her.

They lay that way for a long time. She stroked his back with her hands and placed light kisses on his shoulders. Even if he crushed the air out of her lungs, she'd stay there as long as it took. Her neck felt wet and she thought it was drops of sweat. But then he quivered beneath her hands and she was stunned to realize what she felt was his tears.

"Gabe?" She threaded her fingers through his hair.

At last he moved his head and looked at her, his eyes filled with self-loathing. "God, Jill. Oh God. I don't know what the hell I did to deserve you, darlin', but I must have done something right sometime. Somehow."

She kissed her way across his chest, teasing his flat nipples with her tongue and scraping them with her fingernails. "And you aren't getting rid of me again, either. Don't you forget it."

"Are you sure about this? A baby?"

She giggled. "It's a little late to worry about it now, but yes. It was my idea, remember?"

"But are you really sure? I don't want to take the choice away from you. We haven't even discussed it. You've got a career, a professional life — "

"None of which I plan to change. Just work around things, you know?"

He kissed her with such tenderness she felt she'd shed tears herself. At length he lifted his head and placed very gentle kisses on her cheek and mouth. Then he rolled to the side, taking her with him, their bodies still connected. She pressed her head into his shoulder and touched the pulse at the base of his throat. The erratic beat of anxiety was gone, replaced by a slow, heavy thrumming against her fingertips.

"I love you." His voice was warm and deep, the trace of anxiety gone.

"I love you, too." She managed to lever herself up on his chest and give him a direct look. "Better now?"

He smiled and gave her a hug. "I'd have to die to get better than this, darlin'."

She gave him a slow smile. "I think we might just have made our baby, Mr. Carter."

He grinned at her. "You think so, Miss Danvers? I sure as hell hope so, because a child with you would be a precious gift."

Jill cuddled closer to him. The room reeked of sex and she inhaled it, the sweetest scent she could imagine at the moment. "I know there are things you have to do — things we both have to do—to wrap up what's happened, but right now I'd be happy never leaving you and this bed."

"I think that's supposed to be my line," he chuckled, then lifted her face for his kiss.

His taste invaded her senses as it always did. She drew on it, wrapping her tongue around his and welcoming his invasion into her mouth.

Chapter Sixteen

"Wow." Jill bent over the magazine in front of them. "Reed said he'd give me credit on the story, but I never expected a shared byline."

"You damn sure deserved it."

They were sitting at the table on the balcony of the villa where they were honeymooning. Gary Armstrong, so grateful Gabe had been able to retrieve most of his money, had lent them his private island in the Florida Keys for two weeks. Jill's editor had sent the new edition of *Life in America* by special messenger and they were reading the article she and Reed had written together.

They both were happy to step out of the eye of the storm into some permanent calm. In the ten days before the wedding, the newspapers had been full of the scandalous Bluebonnet Falls story. The collapse of a major development company and the people involved in the fraud had been too juicy not to give major attention to. Add to that the fact that everything had come to a head in a town that could serve as the poster community for utopia and the media had gone wild.

The town had been in a total frenzy, a mixture of avid gossip and desperate hand-wringing. No matter where they were, the story had been the single topic of conversation. The weekly newspaper had even put out a special edition.

Brian Fletcher had cursed everyone, Gabe most of all, as he'd been taken into federal custody. In an effort to spread the blame around, he'd implicated the chairman of Planning and Zoning as well as the mayor, to the embarrassment of everyone in town. Trey Howard had had to answer for the bank's role in it all.

They'd all had one thing in their favor. None of them except Fletcher had known Dolman was using the setup to launder his drug money. Fletcher had started out helping Dolman swindle people out of money by manipulating land sales and skimming money from investors. After a year or two, however, he'd figured out where Dolman's 'private' funds were coming from and had insisted on a cut of the profits from that source. He'd had very little to offer in the way of a deal so he'd hired the most expensive lawyers he could find to see if there was any way around the mess.

Harriet had gone into seclusion and Robin had been staying with Missy Spellman. Missy had closed up her shop and sent her husband to the local bed and breakfast to consider his sins and wait for his own arrest. None of the women had ventured out where people could descend on them.

Jill and Gabe had avoided most of the public places. Jill had holed up at their house writing her article while Gabe had barricaded himself in his office with Christy as watchdog to take care of all the business on his end.

But on the third day after the scandal broke, Robin had showed up at the house and threatened to hammer the door down if Gabe didn't let her in. She'd looked like the bad end of a nightmare and had been screaming the roof down. Jill had listened from the kitchen, trying to stay out of the way.

"You have to help me," Robin had told Gabe. "I need a good lawyer and you're the best I know. And I have no money."

"Do you think I'd lift a finger to help you after what you did? After your very phony pregnancy?"

"W-What do you mean?"

"Did you think I wouldn't find out about it?" Jill had never heard such controlled fury in his voice. "I know all about it, Robin. Get out of here. You disgust me."

"Gabe. Honey." Robin's voice had taken on a seductive quality. "Don't believe everything you hear. I had a miscarriage. I—"

"You lied to me. About everything. Right down the line. And stole ten years of my life in the process. Get the hell away from me."

"I didn't steal anything." Her voice had risen again. "I saved you from that little nothing Jill Danvers. You would have wasted yourself on her."

Jill had peeked around the corner and seen Gabe dig his fingers into Robin's arms. "Get out of here. Now. And don't let me ever hear you say anything about Jill again. That's my future wife you're talking about and nothing's going to stop the wedding this time."

"She's nothing." Robin's voice had been venomous. "Just a bitch in heat who sees a good thing with you."

Jill hadn't been able to contain herself a moment longer. She'd marched herself out to the hall and without pausing walked up to Robin and slapped her face.

"Get the hell out of here," she'd spat. "You've done enough damage already. You are a despicable human being and I never want to see you around Gabe or me again."

For good measure she'd slapped her once more.

It was a toss-up who'd been more shocked, Robin or Gabe. The woman had raised her hand to her reddened cheek, stared with wide eyes and turned on her heel.

Gabe had broken out laughing so hard he'd collapsed on the floor. "Remind me to take you with me whenever I'm expecting trouble. Come here, little spitfire." He pulled her close to hug her tight.

They'd taken a quick trip to San Antonio for Jill to wind up her business there. She'd changed her contract with the magazine and made arrangements to close up her condo and list it for sale. But the newspapers had somehow sniffed them out. Gabe had rented a suite at the new Watermark Hotel, paid a king's ransom to keep the media away and they'd locked themselves in and conducted business from there.

The wedding at the Wolfe ranch had turned out to be more than Jill could have imagined. The guest list had grown to such enormous proportions she'd thought about cutting back to just the immediate family. But her Aunt Karen and Sarah Wolfe had brushed off her objections and simply gone to work.

The day had been perfect—a blue Texas sky with a golden ball of sun hanging between puffy white clouds and a breeze faint enough to cool the air but not disturb the white cloths on the tables or the huge white bows on the urns holding roses of every color. When Jill had walked down the white runner the florist had placed in the backyard, holding her Uncle Joe's arm, the sight of Gabe, tall and sexy in his dark suit waiting with the minister, had taken her breath away. A sudden film of tears had clouded her eyes and she'd gripped her uncle's arm.

"Easy," he'd whispered. "You're almost there."

Then she'd been standing beside Gabe, his eyes on her, so full of love she'd almost broken down again. The trip down the aisle had taken ten years but it had been more than worth waiting for. When the minister had pronounced them man and wife, Gabe had kissed with such thoroughness it had provoked wolf whistles and catcalls from the guests and Jill had blushed to the roots of her hair.

But now they were alone, the hot tropical sun reflected in the clear blue water of the pool below and the Gulf further out. A soft breeze ruffled the pages as they turned them.

"They did a good job with my story, too," she commented. She'd studied all four pages several times.

"They know how good you are." He nibbled her ear. "I watched your editor when you renegotiated your contract with him. He'd rather be flexible than lose you altogether."

She laughed. "Do you think the fact I had my attorney with me had something to do with it?"

"I was just backup, darlin'. You did just fine."

As they talked, he stroked her arms and shoulders and trailed kisses along the nape of her neck. They were both naked. He refused to let her wear clothes most of the time except when the housekeeper came in to clean each day. She and her husband lived in a tiny house at the other end of the island.

"I want to be able to ravish you any time the mood strikes me," Gabe had told Jill.

Last night, after a gourmet meal prepared by the housekeeper's talented husband, they'd made exquisite love. Afterward, he'd bathed her with incredible tenderness and put her in bed between cool silk sheets. Now they sat on the balcony in the warm sun, drinking orange juice and watching the boats on the water.

"I love you, Jill." His mouth was a fraction of an inch from hers. "And I pray that somewhere in here, we made a baby. Because I want that with you more than I can tell you."

Her eyelids flew up as he settled her astride him, his cock slipping easily into her pussy. "You think I'm pregnant already?"

He shrugged. "When was your last period? You haven't had one since that…since that day."

The day they never discussed anymore. The first time they hadn't used any protection.

She frowned. "I…I don't remember."

Gabe grinned. "Aha. I know I'm right. So we're going to shelve the rough stuff for a while, Mrs. Carter." He brushed a kiss across her lips.

Later, lying on the lounger wrapped in each other's arms, the sun warming them and Gabe still buried inside her, she placed a gentle kiss on the side of his face. "I love you, Mr. Carter."

"And I love you, Mrs. Carter. This time nothing's going to get in our way. Ever."

"You know I always wanted a Happily Ever After." She smiled. "I finally got it."

She snuggled against him and as the tropical breeze cooled their bodies and they fell asleep in each other's arms.

About the Author

A multi-published, award winning, Amazon and USA Today best-selling author, Desiree Holt has produced more than 200 titles and won many awards. She has received an EPIC E-Book Award, the Holt Medallion and many others including Author After Dark's Author of the Year. She has been featured on CBS Sunday Morning and in The Village Voice, The Daily Beast, USA Today, The Wall Street Journal, The London Daily Mail. She lives in Florida with her cats who insist they help her write her books, and is addicted to football.

Desiree loves to hear from readers. You can find her contact information, website details and author profile page at http://www.totallybound.com.